THE MAN WITH THE
NOTABLE FACE

THE MAN WITH THE NOTABLE FACE

JAROSLAV (JERRY) PETRYSHYN

IGUANA

Copyright © 2022 Jaroslav Petryshyn
Published by Iguana Books
720 Bathurst Street, Suite 303
Toronto, ON M5S 2R4

Publisher: Meghan Behse
Editor: Paula Chiarcos
Front cover illustration: Melissa Novak
Front cover design: Jonathan Relph

ISBN 978-1-77180-547-6 (paperback)
ISBN 978-1-77180-548-3 (ebook)

This is an original print edition of *The Man with the Notable Face*.

This is a work of fiction with the characters, names, places and incidents a product of the author's imagination. It is set, in part, against historical events. In marrying fictional characters with actual personages, the author has tried to be as accurate as possible to the latter. There are many biographies of Stalin, and Adam B. Ulam's *Stalin: The Man and His Era* is particularly enlightening. The manmade famine in Ukraine (known as the Holodomor) is well documented in Robert Conquest's *Harvest of Sorrow*. Any resemblance to actual events, locales, organizations or persons living or dead is entirely coincidental.

For my parents

PART ONE

CHAPTER 1

June 22, 1941

They gathered at the Commissariat Defense Headquarters in the Kremlin, a collection of ruddy-faced, sullen, and somber men intently focused on one individual in the throes of realizing the gravitas of the situation. Remote, taciturn, minutely alert to the smallest gesture or word inflection, Vyacheslav Molotov, his oldest comrade in arms from the prerevolutionary days, sat erect, formal, like a schoolteacher, his pince-nez firmly in place. Next to him sat Lazar Kaganovich, ruthless, hard-driving, and implacable — his number two. He stroked his bushy mustache apprehensively. Plump, round-faced Georgi Malenkov occupied another chair, a Buddha-like form, the dark, hooded eyes inscrutable in the folds of fatty tissue. A comparative newcomer to the inner circle, he stared blankly across at the squinty-eyed, fidgeting Lavrenty Beria, overlord of the Secret Police.

Although no less prominent, the others seemed more remote, shrinking into the shadows. They included the portly Andrei Zhdanov, his loosening jowls set in a deepening scowl; Andrei Andreyev, the powerful Ukrainian "fixer" who rooted out "disloyal" party members; Anastas Mikoyan, the wily Armenian fox with the empathy of a stone; and the "loyal to the core" Mikhail Kalinin, whose bespectacled, narrow face, complete with a supporting goatee, reminded his boss (mostly in a benign way) of Trotsky, his most feared "intellectual" rival — now vanquished for good...

At the end of the long oak table, deposited on either side, almost as an afterthought, were the two generals, Semyon Timoshenko, recently appointed war commissar, and Georgi Zhukov, chief of staff and commander of the Kiev Military. Both were tough Cossacks who miraculously survived the purges. At the moment, they were the best he had. Like the collected coterie of men, their eyes were riveted to the head of the table. They were expectant, nervous, and above all, fearful.

The object of their attentiveness was Joseph Dzhugashvili, the eldest surviving child of a Georgian shoemaker and supreme ruler of the Soviet Union. His mother, Catherine, affectionately called him Soso; during his revolutionary days when he organized bank robberies for the Marxist cause, he took the name Koba, a fabled Georgian pirate; later, when he felt the taste of power, he changed it to Stalin, which meant steel hardness. It conjured the appropriate image and seemed to suit his character.

Physically, he made little positive impression, a diminutive man who bore the scars of smallpox from his boyhood: a pockmarked face and slightly withered stiff left arm. It was his pathological mind that inspired terror with a heavy dose of loathing. For the last twelve years, his whims were the nation's commandments, and anyone who stood in the way (intentionally or in many cases not) was eliminated by the stroke of a pen. At the moment, however, he was visibly distraught.

Stalin had just received information that shook him to the core. "I-I can't believe it!" he shouted, his face turning a pasty crimson. "I just can't — I will not believe it! It must be the work of agent provocateurs hoping to—"

"It is true," Molotov dared to interrupt, speaking in a quiet, subdued voice. As his master's right-hand man — his bludgeon — he felt compelled to relay the harsh reality.

After all, it was he who listened in stunned silence while the German ambassador delivered Hitler's declaration of war at 4:00 a.m. that morning. "Hitler has deceived us. German armored columns are cutting deep into the motherland. Communications with many frontier units are lost. Our airfields are being bombed, planes have been destroyed, many on the ground—"

Stalin exploded; the fearful little man could stand it no longer. "If this is true, then why are we not counterattacking? Why are we not taking the war to the enemy?"

A silence shrouded the room; everyone present knew the answer to their leader's rhetorical outburst. Despite irrefutable intelligence reports of massive German troop buildup along the Soviet border, Stalin had refused to authorize countermeasures. He did not want to "provoke Hitler unnecessarily." Thus, there was no counterattack because he had not thought it necessary to plan for one.

Molotov, for his part, said nothing but stared at some fixed point on the far wall. The bad news had been delivered, and he knew better than to venture a comment at this point. What could he say? *I told you so. You shouldn't have trusted Hitler. You were duped, sucked in. We are totally unprepared to counter the invasion.*

That would only aggravate their irritable leader's mood. And he was aggravated enough! Indeed, Molotov had not seen his boss in such a state of agitation since Nadezhda, his young wife, unable to stand living with the man she once adored, had committed suicide. That was over ten years ago. Molotov remembered it well, since Stalin's rage almost sent his own wife, Polina — a close friend of Nadezhda — to prison for her "nefarious influence" and for allegedly supplying the pistol! Molotov stoically turned the other cheek. Polina escaped incarceration, but Stalin's wrath was barely contained. He never forgave her and always remained suspicious of her. Now was not the time to advise Comrade Stalin on what he should do or challenge the wisdom of his shrilled orders. If ever there had been such a time, it was well past.

***

Stalin had been restless and anxious since Sunday, when he first learned from intelligence reports of the possibility of a sudden German attack. He instructed his Moscow party officials to spend the night in the Kremlin, although he, himself left at midnight to go to his villa in Kuntsevo — his usual routine — leaving Molotov to tend shop.

But he was uneasy, unable to sleep. At two o'clock in the morning, to reassure his troubled mind, he telephoned Ivan Tyulenev, commandant of the Moscow District. "Have the anti-aircraft defenses at seventy-five percent of war readiness," he instructed.

Feeling a little better, by three o'clock he lapsed into fitful slumber. At four o'clock the phone rang, disturbing General Vlasik, who was in charge of security at the villa. It was General Zhukov. "Wake Comrade Stalin up immediately — war."

Now, surrounded by frightened men, Stalin was clearly becoming unhinged.

While Hitler's war machines gobbled up Soviet territory and German soldiers drove eastward, he seemed immobilized, shouting silly orders. "Marshal Timoshenko — the Fascists are to be surrounded and annihilated!"

Timoshenko, a seasoned veteran, who a few short months before smashed the Finnish defenses in the brief but bloody Russo-Finnish War, was appalled. Given the circumstances, it was a blind, stupid order. "Comrade Stalin, I think it not wise until we appraise the damage, regroup our forces, and map out our strategy—"

"I will not be second-guessed!" cut in a frazzled Stalin. "We will not be like the fucking French and Poles. They couldn't put up any resistance at all. Not this much!" He placed his right index finger over his thumb. "Not this much!" He gestured again. "Attack!"

Zhukov, his square jaw set in firm resolve, supported the other military man. "With all due respect, Semyon is correct. It would be suicidal to advance westward without an adequate assessment of the situation. We have been caught off guard. At this point we should husband our personnel and resources, plot out with extreme care our next move."

Zhukov, too, spoke from hard, battle-earned experience. In 1939, he led a brilliant counteroffensive against the Japanese in Outer Mongolia near the Khalkhin Gol. Stalin, overwrought, suddenly detested his illustrious senior generals. "Enough babbling! We shall attack and drive Hitler's horde out…"

After a short, intense argument, the two officers acquiesced. Their objections did not penetrate the rage of Stalin. And they found no support from the others. None of them dared raise an eyebrow to Comrade Stalin, let alone question a directive from the dear father of the Soviet people.

***

Two days later, Timoshenko issued an order that he knew deep within his bowels was sheer lunacy. Soviet armies stationed in the north and center of the country were to march westward and seize strategic positions within German Poland. The action was premature, embarked upon without a realistic appraisal of the situation. The results proved a disaster. It enabled the Germans to encircle Soviet Russia's second line of defense.

Stalin, meanwhile, disappeared after the scene at the Commissariat of Defense. He returned to Kuntsevo where, prostrated with anxiety, he drank vodka and slipped into a dark, fearful abyss of inactivity.

CHAPTER 2

June 24, 1941

Inside the squat gray concrete edifice of the Marx-Engels Institute, Timoshenko and Zhukov had a very private tryst. What the generals discussed they could ill afford anyone to overhear. Both were under tremendous strain. The day before, the High Command had officially been formed. Included were all manner of military and political personnel, but with one notable exception: Stalin himself. Timoshenko, chief and supreme commander, drew his own conclusions: "The man is a coward, a cockroach who deserted his post. We might as well be in the hands of Rasputin."

Zhukov raised his hand like a policeman stopping traffic. "Restrain yourself, Semyon, please. That kind of talk—"

"You do not agree?"

"Of course I agree, but what can we do? We are soldiers, not politicians. We simply follow orders—"

"Orders!" Timoshenko's voice rose a notch, his large oval head bobbing in indignation. "What kind of orders would allow what we witnessed these last two days? It can't be done, you know — how can I defend the corridor to Moscow when I am commanded to rush like a rabid dog against at least nine Panzer divisions — if our intelligence reports are correct — and thirty-four infantry divisions, supported by the Luftwaffe at that?"

"I understand, Semyon. Nevertheless, you heard the news. Vilnius is on the verge of falling — if it has not done so already — and Minsk is next. Action is necessary—"

"But to blindly commit our second line into battle..." Timoshenko shook his head again. "These orders put us in great danger; we could be encircled..." He let his voice trail off then added an afterthought. "Budenny will probably hold his own in Ukraine, but I would feel better if Voroshilov were not responsible for the defense of Leningrad. He is an incompetent asshole who has eaten too much of Stalin's shit... No, my friend, we have lost too many men and too much equipment as it stands. If we keep following orders, we will lose the war — if we have not done so already."

"Semyon..." Zhukov interjected, stroking his dimpled chin nervously. He sensed that the general needed to get something weighty off his mind.

"Tell me, Georgi, what are our political leaders — those infallible men in the Politburo — doing now? I'll tell you. Nothing! They are too petrified to make a coherent decision. They are all waiting for Stalin to pull himself together. They do not want to anger the master by any act of independent action... Oh, they are good at licking his boots, groveling at his feet, doing his dirty work, but what do they do when he is incapable of giving directives? They turn to us, dumbfounded like sheep, asking for deliverance from the slaughter. Where were they when the madman purged our military? When he tore the soul out of our defense? I checked the figures. It's there in black and white. Think of it! Our beloved leader murdered 3 out of 5 field marshals, 14 out of 16 commanders, all 8 admirals, 60 out of 67 corps commanders, 136 out of 199 divisional commanders, and 221 of the 397 brigade commanders, not to mention all 11 vice-commissars of defense... We could now use Tukhachevsky, Yakir, and Uborevich instead of the political peacocks like Voroshilov we have now dressed up as generals."

Zhukov wearily pulled out a battered cigarette case and offered his friend a smoke. As they lit up, he said, "You didn't bring me here just to give a lecture. What are you leading up to?"

"The country needs decisive leadership. We are the only ones that can provide it."

"I don't quite understand." Zhukov frowned, expelling a wispy trail of smoke.

The protuberant forehead of Timoshenko's balding cranium furrowed as he spat out a rush of words. "A fate deserved by any leader who, through criminal negligence and cowardice, is responsible for military catastrophe—"

Zhukov's eyes widened. "Do you realize what you are saying?"

"He is to blame, you know. He had our best generals killed! Now…" Timoshenko threw up his hands in a gesture of hopelessness. "Now what do we do? He left us at the edge of this unbelievable cataclysm… Look, Georgi, we are professional soldiers — for the good of our military, for the good of Mother Russia, as patriots — the generals, what's left of us, must take over. The nation is rudderless. The Germans will not disappear like the kulaks or our commanders that the People's Commissariat of Internal Affairs butchered. We must act now. Russia's destiny, its very existence, is in our hands."

Zhukov glanced around the little nondescript office as if anticipating a squad of those same NKVD agents ready to burst through the door. Nervously, he wetted his lips. "What do you have in mind?"

Instinctively, Timoshenko moved closer to the veteran general. "Destroy the head and the rest of the corrupt carcass will follow—"

"But this is treason—"

"No!" Timoshenko admonished harshly. "The bastard has lost his nerve. Right now he is in his rat hole, drunk, raving like a lunatic. He is the one who has committed treason, and we are accessories if we do not act. He must be eliminated."

"Semyon… What you are proposing is … is beyond comprehension. I—"

"Just hear me out, Georgi. Just hear me out."

Zhukov sucked deeply on his short fat cigarette again, letting the acrid smoke escape slowly through his nose. "We have been in too many fights together for me to just walk away. I will listen, but—"

"Good! I knew you would." Timoshenko suddenly brightened. He snuffed out his cigarette butt in a tin ashtray on the nearby desk and rubbed his large rough hands together vigorously. It seemed exceedingly cold in the office. "Recently, I received an interesting intelligence report — at least it was curious enough for the decoding section to slip it to me."

"What kind of intelligence report?"

"It appears that Stalin has developed a sudden health problem."

"Health problem?" Zhukov was surprised. Stalin seemed to be in robust shape, but then such information was rarely leaked, even to senior officials.

"Yes — a specialist from Leningrad, of all places, has been summoned to examine him — an internal disorder of some sort. There are no details. Probably nothing more than too much rich proletarian food and drink producing discomforting gas!" Timoshenko attempted a short laugh that didn't quite succeed.

"I see." Zhukov spoke hesitantly. "But I still don't follow. How—"

"Simple. We make sure Stalin does not recover."

Zhukov opened and closed his mouth, staring blankly at Timoshenko. Finally, he said, "Is this doctor to—"

"No. He has not been approached. And the risk would be too great. No, I propose we make a substitution."

"A substitution?"

"Our own specialist for the one coming from Leningrad. With the correct documentation, he would have no difficulty getting into Kuntsevo. Once inside..." — Timoshenko paused and clasped his hands behind his back — "he would administer the necessary drugs. Comrade Stalin's ailment would prove fatal."

"My God, Semyon — poison?"

"Why not? He has a particular affinity for deadly potions. It would make for ironic justice."

Both generals were aware of the rumors that Stalin had poisoned Lenin. True or not, Stalin was attracted to nasty substances ingested or otherwise administered, ordering the NKVD to establish its own toxic-materials development laboratory.

Now it was Zhukov's turn to butt out his cigarette. He did this deliberately and slowly. "Is your information reliable?"

"As reliable as it can be. I have the doctor's name, his time of departure from Leningrad and arrival in Moscow. Being the supreme commander of our armed forces in time of a national emergency has its advantages," he added wryly. "No questions are asked when I require information."

Zhukov nodded. "And this Leningrad doctor?"

"He will be intercepted and detained."

"Detained?"

Timoshenko shrugged. "For now. That is subject to further discussion as we proceed. He may prove to be a liability."

"I see." Zhukov rubbed his cheek and chin, digesting the full impact of Timoshenko's statement. "And who would be the substitute?"

"Ah ... providence, it seems, has come to our aid. There is a certain Ukrainian, a nationalist patriot, I suspect, maybe even a Petlyurist, who has an uncanny resemblance to this doctor and who has medical training, albeit as a veterinarian..." He shrugged again as if to say this was what fate gave them to work with, and it was better than could be hoped for. "He has a score to settle with Stalin."

In spite of himself, Zhukov gave a short laugh. "Who doesn't! Three quarters of the population would gladly face a firing squad to have a chance at Stalin. The other quarter would cheer on the sidelines... How did you find him?"

Timoshenko smiled. "As I said, providence. It started as innocent talk over a bottle of vodka after the meeting at Commissariat Headquarters. My officers are a loyal lot — most of them... And I suppose I was overly frank with my assessment of Stalin. They agreed that something had to be done, especially Yuri, whose father was a good officer whom I knew personally before he fell in the purges. Yuri is very bitter, but like his father, he is a loyal soldier nevertheless... At any rate, our discussion seemed pointless, an exercise in venting our feelings, until the next day, when Yuri delivered the decoded messages of Stalin's illness, along with the photograph of the doctor summoned to attend. He was very excited, explaining that his friend — the Ukrainian — not only bore a striking resemblance to the doctor but also had medical training of sorts — as I said, a veterinarian, although I don't think he ever completed. Yuri vaguely suggested that this information could be useful to our discussions from the day before, if we were serious. Georgi, Yuri provided a photograph. He could be the doctor's twin brother! Admittedly, he's a few years younger, but that can be fixed."

"Who knows about this?"

"Just Yuri and my trusted personal attaché, Andrei — and now you. The three of us sketched out a scheme that will be presented to the Ukrainian. It seemed impossible at first, but now I am convinced it can work, Georgi." Timoshenko laid his hand on Zhukov's shoulder. "Your prestige and talent will be needed to make the transition after Stalin is gone. And to beat the Germans. Do we really have a choice? What do you say?"

"Can it really work?" Zhukov sounded skeptical.

"Yes," replied Timoshenko emphatically. "The Ukrainian is in Moscow. He can be approached and given the necessary documentation and instructions."

"Who would approach him — Yuri?"

"No. Unfortunately, he has just been ordered to Smolensk, a directive I dare not counteract at this point without ruffling political feathers and raising some eyebrows. No, Yuri has passed word on to his Ukrainian friend that my personal attaché will meet with him. Andrei is a bright young soldier in whom I have full confidence. It may be better that way; there is no possibility of Yuri's friendship with this Ukrainian affecting the course of events… Georgi, I need your support. Are you with me?"

"Will this Ukrainian actually go through with it?"

"I am assured that he will — Yuri believes he will." Timoshenko spread his hands out like a priest before communion. "We can only hope and have faith."

Zhukov took a full minute to think, pacing back and forth. "It's a long shot," he finally said.

"There are grave risks," admitted the supreme commander, "but they must be taken. There is no other way. I must know. Are you in?"

Zhukov's mind flicked back to his circle of colleagues purged just a few short years before. Stalin spared him then, but what about the future? Perhaps Timoshenko was right; now was the moment. In all probability, there wouldn't be a better opportunity… He gave a faint nod.

"Good. We have very little time to work out the logistics. Here is what I have in mind…" For the next hour, Timoshenko in a hushed and somber voice explained the details of the assassination plot. Zhukov was aghast; even a gambling fanatic would balk at the odds against success. But then again, there was always a chance — perhaps the only chance to save the country before Stalin led it to total defeat.

CHAPTER 3

June 26, 1941, Gorky Park

The late afternoon sky was dark, replete with menacing clouds hanging over the Moskva River, but the rain held off. The two men, both in their early thirties, seemed oblivious to the threatening heavens. They were preoccupied with more pernicious matters.

From a distance, they were a study in contrasts. One was a tall, lean stalk, fitted in panoply denoting the Red Army. The other stood much shorter, more proportioned, dressed in a white peasant smock and crumpled trousers. He had the bearing of one who was used to hard labor, plank beds, and little else. There were hundreds like him in Moscow. He had been instructed to get off at the Park Kultury Metro Station across the river and make his way to a certain bench near the seedier shadows of the huge park, where he would meet an army officer with a blue ribbon pinned on his lapel.

They walked slowly but alertly, steering a wide, evasive course from other strollers in the park. Timoshenko's attaché had a difficult task; he pursued it diligently. The conspiracy would die in its embryonic stage if they could not conscript this Ukrainian to their cause. There was no time for alternative plans or to find anyone else with the appropriate physical characteristics and professional background. "It must be done within the next forty-eight hours," he said tightly.

The Ukrainian stopped in his tracks. "That's not possible. I would need time to prepare, to—"

"A plan has been formulated."

The smaller man cast his eyes over the verdant expanse of the park. He thought of his youth and of the once prosperous village in the Dnipropetrovsk Oblast where his mother, father, and sister died, victims of Stalin's war against the kulaks. It was through the winter of 1932–33 that the famine consumed them and millions more in a way that was embedded forever in his consciousness. So hideous because it was man-made, a deliberate policy of genocide by a diabolical mind.

They came in the fall of '32, so-called party activists and young Komsomol members from the towns and cities. Like locusts, they advanced into every peasant village, pillaging the homes, abusing the inhabitants, and taking the grain from every barn and shed that had any to give. It wasn't only the grain, potatoes, corn, and carrots that were confiscated but also livestock, implements, clothing, and personal valuables — from eating utensils to a favorite icon. Nothing was left. Soon, villagers, at least those in his region, were reduced to devouring leaves, tree bark, dogs, cats, and rodents, progressing to ants and earthworms. They ground up leather and shoe soles into pasty "flour" mixed with dandelions, burdock, bluebells, willow root, sedum, nettles — anything that grew above and below ground. They pulverized skin and bone fragments, threw them into a gristly stew, and cooked glue. And when that was gone, when not a bird flew nor a leaf rustled, then they died — millions of them — in their homes mainly, but also in the fields, on the roads escaping to nowhere, on church steps praying to their almighty Creator, and under bridges in the towns and cities. He still remembered the stench of festering sores and rotting tissue and visualized the dust-gray bodies with swollen bellies, hands, and feet piled high in roving carts, their last journey to hastily dug graves. Stalin and his bureaucratic henchmen had reduced his family, his friends, his countrymen, his nation to a derelict, stinking rubble of corpses. And it was no mistake, no unfathomable misunderstanding or natural disaster but rather a political decision made in a chiding capital by a hateful, brooding, pathologically mad little man with a grandiose agenda and his personal demons.

Here was a chance, an opportunity for him to act. Above all it would be an act of vengeance, an act of personal retribution against the monster who subverted the socialist ideal and left his family dead. That he had managed to escape this fate was another story... Now he could grasp the sword of justice not only on behalf of his kin but also on behalf of millions who fell prey to Stalin's collectivization campaign. But why should these plotters, who, he was certain, supported and participated in Stalin's war on the kulaks, pick him? What had Yuri told them? "Why me?"

From the inside pocket of his uniform, the soldier pulled out a photograph and gave it to the Ukrainian. It profiled a pleasant square face with dark piercing eyes and wavy brown hair whitening at the temples. The Ukrainian sucked in air; he was looking at himself, or at least a striking facsimile, perhaps a few years older.

Noting the startled reaction, the soldier said, "Remarkable, isn't it? Especially the eyes."

"Who is this man?"

"A doctor. You will take his place when he comes to examine Stalin."

"Take his place?"

"Correct." The soldier went on to explain more fully, concluding, "Your physical characteristics and the fact that you have medical training make you the only choice for this task. Our fate is in your hands."

"Did you know that the state and party purged veterinarians during the famine? Because of livestock mortality..." The smaller man gave a twisted chortle, adding, "Of course, I wasn't an animal doctor then."

Timoshenko's attaché frowned, not quite sure what to make of the comment. The Ukrainian waved off the man's puzzled expression. "Never mind... And you couldn't conscript the doctor to perform this — this deed?"

"It was discussed, but the risks were judged too high. He could betray us."

"And I couldn't?"

"Perhaps." The soldier shrugged. "In your case, the risk was judged as…" — he pursed his lips in thought — "acceptable. You would also be betraying Yuri."

"I see…" The Ukrainian furrowed his eyebrows. "It will be exceedingly difficult."

"But not impossible," cut in Timoshenko's attaché. "As I said, we can get you into Stalin's villa at Kuntsevo."

"We?"

"Outside of Yuri, you need not know names. Who we are does not concern you, just the whom."

"But you are General Timoshenko's liaison. He sent you here, yes?"

The attaché hesitated as if there was more to the question, just below the surface. Of course the Ukrainian would know or would have a good guess, given Yuri's connection to General Timoshenko, even if he didn't actually mention his name. "Yes, I was sent by the general."

The Ukrainian nodded, seeming satisfied. "I saw your general once — probably only a corps commander then. His train pulled into our village — May of thirty-three, I believe it was. He was horrified, I think, as were a great many of the troops, to be greeted by a sea of starving men, women, and children who stood and begged. He deployed his men on maneuvers, and when field kitchens were set up and food was served, the soldiers gave their portions to the famished. His kindest act was to walk away along with his officers and political commissars and not notice…"

The attaché chose not to respond. That Timoshenko was born in Ukraine and showed leniency to wretched kulaks a few years ago had little to do with the present situation. "Stalin must be liquidated. You are being offered the opportunity." He paused, collecting his thoughts. In more measured and intimate tones he said, "Think of yourself as an instrument of retribution for the death of your father, mother, and sister. This is your chance."

The Ukrainian looked up sharply. "I see you know of my background. Yuri, perhaps, told more than he should or intended. Either way, I do not care to be patronized."

Timoshenko's attaché shrugged indifference. "Justify it any way you wish, but I need your answer — yes or no."

The Ukrainian studied the photograph a moment longer before handing it back. Finally, he spoke. "What do you and your superiors get out of this?"

"Immediate gains. It would be an understatement to say that the war is going badly. For the salvation of the Soviet Un — for this Slavic nation, it is imperative that Stalin die."

"I see ... and who would replace him?"

The question annoyed Timoshenko's attaché. The practical matter now was fighting a war, with the niceties of politics a secondary issue to be resolved afterward. "It doesn't matter as long as those who conduct the war do so on a rational military basis, avoiding the military disasters we have witnessed. You, of course, realize that Stalin butchered our first- and second-rank officers. The military staff has undergone two, three — even more changes of command. Wanton destruction of loyal, competent men has resulted in this tragic state of affairs. Besides, he has now shunned his duties as head of state. In our perilous position, that's treason. He must be removed. There still are leaders ready to lead who would command unquestioning loyalty and obedience from soldiers and civilians alike."

There was a long silent interval; a light shower had begun. The Ukrainian asked, "How long before the medicine I am to administer will have an effect?"

"Oh, you will have three to four hours to make your escape before the alarm is sounded."

"Yes, but what of me should I successfully accomplish this deed and live?"

Timoshenko's man gave a short, snorting laugh, understanding fully the implications of the Ukrainian's question. "Perhaps you will receive a medal—"

"Or disappear at the hands of persons unknown."

"Or that too," Timoshenko's attaché responded bluntly. "You already know too much. So do I. We are all implicated — I can give you no guarantees. All I can say is that if the mission succeeds, you will be safe. It will be assumed Stalin expired naturally."

Again, nothing was said for a few moments. They continued walking toward the Moskva River that straddled the park's northern boundary. The light drizzle was turning into a more sustained downpour.

"Will anything change in this socialist paradise if Stalin is killed?" the Ukrainian demanded. "Will I get back my father's land, stolen from him? Can I live in my home, in my country unafraid, unmolested, free from this hell that your politicians, your police, and your army created? What can you offer me if I kill your dictator?"

Taken aback somewhat, Timoshenko's attaché recovered quickly, assuming a self-assured tone. "Comrade, there are no guarantees. I realize we have different feelings and diverging points of view. I am doing what I consider is my patriotic duty. Your actions will be governed perhaps by more personal motives. But if we do not act, then all will be lost, and it will be Herr Hitler and his generals who will chart our future."

A sad yet otherwise inscrutable expression slid over the Ukrainian's face. An almost imperceptible ripple of his jaw muscles perhaps revealed a hideous inner joke. "Maybe that would not be so bad," he mumbled.

Timoshenko's attaché chose to ignore the remark. "Look, we cannot stand here in the rain amusing the pigeons and discussing injustices." He hardened his tone. "Either walk away now, in which case this conversation never took place, or let us proceed with the objective."

The Ukrainian clenched his fists and hissed back, "You are all the same — the same godless bastards shaped from Stalin's mold—"

"True or not," retorted the lanky man, "it does not alter a thing. Now decide."

CHAPTER 4

Leningrad was quite beautiful in June, especially from the vantage point of his apartment overlooking the Neva River. *We possibly have the best view of anyone*, Doctor Dimitri Bodrev thought as he spread apart the heavy brocade curtains and took in the vast expanse of simmering green-blue water symmetrically divided by the tip of Vasilyevsky Island. A month or so before, he watched in awe the ice floes of Lake Ladoga majestically winding their way with the current into the Gulf of Finland. Old St. Petersburg, renamed Petrograd during the Great War, only to become Leningrad shortly after the death of the country's chief Bolshevik in 1924, was not a particularly warm city, even in July, nor was it overly blessed with an abundance of sunny days. Yet for him, whatever nomenclature those in the dreary capital devised, it truly was a magnificent citadel not only for its historical outward window to the west but also its inward perspective of a prevaricating and increasingly isolated center.

He and Tanya made a ritual of sitting well into the evening, absorbing the panorama by candlelight. It brought out his romantic nature and Tanya's passions. She loved to make love by candlelight. "Why not?" she once said. "Only the proletariat and peasants fuck in the dark." He couldn't argue — not when the flickering flames exaggerated her bouncing buttocks.

They were, if not nobility, at least the gentry, and although the revolution had leveled most of their kind to a smoldering ruin, they adapted and survived, carving out a comfortable niche, flanked on one side by the gilt towers of Peter and Paul Fortress and on the other by a grandiose row of splendid palaces, reminders of past tsars and their courtiers…

Doctor Dimitri Bodrev had been dozing. He was tired, very tired after his long train ride from Leningrad to Moscow. *The price of competence*, he thought, and perhaps a modicum of ambition. He had no wish to leave Peter's city or Tanya — certainly not to go to the sordid reality of Moscow. Who knew what awaited him; but then, he had no choice.

The internal specialist was on an extraordinary house call. In his pocket he carried a document signed by the great vozhd himself, abruptly summoning him to Kuntsevo. He was to give the nation's leading comrade a full medical examination and determine the cause and nature of his gastrointestinal problems.

Understandably, the prominent member of the Leningrad Medical Institute, author of an important work on gastric disorders, and renowned lecturer at Leningrad University, was apprehensive. He hoped that he would not be the bearer of bad news, but only disagreeable — some temporary condition resulting in nothing more than excess flatulence, and that the general secretary should cut down on the kapusta and beans. Above that, there was a larger issue — at least from his perspective. That war had come was abundantly evident in the frantic activity to fortify Leningrad's defenses. An attack on the city, the authorities announced, was a real possibility, although full confidence was expressed in the glorious Red Army's ability to repel the aggressors. It was also evident on the train trip, which took a full fifteen hours to Moscow. Disruptions and delays occurred at every stop as troops and supplies were constantly loaded and unloaded, seemingly in chaotic fashion. But what worried Bodrev most were all the rumors — ominous rumors about Stalin. Why had he not been heard from? It did not go unnoticed that Molotov was the one who broadcasted the grim news of the German invasion, not the Soviet Socialist Republic's leading comrade. Newspaper headlines, too, were unnerving in their omission of Stalin's name. How serious was his illness? What really awaited him at Kuntsevo? It was useless to speculate, Bodrev decided; he could only fervently pray that, whatever happened, he'd ultimately make it back in one piece to Leningrad and Tanya.

The train arrived in early evening, and he expected to stay the night in Moscow (at the Metropol Hotel, as arranged) and be escorted to Stalin's villa in the morning. It did not quite work out that way. Just as he was about to retire for the night, there was a knock on his hotel suite's door.

"Yes?"

"Doctor Dimitri Bodrev?"

"Yes."

"Comrade Stalin awaits you — tonight."

The doctor opened the door to show a relatively young, tall, rather brash-looking uniformed official. "But my understanding was that a car would come for me in the morning."

The man shrugged. "Comrade Stalin has changed his mind. My orders are to take you now."

Perturbed, Bodrev let the man in. "Very well, let me get my coat and bag, please."

Traffic was light along the Moscow–Smolensk Road. After a few kilometers of skirting the edge of the Moskva River, the automobile slowed and the chauffeur made a right turn. They were now climbing up a narrow, winding road with tall pines on either side. The light was fading when Bodrev spotted the dacha — *more like a rustic cabin in the woods*, he thought.

"We're surely not at Comrade Stalin's villa?" he asked.

"No… You will be here for the night, however — as my guest."

"I-I don't understand."

"It is quite simple, Dr. Bodrev. You have been temporarily detained."

CHAPTER 5

June 28, 1941

The Ukrainian fantasized once or twice on how it was to be done. He would pick Stalin off as he traveled back and forth from the Kremlin to Kuntsevo. But it was a silly fantasy; it could never work. To get a shot or bomb his car would be near impossible (although he went to the trouble of carefully, over a period of time, observing Stalin's transport entourage). The general secretary's convoy included five ZiL limousines and one Packard; the paranoid dictator sat in a different vehicle each time. Besides, at the moment, he wasn't traveling but remained secluded in his dacha!

As a student of history, the "how to assassinate" problem reminded him of the People's Will hunt for Tsar Alexander II. They shot at him and missed; they mined the track on which his train was traveling and blew up the wrong train; they put dynamite under the dining room of the palace — it exploded, killing eleven servants, but no tsar.

They finally got him, though, on the Catherine Canal embankment, on his way home to the Winter Palace. Like Stalin, Alexander II was well protected, including a bomb-proof carriage. A bomb was indeed thrown, producing minor damage to the royal transport only. But then the tsar made a fatal mistake: He let his guard down, emerging from the carriage to survey the damage. There was a second bomber six feet away... *Will Stalin let his guard down?* the

Ukrainian idly wondered. And, of course, there was the problem of getting away. The crude homemade device that blew up Alexander II also killed the assassin.

If the NKVD didn't get him, then those who conscripted him as the instrument of retribution might. He didn't even know who they were exactly — other than, it appeared, a military coup in the making. This mission was too desperate, too hastily conceived to have a chance of success.

And yet here he was in front of Vlasik, showing him Bodrev's identification papers. Stalin's security chief was all business. "Doctor Dimitri Bodrev." He glanced sternly at the accompanying photo and then the face. "From Leningrad?"

"Yes, yes — no doubt you are aware that Comrade Stalin sent for me. He's in need of a medical specialist — I am expected." He realized he was babbling. Of course, he was expected; they had sent a car for him.

Vlasik grunted his confirmation. "You will not be detained any longer than necessary — please, you must be searched." With that, the crusty man stepped back and a young uniformed guard hurriedly moved forward. He thoroughly frisked the Ukrainian, giving Vlasik a curt nod. "And the medical bag? Please open it, Doctor."

The black leather bag contained what Bodrev had brought with him on his ill-fated journey: an assortment of delicate instruments, little bottles containing various pills and liquids, three syringes, gauze, cotton, and a stethoscope. There had been two additions: a tiny container of capsules and a vial of clear fluid.

It was a simple plan, really, and simple plans are supposed to work. The Ukrainian was told that the real Doctor Bodrev was "detained" en route to Moscow. He didn't know any of the details. In fact, he knew very little. Stalin was having stomach and digestive trouble, and his personal physician advised an expert diagnosis (although Timoshenko's attaché suggested contemptuously that Stalin's problems evolved from vodka and fear). No matter, the conspirators somehow intercepted a telephone call to the exclusive hospital at Fili, on the main highway to Minsk, where, after the appropriate consultation, it was agreed that the brilliant young doctor from Leningrad be beckoned with dispatch. From there it was simply a matter of obtaining the travel itinerary, intercepting Bodrev, and substituting a reasonable facsimile.

Palms sweating, adrenaline pumping, the mind alive to impending danger, the false Bodrev was led down a long oak-paneled corridor. *The hardest part*, thought the Ukrainian, *will be to convince Stalin to take the capsules* — if not the capsules then the injection. The trick was to put him at ease — convince him that he had nothing to fear; that the good doctor would take care of him. And to believe that he could pull it off; after all, he did have medical training of sorts... On the other hand, there had been time for only a scant briefing on the real Bodrev. Suppose Stalin asked questions? Suppose someone knew Bodrev? Not likely, he was told. It was a chance he had to take. Above all, he would have to be careful of his Ukrainian accent, not to let anything slip. But that was not likely to be an issue; Moscow had "Russified" him most sufficiently, as it had Stalin.

The capsules or syringe would become effective within forty-eight hours of administration. By that time Stalin would be running a fever, followed thereafter by convulsions, and finally, it was fervently hoped, a wrenching death. Meanwhile, he was to leave the villa and promise another visit within a couple of days to see if Stalin was feeling better. Once escorted back to his hotel in Moscow, he was to disappear.

Everyone knew the suspicious, Machiavellian nature of Stalin's mind. He might ask Bodrev to take the capsules or give himself the shot as a safety precaution — for reassurance. But that contingency had been provided for. The Ukrainian was given counteracting pills for whatever poison he was to administer (he wasn't told what it was — only that it had been recently developed). Could he trust his coconspirators? *No guarantees...*

What if Stalin insisted that he stay at the villa rather than in Moscow — as his guest? It was a chance he had to take. If all came to worst, he could always swallow the cyanide capsules provided. *Don't think about it — too late to back out now.*

Vlasik came to a massive oak door with two rigid guards on either side. "Wait here, Doctor," he ordered. He knocked on the door twice, opened it slightly, peered in, and disappeared. A minute and a half later, he came out. "Comrade Stalin will see you now."

Stalin was not the imposing figure he seemed in the portraits and posters. *But that*, thought the Ukrainian, *is only to be expected.* He was, after all, only human — *yes, very human.* The general secretary stood immobile in front of a large ornate desk with a green felt top. He was dressed in a plain white open-collar field shirt that came down loosely to his khaki trousers, hiding somewhat his protruding but diminutive form. The hair was whiter than his public profile and thinner; the face seemed sunken, yellowing; the eyes were glazed, worried; and the nose blotched with deep pores and concentric veins. A supercilious smile was frozen on his lips.

The would-be assassin wanted to scream an obscenity and strike the little man down for his mother and father and Anna, his sister, and all those others wasted by the smiling monster. Here was a creature that did to a nation what an enemy could only conceive in a most hideous dream. If he had a pistol, he would have thrust it between the general secretary's legs and emptied the chamber into his dangling testicles and intestines... Now he needed control.

"Sit down, Doctor." Stalin motioned to a leather chair a few feet from the prominent desk that obviously was his work station. "Would you care for some refreshments?" The lighting was subdued, with little else in the way of furniture for such a large room. The walls were paneled with darkly stained wood; there were no paintings, photographs, or mementos of any kind. The only other item of note was the discreet liquor cabinet in one corner with an assortment of bottles outlined through the glass doors.

Easy, easy now... The Ukrainian took his seat, setting the medical bag down beside him. "No th-thank you, Comrade Stalin. I came as soon as I could—"

"Yes, from Leningrad." Stalin abruptly turned and strolled to his chair behind the desk, dropping down with a grunt. The Ukrainian noticed a crystal glass with a generous amount of golden liquid, which he presumed was either whiskey or more likely cognac. "I trust the trip was not too difficult — given our war preparations?"

The false Bodrev imagined it wouldn't be, not if he carried documents signed by the vozhd himself. "No, not difficult at all — under the circumstances."

"Did you see any Germans?"

The Ukrainian momentarily stared at the little man behind the desk. What kind of nonsensical question was that? Of course, Bodrev would not have seen any Germans, at least not German troops. Stalin's odd, twisted smile, which even his full mustache could not subsume, lingered as he awaited an answer. *Demented*, thought the Ukrainian, feeling the hairs on the back of his neck going prickly. Was Stalin being funny? Was he somehow testing him? Or did he know? He half expected the tyrant to point a bony, accusing finger at him and declare that he had been found out, that the game was up, that guards would suddenly appear and haul him away.

"No, Comrade Stalin, I saw no Germans."

"Good! Then we have not been overrun. The rumormongers are wrong."

"Leningrad is safe." As far as the Ukrainian knew.

Stalin exhaled a nervous laugh. "That's encouraging news — from someone who has actually come from there…" He reached for his drink then thought better of it. "The Germans are cunning, you know. Their counterintelligence has set up special commando units to sabotage vital supplies and spread chaos within our ranks — especially in our major cities. There are German agents everywhere."

"I know of no such activity. I have witnessed nothing unusual."

There was an awkward pause. Stalin did not respond; instead, he seemed to have drifted off in thought, ignoring the man seated before him. The Ukrainian sought to fill in the oppressive silence. "Your illness, Comrade Stalin—"

"Yes, well, it seems my physician is somewhat concerned over an occasional pain in my gut — thinks it might be gastritis and suggested, as a prudent measure, your authoritative opinion. Are you acquainted with my physician, Doctor Sansov?"

The Ukrainian thought quickly. In his instructions, no one thought to include Stalin's personal doctor. Where was he? Did he know Bodrev personally? Suddenly, everything hinged on the correct response. The would-be assassin suppressed rising panic. "No, I-I don't think I have ever met him."

"Oh?" Stalin expressed mild surprise. "Nikolai spoke highly of you."

The Ukrainian shifted uncomfortably in his seat. "My reputation, no doubt, has been blown out of proportion. Our paths have never crossed that I can recall. But I should like to meet him — to discuss your case."

"Nikolai will come by later. He has been detained unavoidably in Moscow." The general secretary did not elaborate. "He would most certainly want to speak with you."

"Good. Now, Comrade Stalin, your illness—"

"As I said, Nikolai seems to think that it is this gastritis… I think, however, his concern is unfounded…" He waved his arms, one slightly atrophied, in a dismissive gesture.

"Still, a wise precaution…" The Ukrainian smiled, as if he understood Stalin's nonchalant attitude as an exhibition of Soviet manliness regardless of innermost anxieties regarding his health.

"Yes, of course, but first tell me a little more about yourself and Leningrad. It has been a long time since I have had the pleasure of visiting our Venice of the North." As he spoke, Stalin reached for a pipe that lay hidden behind a thick folder on the desk. His voice was calm, disarming, but the Ukrainian noticed he could barely control his hand as he lit the briar; the flame danced wildly. He noticed, too, the glass tray overflowing with ashes and yellowed cigarette butts.

CHAPTER 6

These last few days had not been easy for Stalin. He had panicked, felt himself choking while his world began to crumble. His confidence had oozed away, only to be replaced by nausea and the bitter taste of bile, fueled by a generous consumption of alcohol. Bodrev had arrived at a bad time; the general malaise he endured had only one cure: the defeat of the Germans; and the doctor had no prescription for that.

I do not want to be beaten, thought Stalin as he took measure of the physician. I have worked too long to make this a self-sufficient industrial nation instead of a country of dirty peasants! Now shall I hide behind illness? To hide is to be beaten!

It flooded back to him, like the last seconds of a dying man as his life flashes by. His useless father, a drunken serf, masquerading as a shoemaker who had his throat slashed in a brawl outside a whorehouse... His mother, who adored him and worked herself to shriveled frailty as a seamstress so that her son could attend a religious school in Gori and the theological seminary in Tiflis. She wanted her child to be a priest — a priest of all things! That didn't last long; he was expelled from the seminary when he joined a Marxist society.

There was something psychologically appealing about the Marxist outcasts: their grand vision, their belief that they were right, that they had discovered the path historical events were destined to take; and as a result, their unquenchable thirst for power at whatever cost. It was worth those intermittent years in prison and exile in Siberia to know that they would ultimately be triumphant. Lenin became his idol, a "professional revolutionist" with one single aim: to attain and hold power. He took Lenin and his message to heart, dubbing himself, in a moment of exaggerated importance, the Lenin of the Caucasus.

All went well for the rude, crude, insolent Georgian with no fixed address or occupation when the Bolsheviks took power. Destiny was now being fulfilled. Lenin liked him in those heady days; after all, he labored hard, diligently, and did not argue with his more illustrious and well-known comrades, especially Lenin. An original member of the Politburo, within two years of the Bolshevik's seizure of government, he was made general secretary of the Central Committee. With the aid of his competent but pedestrian colleague, Molotov, he began molding this post into the most influential in government — its nerve center. Soon, he had the practical day-to-day power in the bureaucracy.

Of course, he was also fortunate. When he disregarded Lenin and brutally crushed the self-determination efforts of his countrymen in Georgia and then insulted Krupskaya, Lenin's wife, the older man was outraged. He probably would have deposed the young, immature upstart had he not suffered his third and final stroke... Most fortuitous indeed, thought Stalin with a smile. It allowed him to suppress Lenin's damning testament and, in the process, his emerging opponents who believed he was amassing too much control. Through the 1920s, unimpeded in any serious way, he proceeded to undermine and where possible eliminate his political rivals.

It was quite easy. First came Trotsky, the arrogant Jew who did not stoop to dirty his hands on Stalin because the general secretary was of no consequence, possessing "a third-rate provincial mind." By the time he took serious notice of Stalin, it was too late; he had been isolated, outmaneuvered. Then came Zinoviev and Bukharin; he played one off against the other until both were politically neutralized during the purges. The purges. Yes! A stroke of genius, very satisfying...

He had done away with his internal enemies, hundreds of thousands of them; he had put the nation on the road to becoming a mighty industrial state, and he avoided war, or so he believed until now. He plotted meticulously to turn the West against Hitler. Let the capitalists and fascists square off, and while the two destroyed each other, he would sit back and later mop up the spoils. That was the way he envisioned destiny to unfold. What went wrong? The West had disappointed him; they were much weaker than he could have possibly imagined. That was it! Stalin realized that he had underestimated the Poles and the French and their ability to deter Hitler. He had hoped that Western intelligence reports of the Nazis' impending attack were wrong... Now he grimly, involuntarily smiled — a twisted, reaffirming smile. The Nazi-Soviet honeymoon was over. Yes, it was time for action. But what was he doing while the German forces thrust deep into his domain, destroying his armies? About to receive a medical examination from a strange man from Leningrad!

Why was he caught by surprise? He knew it was coming. Everyone knew about Operation Barbarossa. Churchill and Roosevelt had warned him; They were trying to trick me was his initial thought. But he knew better; he watched the Germans move into Yugoslavia, Bulgaria, Romania, even Finland. He watched and did nothing. That was fatal. The generals would laugh — are laughing. Three million German invaders caught Comrade Stalin with his finger stuck up his ass...

He had not measured up — had deserted his post. But was he not the man of steel? Was he not infallible? That's what he led the country to believe — the great vozhd — or did they?

Yes, the generals; what did the generals think? What of Timoshenko, the supreme commander, or Marshal Zhukov. Surely they were resentful of the purges in their ranks — of him. They were potential Bonapartists! Trotskyites! They were plotting; he could smell their resentment, insurrection. He was in danger of a coup and needed to get a grip.

All these ignominious thoughts quickly raced through Stalin's suddenly lucid mind. He must pull himself together; the voice of authority must be heard again, just as it had been heard for more than a dozen years of supreme power...

Enough! There was nothing wrong with him that a little sobering up and a grasp on reality couldn't cure — the doctor from Leningrad had better go to where he was really needed. Soon, there would be many bodies that he could be patching up.

While the Ukrainian was summing his limited knowledge of Leningrad and the medical profession, Stalin pushed a small red button under the desk. Vlasik appeared immediately.

"The examination is over," Stalin informed his security chief. "Make arrangements for Comrade — Doctor Bodrev's return to Leningrad, where his services will be required."

Stunned, the Ukrainian tried to think. What had occurred? "But I—"

Stalin cut him off with a wave of his hand. "I am well … the nation requires my attention more than I need yours at the moment." Besides, I have never trusted doctors. "Perhaps we shall meet again under more opportune circumstances."

That was it. There was nothing more to be said. Protest was useless or worse… The paranoid leader had abruptly dismissed his would-be assassin.

***

On July 3, 1941, the citizens of the Soviet Union may have been slightly reassured to hear the master's voice again. In dull, raspy syllables laced with a strong Georgian accent, Stalin addressed the nation over radio. First, he justified the nonaggression pact of 1939, which he and Molotov had signed with Hitler. It enabled peace, he argued, for over a year and a half, thus providing the necessary time "for preparing our forces to repulse fascist Germany." He implored the people to "fight our patriotic war of liberation against the Fascist enslavers," even if they had to leave nothing but desert in the wake of their retreat. He reminded the citizens of Napoleon's fate in his Russian invasion of 1812 and also that of Kaiser Wilhelm II in the First World War. Marxist ideology was judiciously dropped. It was an appeal to patriotism — a rallying cry for Mother Russia.

Whatever the precise effect of this particular speech, one thing was certain: Stalin was back in charge again. On July 19, he personally took over the Commissariat of Defense. He now was commander in chief of the army. Timoshenko and Zhukov would do his bidding — whatever was required of them. It was as if the assassination plot never took place. It vanished, like the two Bodrevs.

CHAPTER 7

When he was formally dropped off at the ornate revolving doors of the Metropol Hotel, the Ukrainian was relieved. Since he hastily left Kuntsevo, a gathering maelstrom of dark thoughts had engulfed him. He sat prostrate, could hardly breathe; all the calmness he exhibited earlier with Stalin had evaporated. All he could think of was that at any moment the car would be stopped and he would be found out.

Once inside his hotel suite, he relaxed, lighting a strong, pungent makhorka and greedily inhaling the harsh fumes. He needed to regain his wits and consider his options. Stalin's vagaries — or just a paranoia-fueled sixth sense — gave him no chance to succeed. Should he still go ahead and meet with Timoshenko's murky attaché as arranged? To do what! Deliver the bad news? What would be the point? He was a liability to the conspirators — a link that success or failure, his inner voice told him, made him expendable. On the other hand, what choice did he have? Could he realistically disappear ... hide?

Then there was the fate of Dr. Bodrev. He didn't know what happened to him, but nothing pleasant, it could be assumed. In a couple of days or so, the good doctor would be missed, and almost certainly a search would begin, questions would be asked. *He has my face*, the Ukrainian mused bitterly, and should the pieces ever be connected... Yes, he was in jeopardy — double-jeopardy, in fact.

So what to do? Best not stay in his suite, despite its comforts and soft bed. He was too vulnerable either as Dr. Bodrev or his impostor.

He had to risk a quick trip to his shabby apartment, take whatever personal effects he needed, and flee Moscow if he could. His scheduled rendezvous with the attaché (he started to call him that, since he didn't know his name) was a few hours off, and he could use the time to make some arrangements.

It would be pickled herring and beet salad one last time in his Kholody Street flat — not that he would miss the tiny second-floor hovel or the miserable Yamchenko, who collected the rent.

The telephone rang suddenly, jarring him to the core — an unwelcome disturbance yet beckoning. Should he pick up the receiver? He knew the answer. No doubt, the individual at the other end knew he was in. Too many observant hotel employees and lurking babushkas paid not only to clean and sweep but also to notice the whereabouts of guests.

"*Dobre Vechar*," he said, answering on the third ring.

"A black auto will arrive at the front door in ten minutes. Get in."

The line went dead. The Ukrainian recognized the voice of the attaché. No choice, then, but to prepare for the worst…

"Where are we going?" the Ukrainian asked once the vehicle sped away.

"A place to keep you from the public and the state's eye for a while," the attaché replied, glancing at the rearview-mirror image of the passenger behind him. They were motoring with dispatch on the Old Moscow–Smolensk highway winding along the Moskva River. Traffic was light. "There's a secluded villa where you can stay."

Thirty minutes later, the vehicle suddenly slowed and made a right turn onto a rougher, twistier road. "Almost there," the attaché assured him.

Thus far, the Ukrainian hadn't been asked about his mission. Good sign or bad? Or did it matter? Perhaps it was time to start the conversation… "So what happens now? Am I to get on with life after this?"

The attaché gave a small smile into the rearview mirror. "If only it were that simple," he said. "We're almost here," he repeated. "We'll talk about this inside over a glass of vodka and some Borodino bread."

The big car slowed down and made another right turn up a narrow lane. A low, solitary structure hunkered into the hillside came into view. The attaché stopped the vehicle and turned to the Ukrainian. "Tell me about your visit to Kuntsevo."

"It did not go well..." The Ukrainian told him of Stalin's change of heart and his abrupt dismissal. "It was like he was forewarned — like a switch suddenly flicked on. Administering the poison was impossible—"

"I see... Most unfortunate, bitterly disappointing, in fact. And you gave him no reason to be suddenly suspicious?"

"No ... none."

"And he did not explain himself? Give you any reason to terminate your examination?"

"No. We actually didn't get to the medical part."

"Just the nature of the man, I suppose ... otherwise he wouldn't have survived this long. Well, never mind now: let's go inside."

Both men exited the car. The attaché gestured for the Ukrainian to precede him up the narrow path to what seemed, on closer inspection, no more than a cabin or small hunting lodge.

Halfway up the path, the attaché stopped, and the Ukrainian heard the distinct click of a cocked gun. He turned to confront a Nagant revolver pointed at him, apparently extracted from beneath the attaché's light-gray army tunic.

"I am sorry, Comrade. I truly am, but success or failure was not a factor in regards to your fate. We appreciate your attempt, but as you know, actions of such magnitude eventually leak out — like sewage from a ruptured pipe. You can't stop it. Such leaks need to be minimized. You cannot be allowed to walk away — get on with your life as you put it — especially with your notable face."

The Ukrainian nodded. He had foolishly hoped that it would not come to this, despite his instincts screaming otherwise. He should have been prepared... "So I am to suffer the same fate as Dr. Bodrev?"

"He, like you, will have disappeared. You will be joining him shortly — not far from here, in fact."

The attaché squeezed the heavy trigger as the Ukrainian closed his eyes and imagined steppes and sky meeting on a crimson horizon.

There was a bang and flash, but the Ukrainian was spared his eight grams of lead. The Nagant exploded in the attaché's right hand, propelling bits of metal and lead forward toward the stunned Ukrainian and backward into the shooter. The attaché screamed and brought his seared hand up to his damaged face. The Ukrainian fled into the darkening woods.

CHAPTER 8

July 29, 1941

Leonid Bakinin felt the sepulchral gloom of the Lubyanka as he climbed up the stairs to the third floor and briskly walked down the long hall to his superior's office. It could not be otherwise, given its function and occupants.

To be sure, it was a handsome edifice built just before the dawn of the twentieth century to house the All Russian Insurance Company. Located in the core of Moscow, its mixture of Paladin and Bourque architecture — minute pediments over the corners, a central loggia, multiple cornices, and an impressive façade topped by a center clock — was the company's signature statement of status and wealth.

But then came the revolution, and Imperial Russia crumpled. The structure was appropriated by the "proletariat" as headquarters for CHEKA (All Russian Extraordinary Commission for Combating Counterrevolution and Sabotage). As the new Soviet state's enemies grew in number, so did the ministry and the building. By 1940, it had doubled in size with the addition of another story and extension into the back streets. Bakinin witnessed firsthand the feverous expansion activity as he skirted gray gangs of workmen, ducked under hastily erected scaffolding, and negotiated assorted piles of construction equipment and materials. Only the third floor, where important officials and ministers resided, remained undisturbed, seemingly untouched by the mayhem nearby.

With a stuttered step, Bakinin halted at Colonel General Genrith Pestrov's door, staring at the intricate parquet flooring while collecting his thoughts, and knocked. There was no way around this; despite his best efforts, the investigation had yielded nothing useful, and Colonel General Pestrov would not be pleased.

"Come."

Colonel General Pestrov sat behind an enormous dark oak desk. He wore a simple gray military tunic with a turned-down collar and epaulets, the style of Soviet leaders — not much distinguished from his own soldier's shirt, Bakinin noted. He couldn't see the trousers…

Pestrov capped his pen and carefully set aside the documents in front of him; he raised his head. An imposing figure with a high forehead and receding hairline, eyebrows arched, stretching the crow's feet at the corner of his eyes as he took full measure of his subordinate and waited. Behind him, hanging on the pale-green wall, was a portrait of Stalin with an accusing glare aimed directly at Bakinin, also waiting.

"No results, Colonel General."

"Nothing?" Pestrov's tone was sharp, and the broken capillaries on his nose seemed to redden.

Bakinin stood ramrod straight, stretching his diminutive frame as upright as possible. "No, results," he repeated. "Dr. Bodrev seems to have disappeared."

"I see," Pestrov said, mulling things over. "You had a task, and you failed," he declared in a tone somewhere between anger and alarm. "This does not bode well for you — or me," he added, running his thumb and index finger through a thin, well-trimmed mustache.

"Yes, Colonel General," Bakinin acknowledged, his voice flat.

Indeed, he had failed in his assignment, which had come from the highest level. And now there would be consequences.

Bakinin's mission began with a terse communiqué saying that the medical specialist who had come from Leningrad to see Stalin had inexplicably vanished. Normally, this wouldn't have been of great concern to the NKVD since, on occasion, individuals were known to "disappear" after visiting Stalin. However, this event quickly took on an ominous tone ("odor" was the word Pestrov used) when Stalin personally demanded that Dr. Bodrev be found and brought back to Moscow (assuming he ever left). The reason remained unclear (did Stalin need a reason?) but his "request" was passed down the bureaucratic chain and landed with a thud on Pestrov's desk. Uneasy and chagrined, Pestrov gave the case to his best NKVD investigator, emphasizing to the young man that he needed a positive result. Dr. Bodrev had to be found.

Bakinin did his due diligence. Yes, Bodrev checked into the Metropol Hotel as arranged. Yes, he was picked up as scheduled and taken to Stalin's dacha. Yes, he "consulted" with the great leader. Yes, he was dropped off at the hotel thereafter and was seen going into his suite. Later, he was spotted in the lobby, and nothing after that.

Despite Bakinin's and the *militsiya*'s best efforts, the illustrious doctor was nowhere to be found.

"He went somewhere and never came back," Pestrov declared when he first summoned Bakinin. "No less than Comrade Stalin wants to know why. It is making him suspicious, and when Comrade Stalin is suspicious, bad things are sure to happen…"

Bakinin was thorough. The wife in Leningrad had been contacted, questioned, and detained. Hospitals, railway stations, and train coaches had been searched and were under surveillance. Photographs of Bodrev (acquired from his wife then cropped and reproduced) were posted strategically in public places. The full resources of the NKVD and the Moscow Militsiya had been employed, to no avail. The man had become a ghost.

Pestrov's mild reaction to Bakinin's bad news signified resignation, if not defeat. Berating his subordinate, who had proven quite capable and efficient in his assignments — whether ferreting out plots against the state or finding individuals — would not accomplish anything. For all he knew, Stalin was aware of what happened to the doctor and ordered this investigation as a ruse to redirect or misdirect attention for some unfathomable reason or simply to rid himself of a doctor who diagnosed his illness. Or not! Which meant that the fatherland's leader would not let the matter rest. He'd want to know who was behind this. But then, who could know the truth or read Stalin's mind? The fact remained: He would report "no progress" to his immediate boss four doors down the hall.

That, in turn, would be relayed to Stalin.

Pestrov sighed. "You know what this means?"

"Yes, Colonel General."

"I heard it said that this is the tallest building in Moscow and that Siberia can be seen from the basement. You and I may well have the opportunity to verify such a claim."

PART TWO

CHAPTER 9

June 30, 1974, Moscow

Andrei Drydenko sat rigidly at his desk. With his thick bifocals and high, creased forehead, he had the appearance of a fastidious Marxist Institute professor intently poring over his lecture notes. In fact, he was judiciously studying two dossiers, but not for a lecture on communist dogma. The red manila folders contained data on two men, one of which brought back haunting memories and the faint smell of fear. His right hand instinctively reached for the scarred side of his face; his fingers circled along the rigid, jagged tissue that extended from the jowls to his diminished left eye, which would never properly focus. The surface felt cratered, like the moonscape. Self-inflicted, to be sure, all those years ago, but there was a nemesis who now stared benignly back at him from the dossier folder. Much older, but there was no doubt about the features ... and an opportunity to finally close a chapter.

It took a long time — over thirty years, in fact — to hunt this man down. While, no doubt, it entailed some luck and fortuitous circumstances, success was due to the diligent work of the Orilov brothers, Ivan and Yuri, who identified and located the fugitive. The Orilovs were the linchpin of the research unit in his section. Over the last three years, they had systematically scoured mountains of postwar émigré lists, records from DP camps throughout Europe, ship passenger manifests, and other more nefariously compiled and acquired registries. They traced him initially to London then lost him again. He had immigrated to Canada, as it turned out. *Rather silly of him not to have changed his name,* thought Drydenko; *an odd oversight for a man on the run... Maybe he believed that he got away — that he was safe...* No point in speculating. He had been found, and Drydenko made a mental note to suitably reward the Orilovs.

Still, Drydenko couldn't simply brand him a traitor, enemy of the state, and order a hit. He'd have to build a case and convince the head and possibly other directors of the KGB (and ultimately the Politburo) to "sanction" the target. Like everything else in this bureaucratic country, the Committee of State Security had become hopelessly institutionalized. Consequently, Drydenko had the Orilovs prepare a carefully crafted indictment to justify the elimination of the target. The Orilovs had the necessary expertise and could fabricate almost any story with convincing documentation if need be.

Once he received their thick file, Drydenko hesitated and rethought his approach. It would certainly raise questions — perhaps too many questions. This one, he finally decided, would have to be done unofficially — off the books. *Like James Bond,* he mused, having just seen a dubbed copy of *Diamonds Are Forever* on his beta machine.

Drydenko again, for what seemed the hundredth time, scanned the file. He still needed the Orilov dossier for credible context — in case it came to light and questions were asked. Viktor Glinka's crimes had to be formally noted, if not exposed for full review. Thus, a litany of charges ... former Nazi supporter and hooligan ... disseminated mendacious propaganda about conditions in the USSR ... worked for Western intelligence recruiting his fellow countrymen for the purpose of espionage. Officially, Glinka had to die for past war crimes. For Drydenko, his own personal reasons aside, the issue was more immediate than settling old scores: Glinka was a potential threat, a clear and present danger to him as he was about to emerge from relative obscurity and make his bid for the chairmanship of the KGB.

Still, there were doubts, usually late at night when he lay in his bed, staring into the darkness, his mind racing... He had convinced himself to let sleeping dogs lie. Why dig up old bones that could get stuck in your throat? It was long ago; the other participants were dead, and who would care? But no, he had enemies — and friends for that matter — with ambitions of their own. If there ever was a sniff, a thread of what he was part of during those tumultuous days in June 1941, he would be unraveled — exposed. That knowledge would be massaged, manipulated to totally destroy him. That was just the way the system worked. Any chance of discovery, no matter how unlikely, had to be covered. Moreover, Dr. Bodrev had a younger brother who was now a highly placed candidate for Politburo status. He most certainly wondered what happened to his illustrious older sibling after his visit to Stalin's dacha. The assumption, never fully articulated, was that Stalin gave an order and Bodrev disappeared. Drydenko knew better, and so did Glinka.

Drydenko readjusted his sitting posture, allowing his elongated frame to relax slightly. For almost twenty years he had labored in this elaborate edifice on 2 Dzerzhinsky Square. Here on the third floor, amid paneled mahogany, ornate sofas, and padded chairs, was the center of an organization with tentacles to almost every nation in the world. Lenin had created it as a necessary tool to protect the revolution. Then it was known as the CHEKA. Strangely enough, the more it punished saboteurs, traitors, and a variety of other miscreants, the more it became imperative to punish. The number of enemies both from within and out seemed to grow. *Like rabbits in a breeding frenzy*, mused Drydenko. So the agency continued to expand until, under Stalin, it became a state within a state.

After Stalin died in 1953, his heirs had curbed its independent police powers somewhat, but there had been political compensations. Recently, the KGB chief had been elevated to the Politburo. Of course, one also had to survive within its system. Drydenko was acutely aware of the agency's record of devouring its own.

Drydenko had more than survived; he had reached a position of influence in its upper echelons. But that still wasn't enough. He wanted to be boss. He aspired to sit in the chairman's seat, to stare at the six telephones within his reach, direct lines to the general secretary, to members of the Politburo, and to the Soviet embassies around the world. He would control a vast army of 50,000 career officers and another 150,000 secret foot soldiers scattered throughout the globe. It was within his grasp.

With rumors of the pending retirement of Ivan Yanev, the current chief — ill health, apparently — the path was open. *It might even be true,* he idly wondered. *After all, Yanev is pushing eighty!* There was only one serious competitor, Leonid Bakinin, a tough, shrewd opponent who also had support within the organization and the Politburo. He didn't like Bakinin much, and he was sure that the feeling was mutual; he, too, was ambitious and ruthless. If he should ever find out — Drydenko shuddered at the thought.

No! He simply could not afford to have his part in the "affair" come to light. It would be fatal, and not only to his career. No matter how remote the possibility of such an occurrence, this was one of the nagging details that had to be laid to rest. Lenin said it during his first days in office — the communists' manifesto and Stalin's creed — get them before they get you. He had to get Glinka, the only man left alive who could expose him. Yuri, Glinka's friend who'd dragged him into the assassination plot, hadn't survived the war, and Timoshenko (not that he would ever tell) died over five years ago in Leningrad, while he just recently attended the funeral of General Zhukov.

Drydenko sighed as he reflected on the march of time. It seemed only yesterday. Not that age was particularly against him. At fifty-eight, he was relatively young compared to many of his "senior" comrades, and he kept fit. Didn't Klara just the other day remark breathlessly on his insatiable virility and how he exhausted her in bed? And she was not even half his age! For an instant, he felt bestirred but mentally checked it. He did not want to lose his concentration on matters at hand.

Yes, it took luck, he realized, but also tenacity, energy, discipline, ruthlessness, and above all, driving ambition. Now he was ready. In a system that rewarded patronage, Drydenko had tied himself to the rising stars. First, to those close to Khrushchev and then to confidants of Brezhnev, all the while keeping his options open and head down. It was time to cash in on his long game replete with owed favors.

For the third time, he turned his attention to the second dossier. It contained a detailed profile on one Alexandr Lucovich, the agent he would assign to "neutralize" Glinka. Lucovich appeared to be exactly what Drydenko wanted for this off-the-book assignment. He was at arm's length from Drydenko and, more to the point, was well honed in the English world, from the language to important bits of perspective and culture. All seemed in order. The man's professional record appeared beyond reproach. Nevertheless, he again surveyed Lucovich's history.

Lucovich was born in Borshtshevize, a district near Lviv, incorporated into the USSR after the Second World War. The son of a Ukrainian kulak, he was attending a teacher's training college in Lviv when he came to the notice of the KGB. The young student, eighteen at the time, took a train trip to his native village without acquiring the proper papers. *Or a valid ticket, for that matter*, thought Drydenko, turning to the next page on the document. Caught by the railway authorities, the frightened young man was taken to a local office of the state security police, where an interrogation and investigation followed. Ultimately, KGB officials "persuaded" Lucovich to work for them against a local Ukrainian-dissident movement operating in the area. Drydenko smiled, reading between the lines. He knew well the threats and inducements employed on the compromised youth; he had participated in a good many of these himself. The interrogators would accuse him and his family of sympathizing with the dissidents, possibly aiding and abetting them. After long, intensive debriefing designed to disorient the target, officials then would give him a way out, an ultimatum: Either take an active part in the fight against these nationalistic traitors and hooligans or be deprived of freedom or worse. No doubt they dangled the stick of deportation to Siberia for the whole Lucovich clan.

Lucovich took the offer; he was really in no position to do otherwise.

At any rate, Lucovich infiltrated the dissident movement and exposed the ringleaders. Drydenko skipped the details; he had been through them before. Of course, once compromised, the consequences invariably determined his future. It became readily apparent after this episode that it was no longer possible for him to return home or to continue his studies. He was a marked man for both sides. In a state where it was extremely difficult, if not impossible, to make a living or otherwise survive without government approval, Lucovich had no choice but to remain in the service of the KGB. *Perhaps he even learned to enjoy it!* Drydenko speculated.

In due course, Lucovich was summoned to Kharkov for "special training." In a cluster of low gray nondescript square buildings, he was not only trained in the devious arts of KGB subterfuge and weapons use but also received intensive instruction in the English language. In his case, this included not only the Voice of America idiom but also the proper Queen's English as broadcasted by the BBC. Indeed, he was groomed for assignments in the United Kingdom. Drydenko perused the instructors' reports — a most proficient student. Later, in preparation for his future duties, he absorbed in minute detail the life of his assumed alias, one Adam Woodal, a resident of London and a British national. He took a trip to London toward the end of his graduation to familiarize himself with the territory.

To become Adam Woodal, Drydenko knew, was remarkably easy. Death and birth records were readily available and not cross-referenced. A visit to a British library and a search of obit pages in old newspapers invariably garnered a suitable candidate who fit the time frame required. After a duly paid-for birth certificate was obtained, an alias could be forged... Drydenko smiled. Woodal, it appeared, was gainfully employed as a clerk in the men's attire department at Harrods, no less.

Drydenko skipped a number of descriptive, unimportant pages and read on. The London trip turned out to be one of many. Over a five-year period, the British capital became Lucovich/Woodal's second home, complete with a comfortable flat. He took field notes, engaged in reconnaissance activity and low-level espionage, acting as a go between for more experienced agents. He spied on émigrés from the Soviet Union and their organizations, wherever possible enlisting their cooperation, and in general was a skilled and valuable sleeper — at least according to the reports of his handler.

Lucovich's first real assignment as a trained operative involved monitoring the activities of a certain Ukrainian émigré, Danylo Rabiak. He was to observe his home and become intimately acquainted with his habits. The purpose became clear enough when a high-ranking agent from Moscow (traveling on a phony passport as a Dutch businessman) showed up at his London flat and presented him with a relatively new weapon, an innocent looking hollow cylindrical apparatus that could easily be concealed in one's coat pocket. Drydenko did not need to read the details; he was quite familiar with the device. He had once been privy to a demonstration: Slip off the safety catch, get within range, point it at the face of the target, and squeeze the trigger. Very ingenious and lethal. A spray of prussic acid would noiselessly squirt forward. Death was almost instantaneous; the victim's respiratory organs were completely paralyzed. The beauty of the weapon was that, afterward, all traces of the deadly poison dissipated. An autopsy would reveal nothing; the cause of death would appear natural — a heart attack.

Drydenko rubbed his eyes and ran his fingers through his thinning hair. That was the older, cruder method of killing. Since then, the techniques had been refined considerably.

The important thing for Drydenko was that Lucovich carried out his orders unquestioningly. According to the dossier, it was a flawless mission. Lucovich eliminated his unsuspecting target, took the anti-poison ampoule provided, got rid of the weapon, and boarded a flight to Frankfurt am Main and from there to Berlin to report and be debriefed.

The psychological profile indicated no apparent remorse, guilt, or search for justification. *Good*, thought Drydenko. Last thing he needed was a Dostoyevskian drama of conscience and remorse. It was important that the assassin be Bond, not

Raskolnikov! Lucovich seemed to possess the mentality and temperament for this sort of cold and calculated work. For Drydenko, this was critical; otherwise, potential problems could arise. Suffice it for the operative to know that he had been issued orders that had to be carried out because the state could only act in the interests and welfare of the Soviet people.

Drydenko read no further, satisfying himself that Lucovich could be counted on for discretion, efficiency, and trustworthiness. Glinka would die by the hand of Lucovich.

Yet this mission would also require a certain delicate touch. There was more on the line than just the elimination of a traitor. *No, pondered Drydenko, this is not a straightforward assassination. Not by a long shot. Problems may arise.* Again, he opened Glinka's file and frowned. Parts of Glinka's background were obscured — ever since he suddenly disappeared in '41. True, he reappeared in '43 as a collaborator with the Germans, only to vanish again. His trail was picked up in London after the war. Apparently, he had a liaison with another émigré while in the English capital. The result was a daughter. Drydenko quickly found the appropriate page. *Yes, it is here.* He scanned her birth date, making a quick calculation. She'd be in her early thirties now. Her mother, Galina, died from some undisclosed illness when the child was three so that father and daughter were no doubt close. *Close enough to share secrets best left in the shadows? Something to seriously consider...* This offspring might be of no consequence or might prove quite troublesome.

Glinka and his daughter now lived together in Canada. Drydenko wetted his thumb and turned the pages — in Edmonton, Alberta, which was somewhere on the Canadian steppes, he presumed. But geography had no bearing on the issue. What was important was whether Glinka confided in her. A father might unburden his soul to his daughter. A sudden thought seized Drydenko — *or a trusted friend?* He dismissed the thought; it created too many variables. Besides, friends could be neutralized more effectively than his offspring, if it came to that. If anyone else knew, then it would be her. What to do about her?

Drydenko leaned back in his seat and closed his eyes for a moment. Lucovich would be instructed to make contact with the daughter to ascertain if she was privy to any information "harmful to the Soviet Union." She might even prove useful. Through her, perhaps, he could complete the second part of his assignment: the destruction of Glinka's documents, official records, and memoirs, if any existed. Drydenko shifted uncomfortably in his chair. He really couldn't afford to have any of what Glinka was involved with leak out. His opponents only needed a small clue to piece together the story that would destroy him.

That posed another problem: Lucovich himself. True, ingrained in any field agent was the absolute imperative that whatever came to light was strictly confined to the orders issued. Still, if possible, Lucovich was not to discover the real reason why Drydenko needed Glinka dead. But if he did: could he be trusted? Indeed, would he carry out his orders blindly, without question? *Enough!* He closed the dossiers. He would make the appropriate decision when and if it was necessary. The essential thing now was to meet with Lucovich, feel him out, impress on him the delicate nature of his task, and hint at suitable rewards upon its successful completion.

CHAPTER 10

First came the image of the dog, a German Shepherd tethered on a long leash in the compound. The animal was friendly, raising its muzzle toward him, the tail wagging. Then he squeezed the trigger. The canine staggered drunkenly on his hind legs and fell over dead. *Don't think about it — as easy as killing the dog — routine, an automatic reflex.* At least it was so according to his stone-faced, sour-breathed instructor. At the time, he wasn't so sure; he liked dogs.

Next appeared the image of the man he'd killed, the murder weapon a short tube only as thick as his middle finger, wrapped up in an issue of the *Manchester Guardian*. It was all so simple. No need to take careful aim, just pass by and pull the trigger. No struggle, no scream, no blood, just a low smacking sound and the fleeting look of astonishment and incredulity as the target reeled backward, collapsed, and died, just like the dog.

Alexandr Lucovich opened his eyes with a start, the sweat glistening on his brow. He had relived these images — he refused to call them nightmares — many times over, always with the same hollow feeling when he awoke. They had congratulated him on the completion of his task: He was "the extended arm of retribution," to quote his superior. Possibly in some bureaucratic sense, but out in the field, it was simply sanctioned death by methods that violated his sense of proper form and perhaps morality.

He was a murderer; he snuffed out the life of another person in a most nefarious fashion, which struck him as cowardly, and no amount of official praise or polemical jargon in a report filed away in the archives of a KGB vault could change that fact.

Five years later, he could still vividly visualize the act. His orders were precise. He was to lie in wait for Rabiak near his home and find the opportunity. He followed instructions, but what the files would never show were the chances he let slip by, his inner voice screaming *No! Not now! Wait one more day — maybe tomorrow.* Each time he'd breathed a sigh of relief until the next day, spying anew, waiting and anxiously checking his watch.

After an anguish-filled week of such inner indecision and turmoil, he could stand it no longer. He decided that if Rabiak came by along his usual route, he'd follow through with the plan, if not … perhaps he simply couldn't and would face the consequences. Regular as clockwork, however, Rabiak appeared, taking his usual shortcut between the two apartment buildings before crossing the street to his flat. Lucovich had determined almost a week before that the alley was the ideal spot with little foot traffic — at least late in the afternoons — and allowed for close proximity without arousing suspicion.

Perspiring profusely despite the unseasonable autumn cold spell in London, he proceeded into the alley toward his victim. A sense of desperation was overtaking him… *It must be done. It must be done…* In the end, it was quite mechanical, and in a matter of seconds, the man was down, suffering from an apparent stroke. No one noticed, and Lucovich briskly walked on.

A low moan tore Lucovich away from his thoughts. The whore was awake. He scratched the stubble on his chin and glanced around his surroundings; he was in the usual Spartan, drab room he occupied while in Moscow, on the third floor of the Red Star Hotel. It was erected sometime in the twenties, a heavy, somber structure that no doubt suited well Stalin's concept of durable architecture. He could afford better; he could even rent a villa complete with a high-priced mistress, but his trips to Moscow were infrequent, and he preferred, for reasons not altogether clear to him, to frequent this dive in the more decayed, humble sections of the city. "Maybe it is my punishment or my peasant roots," he muttered to himself, glancing around. Last night was good — a palatable meal, drinkable vodka (although it stank like something between old socks and paraffin), and a working girl to warm his bed.

Now, in the sober dawn of day, he turned to the prostitute. He threw back the covers on the squeaking bed and stared at the nude female sprawled beside him. *Pretty*, he thought, *fleshy but not fat and generously endowed*. "Good morning."

"Good morning to you too." She rolled over to face him and smiled.

"Sleep well?"

"Fine." She stretched and suppressed a yawn. "What time is it?"

Lucovich peered at the night table, reached over, and fumbled with his wristwatch. "Eight — I think." He had trouble focusing on the Gruen watch dial.

"Should I be leaving soon?"

He strapped his watch on and turned more squarely toward her. His appointment wasn't until eleven. "Not necessarily. There is no particular rush… Why? Are you in a hurry?"

"I can be detained," she said in a flat, matter-of-fact voice.

"Good… Do you live nearby?"

She studied him carefully, and Lucovich noticed the crow's feet around the eyes and the sagging cheeks, which he had not the night before. No doubt the light of day sharpened the perspective. "Why do you ask?" She suddenly sounded suspicious.

"No reason — making conversation."

"No — no, I don't."

"You just work the Red Star?" Of course, she did. He picked her up at the bar lounge, or was it the other way around…

"Sometimes."

"It's a shabby hotel."

"Yes, but the management is … amenable."

"Ah … I see. You are part of the 'in-tourist' service package, without the tourists."

She did not answer but shifted uncomfortably on the bed. Sensing her growing unease, Lucovich realized he should have stopped his indiscreet questioning, but he was curious. "Nadyezhda…" He hoped he remembered her name correctly. "Do you enjoy this kind of work?" It was a stupid question in many ways, but still…

"It depends on the customers. Some are pleasant; some are not," she said with a slight shrug.

"Which am I?"

"You were pleasant but are becoming personal."

"My apologies. I was just interested—"

"Personal questions make me nervous — you understand?"

"I understand."

Officially, call girls were not supposed to exist. Unofficially, it was a fringe occupation. As long as there was a need and the guardians of socialist morality could be induced (or seduced) to turn a blind eye, the profession would continue to exist. Lucovich knew that prostitution, along with alcoholism, urban crime, broken homes, and drug abuse, was viewed in certain quarters as a great threat to socialist stability — certainly, it was growing rapidly in every major city in the USSR. But strangely enough, unlike the other vices, it was kept out of the limelight. Public campaigns had been mounted against the demon drink, especially in the workplace, where its effects were evident in the absenteeism and poor quality of products. Also, much was said and written of the threat to the family unit; Lucovich read the statistics in the *Economist*, of all places. One out of three marriages were annulled in the first year, and Soviet women, on average, had six abortions during their lifetime. All this was general knowledge, but little was known about the young (and not so young) ladies of the street. They were a rarely mentioned commodity in a burgeoning, albeit unsanctioned, private economy. *Thank God the state hasn't collectivized the prostitutes*, he mused. These women made his visits to Moscow that much more bearable…

Nadyezhda sat up, making no attempt to cover herself. "Let's talk about other things."

"Okay, if you don't want to talk—"

"Of course, I don't want to!" she said rather emphatically. "It's black-market business that is frowned upon. I am not like the high-class Gorky Park girls who are protected," she added.

"Then why do it?"

"That's a silly question. Why did you approach me?"

"I didn't want to eat dinner alone, and I wanted to get laid."

"You wanting to get laid pays for my flat."

Lucovich decided he liked this earthy woman. "In that case, I will ask no more questions… I did enjoy it last night, by the way."

"You paid for it."

Straightforward — that's what Lucovich appreciated about the more ordinary Muscovites. Nadyezhda had no illusions. In his complicated lie of a life, she was a refreshing interlude. He appraised her more critically. A wide, generous face capped with thick black hair carelessly parted down the middle. He hadn't thought of sex before breakfast, but what the hell. He moved closer and his hands wandered. She responded in kind.

"Same as last night with cab fare and breakfast thrown in?" he said.

"Why not."

Why not indeed, he thought. It was a good way to start what would no doubt prove to be an anxious day. Soon he would be making his way to Dzerzhinsky Square.

CHAPTER 11

Drydenko thought Lucovich a rather striking figure. Thick brown hair peppered lightly with gray; a firm jawline; straight nose; about five foot ten; trim and possessing expressive eyes, which were brown, like his hair. For a fleeting second, Drydenko could feel kinship toward him, followed by melancholy and resentment. *Ye gods*, he thought, *to be in my thirties again...*

By nature, Drydenko was not overly loquacious. Whether this was due to his nature or profession, he wasn't sure — probably a combination of both — but this characteristic was evident now. In the deafening silence, his mind raced. He needed to communicate, but only in precise, measured amounts. It would be a message — between-the-lines talk, an art he had practiced diligently for years.

"Care for some cognac?" he inquired of the younger man. Lucovich took his wandering eyes off the portrait of V. I. Lenin and refocused on the lanky human with the scarred, leathery face before him. *What does this doyen want? This does not bode well...* For over five years, he had avoided any more "kill" assignments. But then he received an ominous brown envelope containing a document for his eyes only, and he was surreptitiously summoned for an interview with one of the KGB's top honchos. "Thank you, a cognac would be nice."

Drydenko pulled out a bottle of Courvoisier VSOP and two balloon snifters from a standing cabinet on the far side of his desk. He proceeded to pour generously into the glasses and handed one to Lucovich, seated in the leather chair before him. "This is a rare batch that I had ordered specially. I fancy myself as a bit of a connoisseur," he said with great satisfaction, moving around the desk to his swiveling chair.

He raised his glass. "*Nazdarovya.*"

"To your health as well," replied Lucovich, following his host in taking a smooth, warming sip. "Very fine drink." *Especially when compared to the vodka I sampled last night,* he thought.

"Yes, well…" The niceties over, Drydenko got down to the business at hand. "I have been reading your file. You are performing important services for the Komitet."

"*Spasibo* — I try," Lucovich said, feeling apprehensive. He did not like dealing with the upper echelon.

Drydenko continued, "I notice from your file that recently you have spent most of your time in London engaged in … ah … surveillance work of various kinds. Somewhat routine, I imagine, given your assignments in the past?"

"Suits me very well, sir. I have a knack for it."

"Yes, you have made valuable contacts and a number of new recruits…" Drydenko paused for a few seconds, swirling the cognac in his glass. "Now, however, you have been called upon to perform a more substantial task. You received the envelope?"

"It was delivered." *But contained a dearth of information,* he added silently.

"Good… I must ask, do you have any reservations?"

"The details were not entirely clear—"

"Yes," Drydenko interjected, "but nevertheless, even if the details are yet not entirely clear, I need to ask — do you have any reservations?"

It was a blunt, loaded question, demanding, Lucovich sensed, the expectation of an unequivocal answer.

"None that comes to mind."

"Good, there can be no doubts or vacillation on a matter such as this." Drydenko paused and asked, "I suppose you are curious why I requested to speak with you directly and not through the 'normal' channels?"

Requested? thought Lucovich. It was more like a clandestine summons — one which was not to be refused. On any new mission, he would usually be briefed by his immediate superior, Colonel Chernev, who evidently had been bypassed. "I admit the thought crossed my mind."

"Yes..." Drydenko nodded and lowered his voice as if to share a nefarious secret. "There are certain delicate intricacies involved in this particular case that I have personally taken an interest in and that necessitate not going through the established protocol."

Lucovich noted the word *personally.* That was the key. This KGB big cheese was about to deliver a cryptic yet unmistakable message. He'd better listen well.

"The man identified in the document, Viktor Glinka," continued Drydenko, "is an enemy of the state — of that there is no question. He has been found guilty by the highest authority. It is in the state's interest that he should expire."

Lucovich nodded uncertainly.

"Yes ... there are, however, possible pitfalls..." Drydenko wetted his lips on a sip of cognac. "To begin with, he has a daughter who may present a problem..." Drydenko paused and set his glass down on the desk. "She may be privy to certain information harmful to our interests."

Lucovich frowned slightly, even while keeping his expression neutral. *How did this go from the state's interests to our interests?* Moreover, there was no mention of another individual involved in the materials he received. What was this old KGB director driving at?

"It is extremely important," elaborated Drydenko, "to make contact, to — how shall I put it — befriend her, win over her confidence sufficiently to ascertain if indeed she knows anything damaging — perhaps libelous to certain members within our party."

So now it's been narrowed to you, deduced Lucovich, although he dared not ask directly to whom specifically Drydenko referred. The message was received and understood. "What sort of damaging information would I be expected to look for?" *Without actually looking for it.* That seemed to Lucovich a reasonable question, skirting the edge but not too close to a potentially fatal vortex. After all, he needed something concrete to go on.

"Ah…" Little lines of mockery formed around the corners of Drydenko's mouth. "For the moment it is best that you not know the answer, but" — he raised his right index finger — "be aware that such information may exist. If she knows nothing, then it is as it should be and of no consequences to her — or *you*."

Another quite clear message received. "I see…"

Drydenko shifted uncomfortably in his chair. Lucovich took the opportunity to gulp a healthy portion of his drink, perhaps wash down the unsavory nature of his task and their equally unsavory tacit understanding.

As if to underline his thoughts, Drydenko said, "I hope we are beginning to understand each other."

Lucovich nodded. Some sort of conspiratorial pact was in the offing. He could sense it; indeed, read it in the ambiguity etched on the older man's face. *And the one fully functional gray eye…* "What am I to do exactly with this information — should I come across it — and what of this woman?"

"With Glinka's daughter, nothing except make acquaintances, solicit information on her father, find out what she knows and … monitor. It may even prove a pleasant diversion." Drydenko gave a small, crooked smile. "Again, I emphasize she may not be privy to her father's twisted secrets, in which case, all is well. If you do discover that she may have been exposed to highly sensitive material that could injure our work — await further instructions from me." In truth, he hadn't worked out how to deal with such a contingency, although he could order it unilaterally and chalk it up to collateral damage. In his experience, however, such precipitous actions often led to complications.

Drydenko suddenly found himself furtively searching for the correct words. It was proving a bit taxing to issue instructions without divulging compromising information. It was, he recalled, like Khrushchev's secret speech in 1956, when he delineated the crimes of Stalin. It wasn't that what he said were lies — quite the contrary;

nonetheless, the more he listed Stalin's horrors, the more he implicated himself and those comrades around him. They were part and parcel of those horrors. What were they doing when the atrocities against the party and people were taking place? He shook off his wandering thoughts. "As for intelligence-gathering, again I must strongly suggest — *insist* — that you not involve yourself too directly. There are substantive rewards upon the success of this affair. At the same time, curiosity is sometimes dangerous; in this case, ignorance is the best policy."

Lucovich stared blankly at the man behind the huge green felt-top desk. Drydenko was delivering a crystal-clear message in a very obscure way.

"You are puzzled, I see," noted Drydenko.

"I understand the 'sanction,' but how I am to confirm or extract materials of concern to *our* interests without actually knowing what it is?" It was a question that needed to be asked, but *tread carefully*, he reminded himself.

"Would you light a match to see if there was gasoline in a can?" The older man sighed and then smiled; he would have to be more direct. "As you may be aware, in the near future there will be substantial changes in the Komitet — a realignment of personnel with the pending retirement of Yanev. Comrades will be promoted and possibly demoted. As far removed and inconsequential as it may appear, Glinka may be in a position to adversely affect this process of … realignment. That must not happen. And to that end, it is not only Glinka himself but his personal files — if they exist — that could do damage. Eliminate such a possibility by destroying his files, memoirs, letters — whatever the documents — using whatever methods are at your disposal. Do not copy or peruse any material, as that, too, may have unintended consequences — *for you*. Am I being understood?"

"Clearly," Lucovich responded, stunned by the nebulous, perilous nature of the mission and the internal ramifications. He had no desire to become caught or otherwise intertwined in a political struggle within the KGB.

"Good." Drydenko seemed relieved. "I am counting on your discretion … and one more matter: You can appreciate that there will be no official report of anything we speak of. In fact, we have never met! The resolution of this matter is of importance to *me* while only of secondary value to others. Thus, all communications you will deliver directly to me. *We* do not want to complicate the paperwork." He let out a little chuckle, along with his sour smile again.

"I understand."

"I sincerely hope so… You know, Alexandr…" Drydenko got up from his chair and made his way to the front of his desk, towering over the seated man, his eyes boring defiantly into the agent's, searching for what lay just below the surface. "If this is handled correctly — in an appropriate, constructive manner between *you and me* — I should envision a significant reward for your services rendered. And I don't mean just the usual decoration with the combat order of the Red Banner, but more practical, concrete rewards. It is with some modesty that I confess to aspire to the chairmanship of the Komitet. I would then be in a position to make the suitable recommendation for your well-being — if this unpleasant affair is properly disposed of."

Lucovich had just been given an inducement; the message had been made perfectly clear. And as if to underline the point, on his departure, Drydenko put his hand on Lucovich's shoulder like an old *tovarish* and declared, "I am personally counting on you to see this to a mutually satisfying end."

CHAPTER 12

Leonid Bakinin told his secretary that he should not be disturbed. That request was treated as if it were his last will and testament. He now lay on a leather couch, staring at the tiles on the ceiling of his spacious office, deep in thought.

Compared to Drydenko, Bakinin was less appealing. He stood five foot four inches in platform shoes, had a noticeably humped back, and spoke in a thin, nasal voice made particularly irritating by its raspy falsetto register. In private — very private — some dared to call him "the dwarf." The title, while not entirely appropriate, had historical merit, for Bakinin bore remarkable resemblance to another dwarf: Nikolai Yezhov, head of the NKVD from 1936 to 1938. Yezhov was universally detested in his day, and with good reason.

Stalin had dug out the bloodthirsty reptile from a provincial gutter somewhere and manipulated him to get rid of the old Bolsheviks. Of course, once this was done, Stalin got rid of him. It was generally acknowledged that Yezhov was of low intelligence, and it was at this point in the comparison that the first dwarf and the second dwarf parted company. There was more to Bakinin than filled the eye. He was bright, astute, and although a couple of years younger than Drydenko, more experienced. Nothing of note got past him within the Komitet; he knew most of the secrets, including, it was rumored, some very intimate, sordid ones from within the Politburo.

Unlike Yezhov, his reputation for ruthlessness did not come naturally; he acquired and honed it by necessity. Within a month of presenting his "disappointing" report to Colonel General Pestrov, he found himself "reassigned" to Norilsk, more specifically to the Norilsk Corrective Labor Camp, or Norillag for short. The terse order came directly from Pestrov and could only be interpreted as backlash for his failure — a failure that did not hit full gravitas until he occupied space on a rough, damp plank of a nameless prison barge slowly working its way to Dudinka and the rail line that would take him to Norilsk and the few thousand prisoners who extracted copper and nickel for the war effort.

He sat huddled shoulder to shoulder with others who suffered the same fate, knees up, head down. From a rising intelligence officer, he had been demoted to what amounted to a prison guard destined to spend the next three years (at a minimum) on the frigid tundra of Northern Siberia, two thousand miles from Moscow as the crow flies. He took no pleasure in learning later that Colonel General Pestrov followed suit as one of the newly appointed camp administrators.

Still, he was luckier than most; unlike other former intelligence officers he encountered, he was not a prisoner. Their stories were remarkably similar: arrest on sundry bogus charges, torture for good measure, and exile as enemies of Stalin's state. They joined hundreds of other military commanders, journalists, translators, and a legion of poets and writers as inmates of Norilsk Corrective Labor Camp in one of Mother Russia's remotest corners. Yuri, a former NKVD operative who ran amok for offenses he had yet to ascertain, put it succinctly to Bakinin: "This is truly hell — without the fire."

With the first ominous temperature drop in early fall, Bakinin had no doubts. He wondered if Yuri survived (he was still there when Bakinin had been "rehabilitated" and reassigned back to Moscow three years later) but hard labor and the brutality of Norillag's winters took its toll. He presided over men clothed in thinly padded prison garb — hands and feet bound in rags (boots in particular were a black-market commodity worth killing for) — with insufficient rations or medical supplies. Only the most clever and ruthless survived.

Bakinin escaped the worst of such misery; he could dress warmer, eat better, and did not sleep in the drafty, frost-bitten barracks, nor did he have to work to exhaustion in the mines hauling out precious metals for Stalin's tanks. He was an overseer, and after a fashion, a witness to the body count. Whatever else fell in between — assaults, thievery, and unsavory alliances — was best left unheeded. He was spared the physical hardship and abject wretchedness. However, a blackened soul and a scarred perspective could not be so easily escaped. Endless gray on a canvas of stunted and snarled scrubs estranged the mind and set the stage for the true depth of winter's plunge into polar night. In those months men became crazed, animalistic. Bakinin, despite his "advantages," could barely endure, coming to the realization that he needed to harden, to let his humanism recede, be shunned, be kept under lock and key while his cruder, more basic instincts filled the breech. Unbridled nature took dominion over the acquired civility of nurture. Otherwise, he would be lost.

Thus, he steeled himself to all manner of human suffering in order to survive — unlike his boss, Pestrov, who succumbed. On a cold, wind-swept night, the ex–Colonel General marched away from his crumbling concrete apartment and, fortified with a sufficient amount of vodka, sat in an alley just off Lenin Prospekt, Norilsk's main street, and never got up.

"Monsters had been plaguing him for some time," Bakinin heard one administrator explain to another. He didn't elaborate, but Bakinin felt the same monsters arising from the frozen permafrost, reaching through the darkness and whispering destructive thoughts through numbing layers of the sulfur-tinted Arctic air. By the end of the first year, gaunt with a progressive stoop weighing on his posture, Bakinin too encountered the sharpened edge of despair, anxiety, and growing apprehension over nebulous shadows and conspiracies around him. He had become an insomniac, adding to his restlessness and increasing uncertainty.

The moment of clarity and resolution came when he shot dead a well-known Estonian writer. The prisoner in question had been subsumed to what was referred to as "polar light madness." He became erratic, unstable, attacking his fellow workers with a shovel before turning his attention to the diminutive figure in a gray

Napoleon uniform. He charged; Bakinin pulled out his revolver and fired. And there it was — order restored and control maintained. He was in charge, and with that came a power that once truly felt, could never be let go.

In that moment Bakinin made his way back from the abyss; he gained control and bested his circumstances, emerging ... indomitable. He vowed to grab and hold as much of the thorny threads of power as he could. Along the way his motto became "Do unto others, but worse." For many nervous comrades — even those close to him — his actions seemed ... excessive.

He earned a reputation as an efficient but nasty bureaucrat to be feared. Now, in his attempt to attain the KGB's top job, this was proving to be a liability. It was suggested, albeit tentatively, that he outdid himself in unmasking enemies of the state, that he employed at the very least unorthodox procedures and questionable methods in extracting confessions. The most recent case was that of Olga Rak, an outspoken young woman who, besides organizing literary and artistic soirees in her home, criticized Moscow party officials for corruption and violations of legality. Although considered a nuisance rather than a serious threat to the regime, when her file was brought to the attention of Bakinin, he ordered that she be brought in for questioning. A surprise visit in the middle of the night, an unceremonious ride downtown, and two or three hours of continuous interrogation often did wonders to those with rebellious spirits.

Officially, the report stated that Olga Rak had been questioned as to her involvement with dissidents, suitably chastened, and released. But that was the last anyone saw her alive; her body was later discovered in her basement flat on the outskirts of Moscow. She had been brutally beaten and raped.

An investigation ensued where it was determined that her lover, a railway worker with a history of psychological setbacks, was the culprit. The motives were obscure and remained so, since apparently after committing the crime, overcome with remorse and grief, he took his own life. His body was found (in a timely fashion as it turned out) a day later near his place of employment, sprawled over the train tracks, his throat slit. The idea seemed to be not only to kill himself but also to obliterate what remained.

The case was closed, but puzzling questions remained. The Moscow homicide detectives at the scene of Olga's demise wondered (but not too strenuously) why all traces of the crime (except, of course, the body) had been carefully removed. The blood had been wiped up, the apartment was in order, and no murder weapon was found. Surely, a deranged person in a fit of passion would not be so antiseptic! Perhaps the murder had not taken place in her flat but elsewhere, and the body had been deposited there? That could explain the absence of blood and a murder weapon...

By some sort of fortuitous coincidence, meanwhile, it was KGB agents who removed the apparent murderer turned suicide victim. However, it took a full week to identify the corpse as Olga Rak's boyfriend, although he carried various identification documents in his wallet.

It was rumored that Yanev, the chair of the KGB, conducted a secret internal investigation of the circumstances that transpired around the case. After all, no sanction had been ordered against the woman, and even in a police state, there was a certain protocol and decorum to be maintained among the foot soldiers of the organization.

Bakinin and his section were absolved of any "inappropriate" actions. But stories continued to circulate that Olga Rak died at the hands of certain KGB officers during a stressful interrogation.

The suspicion was never fully articulated, but enough hints were discreetly whispered in important enough quarters to reflect negatively on Bakinin. As a result, the more moderate members of the Politburo leaned toward Drydenko as Yanev's replacement at the top of the Komitet hierarchy. It was thought that Drydenko was more in tune with "Soviet legality" and not as likely to overstep his bounds.

Some of his colleagues believed that Bakinin was a sadist. At least one remembered a lecture he gave to new KGB recruits in Kharkov on the evolution of the security service. Included in the lecture (perhaps with a little tongue in cheek, it was noted) were historical footnotes on various effective methods of loosening traitors' tongues.

He listed the usual, from simple beatings administered on sensitive parts to sleep deprivation, but his favorite, he admitted, was the rat-in-the-pipe trick practiced in the Muslim borderlands. A hollow metal pipe would be sealed at one end and a rat dropped into the other. The open end would then be firmly secured to the prisoner's lower abdomen, the prisoner tied or chained, usually to a wall, but there were other variations. Then, the sealed end of the pipe would be heated until the terrified rodent, trapped in an unbearable inferno, would start to frantically gnaw its way through the stomach or intestines, depending on the exact location of the pipe. "Confessions," he concluded with a smirk, "were quickly extracted."

At the same time, he emphasized that such methods were no longer in vogue. That was during the heyday of the security services. Now, procedures were much more humane, with a "rehabilitation" component. In fact, Bakinin helped pioneer the use of intensive drug and psychiatric therapy on political deviants and malcontents. The premise was simple, although the techniques employed were sophisticated: Failure to endorse Soviet communism could only be in itself a sign of serious mental illness that had to be treated. Be that as it may, Bakinin appreciated that the Rak case, no doubt overzealously pursued, cost him some standing and influence, which he hoped to address once he assumed the chairmanship.

Bakinin looked forward to becoming the head of the Komitet, constraining as best he could his mounting impatience and relish. Increasing insidious political, religious, and ethnic dissent dictated that the powers and prerogatives of the agency needed to be greatly enhanced. And he was dedicated to doing just that. Moreover, as boss of the entire KGB network, he would be assured automatic membership in the Politburo, a position he coveted almost as much.

Whatever other deficiencies Bakinin might have harbored, organizational talent and political astuteness held him in good stead. He ran his section like a Cosa Nostra boss: diligently, with a healthy dose of suspicion, sniffing out and anticipating trouble areas. It was part of his terrifying mystique, which made up for his physical shortcomings.

He realized that Drydenko was a formidable opponent who, at the moment, had the edge, albeit a small one, in the current struggle for the chairmanship. At whatever the cost, he had to counter Drydenko's advantage.

It was, then, of some interest to Bakinin when, through his well-placed spy (*keep your friends close and your enemies closer*) he discovered that Drydenko had a clandestine meeting with a field agent. One line in passing in the short weekly reports he received. Perhaps it was nothing, but still, highly unusual. Why would a section chief want to soil his hands at that level? Apparently, Drydenko was after some war criminal who had escaped abroad and eluded Soviet justice after the war. But why this particular fellow, and why now? There were many others like him: postwar émigrés, who had also raged and schemed against the Soviet Union, some with a modicum of success… Yet they were allowed to live. The long arm of the State Security Committee had not pursued them… But then they did not have a Drydenko to take a special interest in them… Why indeed?

There was only one logical explanation: Drydenko and this individual, whose name he would know shortly (he ordered, and the informant promised a copy of the document with the particulars within a couple of days) must have a history or be connected in some odd way. Bakinin took a long puff from his pipe, a soothing addiction he acquired only after he returned back to Moscow in late '44. Before taking significant action on this matter, he'd needed to peruse the dossier.

CHAPTER 13

July 20, 1974

Away from Moscow — with its cement towers, huge skyscrapers, and leftover onion-domed churches — lay the village of Zhukovka. Actually, it was no less than three villages: Zhukovka 1, Zhukovka 2, and Zhukovka 3. Its undulating terrain, covered with tall pine trunks, was dissected by the lethargic Moskva River. Here lived the upper echelons of Soviet society: the politicians, trusted academics, scientists, and artists. Every evening they left the large city's granite piles of Soviet architecture and retired to the serenity of the countryside to rest, to stroll, to shop in well-stocked, exclusive stores, and to live the good life, comforted in the knowledge that they were insulated and zealously protected from adventurous citizens and curious others.

The village contained over 150 dachas, impeccably maintained two-story structures complete with carpet lawns, manicured shrubs, and big polished chauffeur-driven automobiles. The country homes were strictly allocated in accordance with rank and protocol. It was but part of the reward of service for those true communists who made the wheels of state grind on. It could not be refused — at least not without puzzlement turning into darkening suspicions; however, just as surely, it could be taken away if one was deemed derelict in his duty or backed the losing side in the ever-festering power struggles that plagued the Kremlin. From rags to riches had a very stark meaning here; reward and punishment were the glue that kept the comrades faithful, diligent, fearful, and most of all, forever anxious.

Drydenko lived here in a comfortable yet relatively modest country home. He was proud of the status he had attained and fond of his dwelling, although he knew that, after he became chairman of the Komitet, rank would dictate that he move into more suitable quarters, closer to the edge of the bluff overlooking the river.

Zina would have been happy here, he thought, had she'd given it a chance, but such was life. "Ladybird," as he fondly called her (because of her delicate, small-boned frame and elfin face) had flown the coop after almost thirty years of marriage. She could no longer tolerate, as she put it, his "obsessions and indiscretions." In truth, they had been estranged for quite some time, but it was less than a year since Zina packed her bags and left. There was little rancor or melodrama; he agreed to provide her with an apartment in the more fashionable part of Moscow and a generous living allowance. Divorce was soon to be finalized. Although they had ceased to communicate on any meaningful level for quite some time, he still occasionally thought of her, even as he moved on to younger, more adventurous women.

Drydenko met Zina under stressful circumstances. February 1943 saw him on the right bank of the Volga amid the ruins of Stalingrad. His work as a military attaché and liaison officer took him briefly to the city that had just withstood the destructive assaults of the German sixth army. He was gingerly making his way through the rubble of wood, brick, and frozen turf to a nearby command post when an explosion deafened his ears. He found himself somewhat dazed, recovering in a makeshift field hospital.

Apparently, an unspent shell had detonated close by, and he was hit by some flying debris. The wound proved superficial; nevertheless, it was painful and in an awkward spot. He had just adjusted to a more comfortable position when a pretty young nurse marched up to the cot. Quite petite, very blond — Scandinavian rather than Slavonic in features — *Ladybird indeed...* Drydenko smiled, and she smiled back, seemingly oblivious of his ruined face. He was smitten and about to indulge in banal conversation when she calmly ordered him to take down his trousers.

"What? Why?"

"How else can I treat your wound?"

The young man was embarrassed, but, he recalled, it was love at first sight. They were married the following year.

For almost twenty-five years she stood by his side, through successes and failures, seeing him through the dirty work that came with the Beria era. He had started his career in the Red Army but ended up in the upper echelons of the KGB, earning his stripes en route as a cold, scar-faced functionary who performed the unpleasant but necessary tasks. It wasn't his occupation that she finally objected to; she was used to his unsavory decisions and actions, although he told her very little of the details. No, it was much more personal: Although no prude, as she put it, she could not abide in his affairs with "tarts half his age" — a need, she surmised, to fulfill his middle-aged erotic fantasies. In the end, he couldn't really hide or deny his infidelity and numerous transgressions...

Nevertheless, Zina still had a special place in his thoughts. Their union, after all, produced two daughters, one now a fledgling journalist and the other... He sighed. *Well, she lost her way...* All that sprang to mind was that she liked jewelry and drugs and now was recovering in a psychiatric ward. That, too, might have been part of the problem. In truth, he had to admit, he was not much of a family man...

Now he was absolutely free to do whatever he desired, and although he was sure he'd never remarry, he wouldn't be without female companionship. Each Saturday at 6:00 p.m., as was his custom in recent weeks, he ate a hearty dinner (one which he would work off in the gymnasium on Sunday), dismissed his felicitous and fastidious charwoman, took an invigorating shower, slipped on his kimono, opened an expensive (usually rare) bottle of cognac, and watched Western movies (mostly), sprawled comfortably on his waterbed. He understood English and German (as the occasion dictated) well enough to follow the storyline — not that that was critical, given the type of videocassettes he often viewed. His sexual appetite had diminished little; nevertheless, while he awaited Klara, who usually arrived around nine or so, he found "adult" movies were stimulating.

Today, he was more restless and moody than usual. That night he had a dream — a dream of portent ... or nonsense. Through a watery veil, he embraced acquaintances he had forgotten about or who had died many years ago. It was truly déjà vu; he tried to recall ... he was in an enormous black skyscraper, on the top floor... Zina appeared, radiant, youthful, but so did other more sinister persons, including the granite face of Stalin, followed by Khrushchev, and the current rival, Bakinin. For some reason, Drydenko tried to hide; he didn't want to be seen by them. He slunk away, mingling with the simpler folk — mistresses, fellow soldiers, drinking buddies — people that his mind plucked from its dormant chambers. Then he saw the stern, furrowed face of Timoshenko from across the room. Drydenko waved, trying to draw his attention. The great general seemed to be ignoring him. Suddenly, the building tilted, all in the room were thrown against one wall, and after a momentary pause, the edifice they were in started to plunge downward, increasing in speed, pressing its occupants to the ceiling with terrifying g-force. Before they hit bottom and he awoke, Drydenko spotted another individual he had not noticed before: Dr. Bodrev — or was it Glinka? Real or his double? The dream didn't tell him. Did it matter? The distorted image of Bodrev/Glinka pointed an accusing finger at him and screamed something that was lost amid the wails of others. There was one last, unified cry it seemed, before a shattering death.

Silly dream — nightmare... *Anxiety, too much on my mind,* decided Drydenko as he switched on his Sony TV and fiddled with the videocassette before inserting it into the Beta Max. Yet perhaps he'd had an apocalyptic vision that would lead him to a cataclysm. Perhaps the past should be left alone; like his father used to say, disturb shit and it will stink! Perhaps Glinka should be left alone to finish his miserable life. Maybe he should concentrate on Bakinin, who, too, had skeletons in his closet — or so it was rumored — specifically a proclivity for younger men. But that would be an internal pissing match that would hit uncomfortably close to home for at least two other directors in the Komitet. Could he chance leaving well enough alone? Should he call off Lucovich — let him get back to his work in London? For the first time in a very long time, Drydenko realized he was not totally sure of his reasoning abilities. Was it a rational, lucid decision? Or one clouded by an old man's paranoia of being discovered on the cusp of attaining his goal, only to lose it all...

Drydenko's somber ruminations were cut short when the TV came to life, a few seconds of wavy lines and white dots and then the title *American Pie.*

American decadence. He chortled as he focused on a rather sensuous blond, her hair bleached to a milky white and her public hair shaved to a narrow dusty strip, glancing up into the camera. One of the KGB's most important bosses was in a state of full arousal by the time his chauffeur, Vasilevich, discreetly knocked and announced that Klara Pavolichna had arrived.

Klara was an extraordinary woman in more ways than one. Originally from a working family in Smolensk, she came to Moscow because that was the place to be for enterprising, ambitious Soviet citizens. Vigorously vetted with no "red flags" from her past, her superior typing and organizational skills landed her a position in Drydenko's section; however, it was her other endowments that ensured a rapid promotion. Drydenko was infatuated from the moment he set eyes on her. Within a year, she became his executive secretary.

It wasn't long before he discovered her extracurricular talents. He hinted, and she let it be known that she was available. A bargain was struck: Klara received a better than average apartment, access to normally unavailable amenities and clothing, extended holidays to the Crimea, and the best that foreign goods shops could offer in exchange for her personal services once a week. The woman from Smolensk had been his mistress for over four months now; he fervently hoped that the arrangement would continue indefinitely.

Klara was lithe, dark, and wicked. Drydenko sometimes wondered what Vasilevich thought as he drove her to and from Moscow.

He'd probably give six months wages just to get into her snatch, he ventured, getting off the bed and turning off the TV. *Time for the real thing!* That thought excited him even more. In public, he was a man who could command unquestioned authority and respect, but in private, well, he didn't know anyone who wasn't a chameleon. Sex, with its endless bourgeois decadence, was much more palatable than the official version of a socialist man who had no sexual fantasies, and women who existed strictly for procreation purposes. The missionary position was the only sanctioned position and, of course, there were no prostitutes.

But there were many Klaras for those who could afford their extravagance. Exotic creatures with shaved armpits, perfumed hair, flashing earrings, black nylons, red garter belts, and pubescent thighs — *right!* Klara could resurrect his manhood quicker than Lenin could sway a crowd.

CHAPTER 14

July 23, 1974

Bakinin was both intrigued and puzzled as he carefully read a copy of the dossier his industrious informant had couriered to him over an hour ago. He had a name, Viktor Glinka, and the "unofficial" report that attributed all manner of crimes to him ... and yet the question remained, who was he really, and more to the point, why was Drydenko so interested?

According to the document, Glinka was a prominent member of the Vlasov movement in '43 and '44. Bakinin sat up on the couch, reached over to the coffee table, and retrieved his favorite pipe, along with a tobacco pouch. As he went through the ritual of stuffing and lighting the contents in the briar, his thoughts focused on Lt. General Andrei Vlasov. A good general — one of the better ones in the Red Army —before he turned traitor. He'd been commanding an army attempting to relieve Leningrad when he was captured in July 1942. The Nazis, Himmler in particular, recognized the potential of Vlasov as leader of an anti-Soviet Russian army. Indeed, Bakinin recalled, a huge Russian Liberation Army was formed, and thousands of German prisoners joined, anxious to fight Stalin. In 1944, much too late to be effective, Himmler promoted the formation of the Committee for the Liberation of the Peoples of Russia (Komitet Osvobozhdenia Narodov Rossi) as a nucleus of a government to supplement this volunteer army. Later that year, this committee issued the nefarious Prague Manifesto, stating that Stalin was a tyrant.

Bakinin chuckled at the understatement. "Like saying Ivan the Terrible had a mean streak!" he muttered as he settled back and once again studied the Glinka indictment.

The purpose of this committee was to destroy the communist dictatorship and establish a "free" people's political system without Stalin and his Bolshevik exploiters. *Old news — well past any relevance, surely,* thought Bakinin. Glinka was a liaison official between the committee and this Liberation Army but not an overly prominent one. No doubt he should have been executed as a German agent a long time ago, but he escaped his fate when the Americans and British repatriated Vlasov, his officers, and the remainder of the army to the waiting arms of Stalin. That was at Plattling, Bavaria, in 1946. By then, Glinka had vanished along with thousands of other displaced persons. According to Drydenko's secret indictment, he worked for British intelligence to undermine the Soviet state.

It would have taken much effort, time, and many resources to produce such a document. So why bother? There could be only one reason for Drydenko to pluck an inconsequential "war criminal" out of air: He and Glinka were somehow connected, and if a hit man was being sent, then Glinka was a long-standing threat who knew something highly damaging.

Bakinin again flipped to a copy of Glinka's grainy photo — obviously dated, showing a younger man with dark curly hair and a pleasant square face. No particular features stood out, yet the profile appeared familiar. Bakinin never forgot a face, and he had seen this one before many years ago. He just couldn't place where or under what circumstances. "Or my memory is just playing tricks on me," he muttered, shaking his head. It was maddening…

Then it came to him. When he was a young NKVD investigator, he'd seen a much younger version spattered on posters throughout Moscow… The missing doctor — the man who sent him and his boss to the outermost edge of civilization. Was he really staring at an older Dimitri Bodrev? He had relegated this unsolved case to a back corner, but it was still there, indelibly etched in his mind. So what did Bodrev/Glinka have to do with Drydenko? Intriguing indeed if this was true and not some twisted coincidental lookalike. There was only one way to find out. He wrote a confidential note to his executive assistant requesting everything available on one Viktor Glinka, all materials from the archives related to the disappearance of Dr. Dimitri Bodrev, and finally, the availability of Arkady Zhutoff, his most trusted operative.

CHAPTER 15

July 26, 1974

Alexandr Lucovich was an unsettled man. The next day, he was scheduled to leave Sheremetyevo Airport for Berlin on one of Aeroflot's late afternoon flights. There he would transform himself into Adam Woodal, British national, frequent traveler, emerging suddenly in West Berlin. Thereafter, it would be a quick stop in Frankfurt and then on to London, where he would set into motion a "business trip" to Edmonton, Alberta, Canada.

While the reasons for his mission were sketchy — and he was encouraged to let them remain so — the expected outcome was made clear: find and eliminate, leaving no collateral evidence behind. The target would be easy to find, probably in the phonebook. In fact, there was an address provided in the file, and it would only be a matter of verifying that he had the right man. Lucovich didn't know how Drydenko managed to locate Glinka after so many years. A combination of diligence and luck, he suspected.

None of this made him unhappy per se; indeed, he looked forward to getting back to London, albeit briefly. Somehow it was never as dour as Moscow and didn't leave him with the taste of bad kvass in his mouth. Perhaps it was the accumulated influence of Russian winters. Unlike optimistic Londoners, Muscovites were instinctively pessimistic, knowing that their summers and falls were but short reprieves from the cold shroud that would descend and, like an unwanted tenant, prolong its dreary stay.

However, what did make him most unhappy was the unannounced knock on his hotel room door and the appearance of a squat, heavily muscled man with a Tatar complexion. Dressed casually, he could be mistaken for a swarthy laborer who drank lots of beer, joked with his comrades, followed the fortunes of Dynamo Moskva, and ruled over a pleasantly plump wife with several kids. Dressed in a cheap seersucker blazer, he could be a used-auto salesman — at least in London; upgraded to a proper suit and tie as he was now, perhaps a Mafia foot soldier. A Komitet agent would have been further down Lucovich's list.

"Deputy Director Bakinin would like to see you," he stated the moment the door opened.

"When?"

"Now. There is a car waiting. You will come with me."

There was no point in arguing. Lucovich knew who Bakinin was and could no more refuse than he could a summons from Drydenko.

Lucovich and his "chauffeur" drove in silence, not to Lubyanka and Bakinin's office, but to what appeared to be a dining establishment on Vasilyevsky Prospekt, which was a little off the beaten path and away from Dzerzhinsky Square. A small, discreet sign — Soviet Hunt Club — hung above a nondescript front façade. Lucovich surmised that it was one of those exclusive places frequented by high-ranking apparatchiks who wanted privacy in their more contentious meetings. Here, payment was probably in foreign currency, preferably American dollars, rather than rubles, he would wager.

"Forgive me for the drama and having Arkady bring you here on such short notice," Bakinin said when Lucovich and his chaperon approached. The deputy director was sitting alone in a darkened alcove. "But I thought it best to meet as inconspicuously as possible. Please sit down." He motioned to a seat across the table from him. "A drink perhaps?"

"Whatever you are having," Lucovich said guardedly.

Bakinin nodded toward Arkady, and he disappeared. Evidently, Bakinin didn't trust any maitre d' or want nosey waiters hanging around in the shadows.

Eyes adjusted, Lucovich noted that this was indeed an august establishment, replete with mahogany walls, ornate high-back chairs, a parquet floor, and heavy velvet curtains drawn on two modestly sized windows. Ebony statues of exotic wildlife sat on the ledge of a dormant fireplace, and an assortment of curios was sprinkled on marble-top fixtures — no doubt objets d'art — here and there. It had the ambience of an English gentlemen's lounge with whiffs of cigar smoke tickling the nostrils.

"Now, Comrade Lucovich, I will get to the chase, as the English would say — or at least that is what I have been told. You can correct me on the idiom."

Lucovich nodded but said nothing, waiting for the shoe to drop. And it did.

"A couple of days ago you were summoned to Deputy Director Drydenko's office, where you were asked to carry out an assignment off the books — go rogue, yes?"

Lucovich didn't see any point in denying it, although "going rogue" was a rather harsh characterization given that his superior — many, many rungs up the ladder— sanctioned it, the politics behind it notwithstanding. "You are well informed," he said. *Too well, in fact!*

"Deputy Director Drydenko requested that you use some discretion on this particular assignment, yes?"

"That is true."

"Yes ... well!" Bakinin exclaimed with a bounce in his tone. "I do not want to dissuade you in any way. Complete your mission by all means, but with a couple of amendments... Ah ... here we are..." A young lady dressed smartly in a sleeveless red dress and thin enough to audition for the Bolshoi emerged with a tray and two glasses of brandy. Arkady was nowhere to be seen.

"Care for some caviar and condiments?" Bakinin asked as she served the drinks. "They also serve excellent roast duck and beef

Wellington." He smiled, an obvious reminder that he knew of Lucovich's time in London.

"No thank you — the brandy will suffice."

Bakinin nodded, and the woman disappeared. "Well then, back to business… I need you to provide me with all the intelligence you uncover. Specifically, why Deputy Director Drydenko is so extraordinarily interested in seeing this Glinka fellow be brought to justice. What secrets do they share? Surely there has to be a connection, or what would be the point of sending you on such an extravagant, clandestine mission? I am sure you have wondered about this too."

"Evidently, my assignment is not so secret after all," Lucovich said. "But yes, the thought has occurred to me."

"Oh, it is still quite secret, but I have my sources," Bakinin replied wryly. "And Deputy Director Drydenko has a weakness that makes him vulnerable… Now, I could have sent Arkady to follow in your footsteps, but that would have been duplication — not much sense to have two Komitet agents tripping over each other in a foreign country, is there? Besides, Arkady is not as well versed as you in the English language, and he also has a dislike for travel. He hates to leave his aging mother in the apartment alone — feels guilty, especially if it is a prolonged trip…" Bakinin sniffed and took a sip from his glass. "Now, so that we are clear, do no harm to Glinka, at least not until you have obtained what there is to know, along with any corroborating evidence — documents if possible. Once you have secured this information" — he shrugged —"I leave Glinka's fate to you… And, of course, this arrangement will be strictly between us."

"I understand," Lucovich said. The message was clear: Get the dirt on Drydenko and keep your mouth shut.

"I'm sure you do… Tell me, Alexandr, is it? What is it you want in life?" A rhetorical question, no doubt, and Lucovich had no ready answer. "Whatever it is," Bakinin continued, "perhaps I can help you…" It was the second time in a week that a KGB director offered him a reward for doing his personal bidding. "I know you are in a bind — divided loyalties and all that. You are asking, whom do I trust?

How do I play this game? Alas, you have to decide on which horse to bet on, so to speak. Two old warhorses to pick from, yes — one wins, the other ... not." Bakinin produced a small laugh. "Let me simplify and reassure you. Deliver what I need to know, and that will be the end of it. No one, including Deputy Director Drydenko, will be the wiser, since this conversation has not taken place..."

***

Each man walked away with a different perspective. Bakinin was well satisfied. He was confident that there was something nefarious to be discovered that he could exploit against Drydenko. He could feel it; there was no other reasonable explanation, especially given the extraordinary tie to Dimitri Bodrev. He hadn't mentioned Bodrev to Lucovich. It would have been premature. *Let's see what he finds out...*

As for Lucovich, it was a matter of evaluating unsavory choices. He was not so much conflicted as chagrined to be put in such an untenable position. He had no loyalty to either man and knew that he was a pawn to be played and sacrificed in an intricate political game. *No one will be the wiser* was a hollow promise that remained as long as it suited Bakinin. Moreover, there was no guarantee that Drydenko wouldn't find out about this double-dealing. In either case, he was disposable.

In such a precarious situation, when one really had no choice, the best course of action, Lucovich decided, was to shake hands with both devils and hope that the "right" horse won.

Part Three

CHAPTER 16

August 1974, Edmonton

"Eat your breakfast, Carli."

"Aw, Mom, I don't like eggs done that way."

"Please, honey, finish your breakfast or you'll be late for school and I'll be late for work." Irene Cohen, née Irina Glinka, inwardly sighed; her daughter would soon be entering a stage where she would become difficult for a single parent. Carli was developing a self-centered, defiant personality that posed a challenge to her mother's authority. *All very normal,* Irene supposed; still, sometimes Carli's protestations and brooding seemed like a reproach. Although Irene tried to suppress her annoyance and irritation, she was not always successful. *Damn, you Stephen,* she ruminated, *our child needs two parents...*

While she lamented the devastating failure of her marriage, the phone rang. She grabbed the receiver from the kitchen wall in midstride. "Hello?... Oh, hi, Jane — yup, we are running a little late but just about ready to go... See you in ten minutes."

Irene glanced at her daughter pushing her eggs around the plate and said, "Okay, Carli, just put the remains in the garbage and the dishes in the sink. No time to lose."

"But I'm still hungry!" wailed the eight-year-old.

"I packed you a big lunch. You won't starve if you don't share it with your friends like you did last week. Now get your coat, don't forget your reader, and shut the door quietly; Grandpa is still sleeping."

It took eleven minutes to deposit Carli at the neighborhood school and pick up Jane en route to work. They were now winding their way down 109th Avenue through stop-and-go traffic; soon they would cross the Saskatchewan River at the 105th Avenue bridge and find themselves in the heart of the province's capital amid enormous concrete and glass towers. Irene and Jane were legal secretaries who were employed in the same building, although for different law firms. They had known each other for two years, ever since they shared a table at the Tim Hortons on the first floor of their workplace edifice. Over that time they had become good friends.

At twenty-eight, Jane was four years younger and, it appeared to Irene, less restrained. A petite, perky blonde with a pleasantly round face, a straight nose, and bubbling personality, Jane seemed alive in ways Irene envied. Perhaps it was because she had not been blighted by a failed marriage. Edmonton-born and raised, Jane had but one passion in life: the Eskimos football team, for which she always bought season tickets — and two goals: to find a man who liked kids and who was rich enough to provide a secure, permanent home; and to become Klondike Kate for the city's annual Klondike Days. The former held promise; after a long string of boyfriends, Eddie, her latest, had all the makings of a suitable catch (with the added bonus of not being a lawyer). The latter remained in limbo, despite her yearly auditions. In both cases, Jane's attitude was "que será, será." Unlike Irene, who attended one year at the University of Alberta before getting married and becoming a mother, Jane enrolled in Alberta College after high school to enhance her typing and office-related skills. In due course, Irene, too, ended up in Alberta College as a practical necessity when her husband left her for someone she euphemistically called "the other woman."

Irene enjoyed talking to Jane, even though at times she couldn't tell whether Jane was being serious or flippant. As they drove, Jane was relating her experience with an irate client the day before. "God, he was mad, and I couldn't blame him — but who am I, the boss or something? I just type, copy, file, and witness."

They stopped at Whyte Avenue waiting for the light to change. "What was the problem?" Irene asked.

"Well, he bought this home in Sherwood Park about three months ago. Everything was fine until last week, when the bank sent him a tax bill that the previous owner left unpaid. Apparently half a year's taxes plus penalties were outstanding, which the builder and realtor did not tell him about. The bank as the mortgage holder paid but now wants its money plus interest. Well, he hit the roof. He couldn't understand why he was responsible for someone else's tax liabilities. The bank said there was nothing it could do but charge him since tax adjustments were supposed to be taken care of by the lawyers. They told him to look at his statement of adjustments — that's when he discovered that there wasn't one in his mortgage documents. Well, he stormed into the office with a copy of Sterk's Alberta Law and Conveyancing Practices under his arm and demanded to know why he hadn't received his statement of adjustments."

"And why hadn't he?" asked Irene as she pushed hard on the stiff Pinto accelerator pedal. "He's supposed to get the taxes adjusted on completion day of the transaction."

"Yeah, I know," intoned Jane. "That's normal practice — he quoted the book. The vendor was responsible to pay the taxes and expenses until completion day, and we were supposed to make sure that that was done." She mimicked what sounded to Irene like a British accent while at the same time rolling her eyes. "Well, I really don't know why he didn't get a certified copy of the discharge on the two prior mortgages. There has been a gross foul-up somewhere. That's when he became excited — I thought he'd have a seizure! He started quoting from the book again, something about a breach of faith and my duty to disclose a defect in the title... Before I knew it, he was going to bring the firm before the Law Society. I'm only the secretary, for poop's sake!"

"So, it was a rough day."

"Yeah, I hope today is less exciting... I hate taking a client's wrath when it's Smith and Associates who screw up. I think Smith had some sort of deal worked out with the builder, since the firm represented them also—"

"Oh, oh — that's not supposed to happen. Conflict of interest and all that," said Irene.

"Well, you didn't hear it from me. But now the builder is in receivership... Anyway, I made an appointment for him to see old man Smith. Let him sort it out..."

As Irene's Pinto rolled down the steep bank of the Saskatchewan River Valley toward the low-level bridge, Jane abruptly changed the subject. "How's Carli?"

Irene let out an exasperated sigh. "Oh, she's fine but growing up too fast. Sometimes I think I'm not on the same wavelength. You know what I mean — daughter-and-mother tension. Sometimes I think she needs her father."

Jane was immediately sympathetic. "How long has it been since you and Stephen parted ways?"

"Two years this July. I don't think Carli can quite comprehend our divorce."

"Doesn't he see her?"

"Every second weekend, but it's not the same."

"The fink! What's he doing now?"

"The same old thing," said Irene with a trace of bitterness. "Playing around, I presume, selling real estate and making money. I don't think he was cut out for marriage, or at least monogamy... Maybe I should spend more time with Carli, but this job — and I come home so drained."

"Yeah, I know what you mean."

They were now on the other side of the river, creeping up the embankment toward the looming skyscrapers, the Pinto's anemic four-cylinder roaring.

"How's your dad?" asked Jane.

Irene bit her lower lip. "He's recovering slowly from his stroke, poor dear. His left side was paralyzed, and he had memory loss, but it's coming back. He tries hard and is good with Carli. Sometimes I feel guilty leaving him alone. I dread a reoccurrence with no one around to help, but he's stubborn and independent and absolutely refuses to have anyone look after him. I suggested homecare, but he wouldn't hear of a nurse — 'nanny' as he put it… So, here we are."

The little car turned right and stopped at the buzzing mechanical gate underneath a gray concrete canopy. Irene rolled down the sticky window and snatched the ticket from the box's mouth. The wooden arm swung up. Irene drove down two levels until she found a cozy spot alongside a scraped pillar. She carefully eased the vehicle in. "The firm should pay for employees' parking," she lamented as she stuck the ticket in the sun visor — the discount notwithstanding. "If prices keep going up, I'll have to use transit."

"Yeah, and I'll have to get a car and learn to drive." Jane laughed. "Eddie thinks I should… It seems I've ridden the buses all my life 'til you came along. I hate buses, especially in the winter, freezing your buns off waiting for them. If it helps, I'll bribe you. How about an increase in my contribution to operating expenses?"

"Forget it, I'm not that desperate yet… How about lunch today?"

"Great! Where?"

"We can decide when we meet downstairs. Somewhere we haven't been for a while."

"Sounds good — if old Smith allows me the full hour."

CHAPTER 17

Viktor Glinka slowly, painfully sat up on his bed and reached for the cane perched against the chair. His spindly arm, laced with dark-blue veins running down to his wrinkled hand, wavered unsteadily before his fingers clutched the source of his support. *God be merciful*, he thought. Once, not that long ago, such a strong Cossack and now a frail, suddenly old creature with even his mind becoming cloudy. Such was life. He remembered the ancient Ukrainian proverb, *Tak bude iak Boh dast*. (It will be as God wills.) But he was not about to give up: *De nema holui tam nema i zhyttia*. (Without pain there is no life.) He had witnessed pain, felt pain, but he also lived — and passionately at that.

By comparison, he was luckier than many others. Instead of wasting away alone in an old-age home (or worse), he was in his house, surrounded by his possessions, with a loving daughter and a granddaughter who brought him much joy. And after a fuller recovery, he still hoped to do those things that inscrutable old men do — least of which was sitting on creaking chairs smoking or having a brew — or both —peering out from an open garage door. A trace of sadness wafted over him when he thought about his poor Irina. He had lost track of time — two years at least since she and Carli moved into his small stucco-clad bungalow. She was so distressed… And her valiant attempts to come to terms with the separation. The one last attempt for Carli's sake, if not her own, to reconcile. He shook his head at the enormous loss and waste Irina must have felt in her life. "She shouldn't have married Stephen," he muttered to himself; he brought her nothing but grief — but on the other hand, there was Carli... And they were both with him, and someday Irina would find a proper husband.

Laboriously, he seated himself on the creaking wooden chair and put on his comfortable flannel shirt; next came the crimplene trousers draped over the arm of the chair. Amazing, he lamented, how life's simple chores became suddenly a major task. Thank God he could still dress himself. The teeth — had he put them on the dresser?

He stood up unsteadily, like a drunk. From a water-filled glass he fished out his upper plate and momentarily stared into the mirror. Today, he felt as if his cataracts had just been removed, and for the first time, he clearly saw himself and wondered what they had done to his face. A scar-puckered, leathery pear-shaped face with sallow, sunken cheeks and rheumy eyes. Thinning whisks of white mane on top and stubble on the sides and chin. The protruding, once noble nose was dissected by irregular red capillaries. His clothes, too, looked wrinkled and baggy; or was it just that the man inside was shrinking? He meandered into the kitchen, pressing firmly on the cane with each step. He was recovering; a month ago this would have been an exhausting exercise.

Dishes in the sink; must have been in a hurry this morning, he surmised. He poured tap water into the spout of the kettle and plugged it in. Since his arrival in Canada, he had acquired a taste for coffee, couldn't do without it, but it had to be instant; for some reason his system did not like percolated or filter-dripped coffee. In the past, he used to have a smoke with his cup. Now that was forbidden. "Damned doctor," he muttered under his breath. How he wished he could light his pipe. What the hell good was his assortment of pipes stuck into two beer steins in his study if they couldn't be used? *A damn waste of briar and meerschaum.* For a fleeting moment he felt like cheating. A few puffs wouldn't hurt, but he decided against it. He remembered the last time he broke down and the subsequent plunge into a coughing spree. *Maybe when I'm more fully recovered,* he consoled himself. He mildly cursed his habit and the incurable Polish smoker who many years ago introduced him to the vice with the words "a woman is just a woman but a pipe is a good smoke!" The sound of the whistling kettle interrupted Glinka's musings.

As was his custom, he would take a walk after breakfast either toward the university or the other way to St. Basil's Ukrainian Church on 109th Avenue. He had become very fond of these morning treks (weather permitting) through the older residential section of the city, especially now, with the sun still warm, the grass green, and the flowers hanging on to the last of their midsummer bloom. The long, dreary winter would arrive soon enough.

Today, he lingered in the kitchen somewhat longer than usual. First, he washed, dried, and put away the dishes — not an easy task. Then he sat down at the kitchen table to gather his strength, leisurely sipping his coffee with loud slurping noises, sloshing the liquid around his mouth before swallowing. During this period of solitude, his thoughts wandered, and he was glad. Immediately after his stroke, he had partial memory loss, and that frightened him more than his physical disability. Like other inscrutable old men sitting on creaking chairs peering out open garage doors, he wanted to ruminate, to remember, even if they were blurry bits of a life lived: triumphs, defeats, joys, sorrows, delusions, and illusions mixed in between. It mattered. For a couple of weeks he tried desperately to reconstruct his past — tears filled his eyes as he fought with the vagaries of a damaged mind that suppressed those things he needed to be resurrected and restored. Slowly, in bits and pieces, a great deal of it came back: his youth, his parents, and, of course, the war.

Yes, the war, he thought. *What irony.* He shook his head as a flood of bitter memories suddenly impaled themselves on his consciousness. Could anyone understand, comprehend, that it was better to fight with the Germans against Stalin than to become part of his sewer system? How sad in retrospect. For those who acted on this conviction, no quarter was given on either side; they were labeled traitors and dealt with accordingly. Yet he had escaped, hadn't he? *Dolia ne pytaie; schcho khoche te I daie.* (Fate does not ask; what it wills, it gives.) He'd simply marched westward, another peasant joining the thousands of deserters, *shtrafniki* (ex-prisoners) and other indeterminate émigrés retreating toward the German lines.

Details were hazy, and perhaps they would remain so forever, blanks never to be filled in. His escape through scorched fields, deserted villages, bogged combines, burnt-out Betuska tanks, and scattered bodies, some blackened, some pristine as if they simply lay down on the roadside never to arise; others twisted, intertwined, partially buried in makeshift shallow rows of furrowed black earth... He remembered this in fragments, all under an extenuated darkened horizon where steppes and sky met.

There could be no retreat — certainly not to Stalin's army. So he moved forward, to the Germans and their Schuma police, trading his Nagant pistol (he couldn't remember how he acquired it!) for a well-oiled Parabellum sidearm, the kind the SS favored. Surrender and defect — it became contagious given the circumstances...

He ended up in a displaced persons camp, somewhere on the *right* side of the German line. Along with thousands of men, women, and children, he awaited his fate, hoping, praying that he would not be sent back to Stalin... Westerners were both naïve and unimaginative regarding the reality that surrounded them. They couldn't fathom why these Slavs did not want to go home; why they didn't want to see the motherland again; why men and women burned themselves alive or jumped in front of moving trains to escape such a fate; why mothers gave up their children to others — strangers — who were fortunate enough not to be repatriated. They didn't comprehend that anything was preferable to returning...

And still, using rifle butts if persuasion failed, they were herded onto trucks for transportation to Soviet assembly points... From there to Soviet territory to be reeducated, rehabilitated, decontaminated — after all, they had come in contact with Western ideas and in the process, no doubt, they told dirty, slanderous stories — lies — about the Soviet Union and Comrade Stalin. They had to be punished. And Glinka knew, they were. Some were summarily executed as traitors (his fate if he were returned) or simply disappeared. Others rotted out their lives in prisons and labor camps.

The reason for such action was simple; if you had been captured or gave up or found yourself behind enemy lines, then you were a suspect — a spy, a saboteur, a collaborator — or all three. There could be no other explanation...

But he was fortunate. He posed as a Ukrainian peasant from pre-1939 Poland and therefore was not considered a Soviet national. Stalin's annexation of Eastern Poland was not recognized by the Allies. Glinka blinked and shook his head slowly. Yes, that was the way it was. From Germany, he made his way to France — to Paris, teeming with forlorn refugees, nameless émigrés, and MVD operatives. From there to Calais and London.

Nevertheless, he knew he was a wanted man — a hunted man — in more ways than his "German" activities warranted. It would be many years before he could feel safe...

Glinka sighed; he couldn't remember many of the details — just the blurry bits. He regarded it as a misadventure that could have changed the course of history, if he'd succeeded. He tried not to think about it — how impossible it was and yet how within reach...

Even more remarkable was that he got away without paying the price for such audacity. He should have died at the villa. He had seen his impending death unfold, then the flash, a scream, and him running through the dense underbrush under a canopy of pines for what seemed like eternity until he emerged onto a highway and saw the truck convoy. The last pulled over, and a bulky figure climbed out, giving him his chance. While the man wandered off to relieve himself, he rose from the ditch and found footing on the back hitch, quickly undoing the loose canvas and dropping in. He knew that he was at least going in the right direction — away from Moscow and toward Smolensk.

He never spoke of "the plot" and his escape, not even to his beloved Galina. He dared not...

Ah, Galina... He closed his eyes and focused on the emerging image: alluring with silky light-brown hair luxuriously flowing over her shoulders; mysterious eyes, the kind that touched the soul; a petite nose; and a wide mouth that spontaneously, although not too often, burst into a dazzling smile. She, too, was an émigré — alone, afraid, the horror of war deeply etched upon her. She was living on a *kolkhoz* (a collective farm) with her parents and younger sister, near Tarnopol, when the Nazis overran Ukraine.

"We saw the Germans as liberators and welcomed them with bread and salt," Galina told him.

But it was soon discovered that the SS and Gestapo regarded the Slavs as subhumans whose fate was to serve the "master race" or die. Her parents and sister perished in the winter of 1941–42 in a way that forever scarred Galina. She recalled the terror and revulsion of her story as she told it with strained fortitude one night in a cold London flat, over thirty years ago. Three drunken Gestapo brutes burst into their home late one evening, pistol-whipped and threw aside her protesting father, and seized her with the command: "Give! Give!" At first, she didn't understand until one shouted in rudimentary Russian that the Führer had given instructions that Slavic women were to be treated as booty and they were there to collect. When Galina began to struggle, they beat her and one started choking her until she was only half-conscious... It was quite some time later that she discovered her mother and father dead — both summarily executed. But that wasn't the worst of it.

Nadia, Galina's sister, suffered a more terrible fate. They found her in the adjoining room. She was dragged outside and taken to a nearby barn. Nadia's screams were heard throughout the village, but no one dared investigate, let alone intervene. Then, in the wee hours of the night, the barn burst into flames. Her charred remains were found the next morning and buried in the church graveyard. That was the end of it.

Local officials, under the watchful eye of their German masters, remained sullen and quiet.

As Galina related the sordid events, Glinka realized that this was the new normalcy of the world; he had heard similar stories and witnessed firsthand the aftermath. Such atrocities were almost commonplace, since given the chance, the Red Army and the MVD did the same. Herr Hitler and Comrade Stalin were but two sides of the same devil's head... *one side of which I had a chance to remove*, he mused with a mixture of melancholy and bitterness.

After her ordeal, like a wounded, hunted animal, Galina ran away from the village, hid in the woods, and would have probably died from exposure and lack of food had not an old parishioner living on the outskirts of the village taken her in. Later, Galina was reincorporated into the collective to work in the fields and ultimately was hauled off to the "Fatherland" as part of the Ostarbeiter program. Some 2,800,000 civilians were removed from occupied territory to work in Germany, where there was an acute labor shortage. One of the ironies of war, Glinka thought. Macabre, and yet how fortunate because many ended up on the Western side of the line, making good their escape from Stalin. Galina was one of the fortunate ones; she made her way to London.

Glinka sighed heavily. Two years he lived with Galina in a run-down London flat — two years of bliss and evolving plans for themselves and Irina, their newborn. Although money was scarce — he was partially employed as the building janitor while Galina worked as a seamstress — still, they managed. Then a suggestion from Galina took root.

She had heard that Canada needed people, that displaced persons were welcome, that jobs were plentiful, and moreover, she had a distant relative in Alberta. Perhaps, she should write...

Events took their course. After obtaining the required travel documents, health certificate, and certificate of sanity, they left Britain on a ship bound for Montreal. A month later, they boarded a Canadian Pacific train for the long ride to Edmonton, where a job awaited Viktor in a tannery. Galina's distant cousin had come through, securing a commitment of employment while convincing a local Ukrainian Catholic Church to help sponsor them.

Within a couple of years, the Glinkas had established themselves, buying a modest bungalow on the south side of the city. But then Galina got sick — *Must have been the latter half of '64*, he thought — and life changed; she became more and more debilitated over the next three years before finally succumbing to her slowly spreading cancer.

He was left with Irina, who grew up to be a reincarnation of her mother.

He wiped salty tears from his eyes. That was over five years ago. It had been some time since he thought about Galina — to actually remember. Yes, he dreaded forgetting; he'd rather have died from his stroke than recover with a blank slate. Without memory, he would have no history. And without his history, there was nothing.

It was a beautiful August morning, cool, refreshing, perfect for a walk. Glinka buttoned up his favorite sweater, put on his Texaco ball cap, and made his way out, carefully closing then locking the door before slowly ambling down the street toward St. Basil's. He spotted the widow Holenski, who was out early fussing over her hostas. The old woman had lost her husband the year before and only now seemed to be emerging from her mourning. Stopping briefly for a chat, he had no reason to suspect that his past was soon to intercept his present.

CHAPTER 18

It seemed to Irene that all of Edmonton had decided to go to Southgate Mall. The parking lot was a swelling sea of automobiles, while in Woodward's people rushed like lemmings, bumping, grinding, darting in and out of aisles in search of their weekly groceries. Irene, with Carli in tow, maneuvered her shopping cart amid other badly steered carts en route to the shortest of the long queues that formed at the checkouts. It was all to be expected on a Friday night. She stopped at the cereal section. "Okay, Carli, but just one box of that sweet stuff. What would you like — Alpha-Bits or Trix?"

"Trix!" shouted the eight-year-old. "Trix are for kids!"

Brainwashed, thought Irene. Too many Saturday morning cartoons. "Fine, as long as you don't gobble them up in two breakfasts."

"Oh, Mom, I won't. I'll mix them up with the cornflakes. I like cornflakes, and they're not sweet."

"Then it's a deal — now, while I take this up to the cashier, could you get me the milk, please? I seem to have forgotten."

"I will." Carli quickly disappeared into the wall of humanity around them.

Irene watched her skip away. She really was a sweet child; perhaps a little more patience was needed. *I have been testy lately, too quick to react. We're both going through a period of adjustment — Carli growing into awareness of the world around, and me...* Irene frowned. *What is it exactly? A period of stagnation and dissatisfaction. It has been almost two years since we parted, and it's the same routine with Carli and Pops providing the staples of my life...* She was grateful but needed more — $86.24, outrageous! And she had bought little meat this week. It seemed inflation was a disease that infected everything except her paycheck...

Irene wheeled the shopping cart to the edge of the sidewalk and stopped. "Now, where did we park the car?"

"Straight ahead, Mom, down at the end." Carli pointed.

"Boy, you have a memory that's better than mine. Lead the way, but be careful when crossing over."

Mother pushing the cart and daughter scampering ahead, both dressed in matching white skirts and polka dotted blouses, were easily observed. It was almost time for contact...

Irene twisted the key in the ignition; the engine turned over freely but did not come to life. After the fourth attempt, Irene became exasperated. "Damn, damn, damn. What now?"

"You shouldn't swear, Mom — it's not polite."

Irene flushed and was about to respond when a knock on her window startled her, making her heart palpitate a trace faster. She rolled down the window halfway and took in a pleasant square face. "Having a spot of trouble, are you?"

Irene recovered and caught her breath. "It appears so."

"Sorry I startled you." The man smiled, revealing an even row of white teeth. He continued in a precise, modulated English accent. "Perhaps I can be of some assistance."

"That's very kind..." she began. The gentleman had already gone to the front of the vehicle, his hand underneath the hood, groping for the latch. *Handsome*, thought Irene as she peered over the steering wheel, down the sloping hood to the stooped figure in a beige corduroy leisure suit and open sports shirt. Red metal suddenly blocked her view. She got out of the Pinto and scanned the greasy engine. It was a confusing tangle of wires and hoses. "I'm afraid I don't know much about mechanics," she said. "It ran fine until now."

"Not to worry. We'll have it right in a moment."

"Be careful — I would hate you to stain your clothes."

The would-be mechanic only smiled. "Hmm," he said, "I believe I have found the trouble. The wire that connects the coil to the distributor has come loose." He pointed to a black cap nestled beside the engine block. He shoved the dangling wire into the middle hole on the top until it was snug. He knew precisely the problem, because, after following her from her domicile an hour before, he had performed the same operation in reverse. "There, try it now."

Irene slid behind the wheel, again twisted the key, and the engine roared instantly to life. The man undid the rod that kept the hood aloft, gently eased it down, and gave it a quick jab until it clicked.

He leaned over the driver's door. "There now, I don't expect you'll have any further difficulties."

"Thank you, thank you so much," Irene stammered ever so slightly. "Both of us appreciate your kindness."

"Not at all." The man's piercing eyes shifted from Irene, and for the first time took in Carli, who sat sideways in her seat, giving him a furtive, shy glance.

There was an awkward pause as Irene's mind raced furiously. What was the matter with her? She felt like a teenage girl struck by the love bug. Perhaps it was the mood she was in, but she wanted to know his name — something about him. Suddenly, she thought of Stephen. Those eyes reminded her of Stephen. Before she could marshal any more conversation, he turned and briskly walked away. She felt a little weak-kneed; blood seemed to rush to her head as she shifted into reverse. It was about time, she thought, that after two years she should break out of her impregnable cocoon and make an effort to meet eligible men. Otherwise, she'd go bonkers…

As he strolled purposefully to his rented vehicle, Lucovich wore a satisfied smile: phase one had gone as planned. Monday would bring phase two. He had some time to complete his assignment. Meanwhile, perhaps Drydenko was right — Irene might prove a pleasant diversion.

CHAPTER 19

Monday started out as a typically hectic day for Irene, a myriad of routine with unexpected twists. Carli complained about her homework but ate her breakfast, Trix sprinkled with cornflakes as promised. She was duly deposited on the school grounds, a little apprehensive about her fourth-grade supply teacher, a temporary replacement for the pregnant Mrs. Sedgewick. Jane was her usual bubbly self, expounding for most of their drive downtown on a wild weekend party she and Eddie attended.

On her arrival at the office, Irene discovered that the receptionist would be a couple of hours late because of an emergency dental appointment — and could Irene please cover for her? By nine forty-five Irene had answered a half dozen phone calls, sifted through a mountain of mail, and made coffee for a coterie of clients who were filtering in and through to the inner sanctum to see Louis Swartz or one of his many associates.

Irene's day, however, took a quantum leap when out of the blue, Mr. Brown Eyes, as Irene labeled him after the episode in the parking lot, walked in. He looked dapper, wearing a blue pinstriped suit and a wine-red tie. "Good morning," he declared cheerfully.

"Good morning," she responded, suddenly feeling her throat constricting.

His face lit up in recognition. "I say … we've met, haven't we?"

"Yes," she hesitated, again squeezed for words. "Friday … in the parking lot, Southgate—"

"Quite right. How's the motor car performing?"

"Good — marvelous. You are an excellent mechanic." Irene observed more closely that square face she had admired; she noticed the deep lines of sadness that it contained. There was something compelling yet frightening about the man, as if those facial furrows possessed somber secrets she would never know...

There was a brief awkward pause; he seemed to be studying her intently.

"Ah..." — Irene cleared her throat — "may I help you?"

"I hope so..." he began and then broke off. "Is that a freshly brewed pot of coffee?" He glanced beyond her to a little table with the coffee maker and steaming pot behind her.

"Oh — of course." Irene disengaged from her low sitting position behind the high counter, all the while aware that his gaze was upon her. Without being too self-conscious, she poured Mr. Brown Eyes a coffee into a Styrofoam cup. She didn't even know his name, although that was about to be remedied... "Cream and sugar?"

"Black will be fine, thank you."

She handed him the cup. "Do you have an appointment with Mr. Swartz?" she inquired while looking down at the receptionist's notations in the appointment book. She noted that today Swartz was in seclusion until 2:00 p.m., preparing for a trial.

"Actually, no... This may be somewhat unusual, but since I may have need of a barrister and I was in the vicinity, I stopped by to make an appointment. Fancy that I should by chance run into the only person I've met informally in Canada. And I was under the impression that your country was so vast that such meetings were an improbability." He laughed; Irene smiled.

"Your name is..." she asked solicitously.

"Adam — Adam Woodal."

Irene studied the appointment book. "Well, Mr. Woodal, Mr. Swartz will not be available until Thursday morning, but if Mr. Humbolt or Mr. Lunacharski can be of assistance—"

"No particular hurry," he broke in. "Thursday morning will be fine."

"Ten o'clock?"

"Excellent."

"What shall I say is the general nature of your business with Mr. Swartz?" Normally, such a blunt question would not be asked, but Irene was curious.

"I represent a small investment firm in the United Kingdom. While I am in Canada, it is entirely possible that I may have need of Mr. Swartz's services."

Cup in hand, Woodal had been peering over the counter at Irene while she jotted down the pertinent information. Suddenly, some of his coffee splattered on the appointment book and quickly dribbled onto her green chiffon dress. "Oh dear, I'm terribly sorry — so clumsy of me."

Irene swiveled out of her chair and procured some napkins from the coffee table behind her. "That's okay," she said as she brushed her dress and laid the napkins on the affected page of the appointment book. "No harm done."

Within seconds the spill had been absorbed, except for a large wet stain on Monday's page and four little amoeba-like marks on the dress.

"Oh, this won't do," he said apologetically. "I insist on paying for your cleaning bill."

"Really, Mr. Woodal, it's quite all right."

"How about lunch while we discuss the matter? Please allow me to make restitution to you in some way."

He caught her off guard; she hesitated. "It really isn't necessary—"

"I insist. Shall I come by at twelve or so? That is when you take lunch?"

"Yes, but—"

"Then it's settled. It shall be a pleasure to take a beautiful woman to lunch." As Irene felt a creeping blush on her neck, he continued, "I'm a stranger in your fair city, so I will leave it to you to pick a place." Woodal glanced at his watch. "I must be off." He drank the remainder of his coffee and deposited the Styrofoam cup in the nearby garbage can. "By the way, what is your name?"

"Irene—"

"Irene, I will see you in a couple of hours then. Perhaps you can tell me about your delightful city…"

***

The Crêperie, a French-style restaurant in the old Boardwalk Building downtown, was crowded as usual, but they did manage to obtain a cozy table in a dark corner opposite an old brick wall with a ledge dominated by a couple of potted plants. Partitions of various sorts separated the clientele into sections while overhead, water pipes and heating ducts gave evidence that the building was originally a warehouse. Indeed, the restaurant was in the basement; when patrons entered from street level, they descended into what might have been mistaken for a wine cellar. It had the atmosphere of an intimate hideaway — the perfect place for each to size the other up, Woodal reckoned. As the maitre d' showed them to their table, Woodal noticed decorative wire wine racks. Punctuated with empty wine bottles, they formed entrance arches to the maze of cubicles that divided what was undoubtedly once a dusty storage space. *A nice touch*, he thought; it reminded him of a quaint eating establishment he had frequented in London.

"I like this place," said Irene after they were seated. "I haven't been here for a while." And, in fact, she hadn't. Her suggestion to Jane to splurge a little and have lunch here the week before had not materialized. Jane couldn't get away from the office at the appointed time.

"Yes, rather charming," he said, leaning a little toward her. "Reminds me of Hernando's Hideaway—"

"Hernando's Hideaway?" Irene asked with a puzzled expression.

"You know the song? Sorry, my attempt of levity has failed."

A buxom blonde with a pretty, smiling face rescued him from further explanation, laying in turn before them the menu and liquor list. A flittering, uncomfortable moment of silence ensued as they studied the menu. "Crêpes, crêpes, and more crêpes. What do you suggest?" he asked.

"Well…" Irene paused. "One can order a combination. I think, for example, I'll have the crêpe chou-fleur and the crêpe Florentine—"

"Ah, I see … in that case, crêpe boeuf stroganoff and crêpe St. Jacques should suit my palette — I am tempted to start with their soupe a l'oignon, but that may be a little heavy. Perhaps a salade Caesar. What about you?"

"A small spinach salad…"

At Woodal's suggestion, a bottle of red house wine was added to the luncheon. Irene protested that she normally did not have alcohol during the day; it made her sluggish and sleepy. And she had to get back to work! But in this case, she made an exception.

Woodal proved an inquisitive fellow, plying her with all sorts of questions. She didn't mind, content to let him initiate conversation.

"I presume that was your daughter I met the other day?"

"Yes, Carli—"

"Is that your only child?"

"Yes."

"Hmm, this stroganoff is delicious — and what does your husband do?"

Irene sipped her wine and stated, "He's a real estate agent. We are divorced."

Woodal put his fork down. "Oh, forgive me. I'm prying. Not very polite, am I? I should not ask personal questions. It's my curious nature…"

Lucovich/Woodal thought himself a good actor — at least in the role of an inquisitive Englishman. He knew only what he had read in the file and wanted to fill in some gaps. The dossier simply stated that Glinka had a daughter who lived with him — nothing about her being once married or having a child. Not that it seemed pertinent… He was relieved that she was divorced; a husband would have made it that much more difficult to win her confidence. He had her at a disadvantage, which he sensed he could easily exploit. Yet there was something about her he liked; he was genuinely interested in who she was at the moment, not just extracting information. He'd have to be careful, though, not to overindulge on a personal level.

Irene responded, unperturbed. "That's quite all right. There's nothing untoward about your question. Divorce is common enough, and after two years I have gotten over both the event and the stigma. What about you, Mr. Woodal?"

"Please call me Adam. No, I have never married. Haven't had the urge — or perhaps, as of yet, I've not found the right woman." He smiled disarmingly, topped off her glass of wine, poured himself another, and changed the subject. "Have you lived in Edmonton long?"

"Practically all my life. My father settled here — it must be over twenty years ago. Actually, I was born in your country — in London."

"Really?"

"Yes, Mom and Dad lived there after the war for about two or so years before moving to Canada. Poor Dad. My mother died about five years ago."

"Oh … so sorry — must have been traumatic for him and you."

"It was… Her death hit him hard. He was quite depressed, and then there was his stroke a year ago—"

"A stroke? Is he okay?"

"He's doing much better now. He's gotten a great deal of his mobility back, and his speech and memory are also almost back to normal."

Woodal nodded empathetically. "Must have been a frightening ordeal."

"That it was — for him, Carli, and me…"

"What was his occupation?"

"In the old country, as he calls it — Ukraine — he was studying to become a veterinarian, but the war interrupted that. Here he obtained employment in a tannery. Didn't particularly enjoy it, but" — Irene shrugged — "as he said, it put food on the table, and fortunately, there were other DPs who worked there and spoke the language—"

"DPs?"

"Displaced persons — refugees from the war."

"Oh, yes, I see… Must have been a terrible experience — war."

"It was, although he doesn't talk about it much."

"Does he live close to you and Carli?"

"With us, actually. Or I should say Carli and I moved in with him after my divorce."

"I'm sure he's pleased having his daughter and grandchild under the same roof."

"It has worked out well. He's retired now after the stroke…"

Woodal hadn't known about the stroke. A most useful piece of information. It seemed that Drydenko's file was not totally up to date. If in fact, Viktor Glinka was seriously incapacitated or compromised, the whole mission might need a reassessment. Conceivably the threat might be deemed neutralized without action on his part. He needed more information.

"Here I am babbling on about my dad and me," Irene intruded into his thoughts. *Why am I prattling on so*, she wondered, suddenly becoming self-conscious. *Surely it's not the wine?* "What about you?" she asked, trying to deflect and obtain some information about him.

"There isn't much to tell," he said, noticing that she glanced at her watch. Her lunch hour was rapidly coming to a close. "Perhaps we can carry on with our conversation tomorrow night — over dinner?"

Irene hesitated for a fleeting second, surprised and pleased. Adam was a charming man, and she was beginning to feel comfortable with him. Besides, she would like to know a little more about him, and her social life had been nil lately. "Yes, I would like that."

"I am delighted. I have rented a vehicle during my stay here. If you would care to jot down your address, I shall come by, say, around eight?"

Irene fished into her purse for a pen and pad and wrote down her address and phone number. She began to give him directions, but he cut her short. "I'll find it. Your city with its numbering system is logically laid out — I'm sure I'll have no problems."

CHAPTER 20

It had been a windy, rain-pelting day — gloomy, depressing to the spirit. Worse was yet to come. By the time Woodal parked his rented Chevrolet, it seemed that God was about to pronounce judgment on the planet's miserable mortals. The prairie sky grew blacker, and the ground appeared to quiver periodically with the Almighty's fitful hiccups from the clouds.

Woodal dashed to the door, avoiding the little puddles that the rain had nurtured during the day. He rang the doorbell; Irene let him in. Again he was struck by her beauty — no, not beauty, exactly — he checked his thought. Appeal. That was it — intangible appeal. Fair, light-brown hair, distinctive but unobtrusive nose, hazel eyes, and a generous mouth — one that widened into a most welcoming smile. She wore a gingham dress with lace at her throat and wrists. Not extravagant or flashy but attractive and certainly well proportioned.

Woodal felt reassured, comfortable with this woman before him, although he couldn't quite put his finger on why. He was attracted to her, and it went beyond just physical attraction, but given his dark purpose, at that moment he was hard pressed to articulate or define his sentiments.

"Hi, come in, Adam. Nasty night out."

"Indeed, and I've forgotten my raincoat. Imagine a Limey without his raincoat — or umbrella for that matter."

"You had no trouble finding our place?"

"None at all."

"Well, come into the living room and have a seat. I'll be another few minutes… Dad has gone to bed; Carli is spending the night at her friend's…" Irene spoke in gasps, moving her hands furtively as if she didn't know quite what to do with them. Her manner portrayed nervousness. "So … you won't have company for a few minutes."

He took three steps through the tiny kitchen and entered the slightly larger well-lived-in parlor. His eyes registered a small Sears TV set, an old Telefunken hi-fi, a dimly lit brass standing lamp, and a brocaded sofa and matching love seat; he wasn't sure what color they were in the diminished light, since both were covered with a brown afghan. His polished shoes, glistening with water drops, creaked on the hardwood floor. *Pleasant but modest*, he thought, at least by the standards of his London persona, although for an ordinary Soviet citizen, it would have represented a mansion — the culmination of three lifetimes of socialist labor.

"Would you care for a drink?" she asked. "Scotch, whiskey — I think there is some vodka."

"Uh … no thank you. I'll just make myself at home. You can carry on. By the way, I have made reservations at the oddly shaped hotel near the river — Chateau something or other."

"Chateau Lacombe."

"Yes, that's it. Apparently at the top it has a revolving restaurant from which one can have an excellent view of the city's core — although tonight with this foul weather, the scenery may not be the best." This was said in that understated British way that he had honed over the years. The particular venue was suggested to him by the concierge at his own hotel. A unique experience, he was told, opened about a decade ago — really a cylindrical tower of twenty-four stories capped by a fine eatery (appropriately named La Ronde), which provided a sweeping bird's-eye view of downtown Edmonton and the North Saskatchewan River Valley while making a full rotation every ninety minutes.

"Wonderful! You know, I have never been up there!" Irene was genuinely enthusiastic. "Well," she exclaimed, "I better get a move on."

As Irene disappeared down a hall into a room at the end, Woodal quickly surveyed the parlor again. There were embroidered pillows on each end of the sofa, a reprint hanging over the Telefunken that depicted a wild Cossack dance around a campfire, and above the love seat, a large painting of the Virgin Mary with a dying Jesus in her arms. Woodal stared at it for a moment. He hadn't been to church for a long, long time — since his youth. *Religion is the opiate of the masses*, he recalled his KGB instructor stating during the basic foundations of a communism course he was obliged to take. It was a direct slogan from Marx. *Maybe*, he thought, but he would feel just as uncomfortable if a portrait of V. I. Lenin hung above the love seat instead. Neither Jesus nor Lenin in retrospect seemed relevant...

Hands in pockets, he strolled to an open archway off to the side of the parlor. Pausing momentarily, he wandered in. There was just enough light to observe the outlines of a tiny study: desk, reading lamp, swivel chair, and one wall lined with books. On further inspection, he noted most of the volumes possessed Ukrainian titles. Curious, he lifted one out — Shevchenko, the bard of Ukraine...

"Can you read Ukrainian?" Irene came in, fiddling with her earring.

Startled by her arrival, Woodal recovered quickly. "Took a little Russian in university, but it's all Greek to me." He slid the heavy tome back into its resting slot.

"That's Dad's little private corner of the house. He used to spend a lot of his evenings here before the stroke, but not much lately."

"Fancied himself a bit of a bookworm, did he?"

"Not really, but he did spend some time writing his memoirs. There's a Cyrillic ball on that old typewriter." She pointed to a Remington on the desk. "I don't think he finished... In some respects, Pop is a private person. I'm not sure what exactly he does while he's in here."

As they made their way into the parlor again, Woodal couldn't help thinking that the secrets that Drydenko so obviously feared, so desperately wanted him to ensure were kept secret, could very well be contained in the old man's memoirs and memorabilia. He would have to give this study a thorough perusal when the opportunity presented itself...

In the car, Irene asked the question that had been on her mind. "How long will you be in Canada?"

Staring through the windshield, which was rhythmically rubbed dry by the swiping blades, Woodal framed his reply carefully. "It depends on a number of things: how quickly I can conclude my business, how much appeal this part of the country has for me, and whom I meet." He gave her a quick glance and smiled beguilingly. "I expect that it shall be a little while yet. I am getting rather acclimatized to the environment, and I have met at least one interesting person..." Then he laughed. "On the other hand, I may cut my visit short for health reasons. I'm having a devil of a time getting used to driving on the proper side of the road. You colonials tend to be rather contrary to good form on the road!"

Twenty-four flights up, in Chateau Lacombe's La Ronde dining lounge, they slowly circled the stormy sky, the lightning creating jagged tears against the black velvet of the night. Neon symbols of wealth and power dominated the roof of the city: the stylized green TD for Toronto Dominion, the glaring Nova Scotia red with a globe in the middle of the S, and the solid, conservative blue M for Bank of Montreal. These stuck out in a jutting forest of trust towers. "Those are our major financial institutions," concluded Irene, having listed the five banks and pointed out their structural manifestations in and around Jasper Avenue. "I'm surprised," she added, "that the Bank of Commerce hasn't constructed an edifice with Anne Murray's cheerful face beaming brightly over the city."

"Anne Murray?" Woodal asked.

"Yes!" Irene said, seemingly surprised that he wasn't acquainted with Canada's international songstress. "The singer. She does their commercials."

"Ah..."

Irene loved Edmonton. It was her city, and as they majestically turned, she noted the landmarks. "That ribbon of black to the east, of course, is the mighty Saskatchewan River. Those lit strips are bridges. You can only see two now. And that," she motioned to their right, "is an expensive apartment complex where the jet set dwells."

Woodal cranked his neck to take in the towering accommodation that rose above the La Ronde. The white concave balconies contrasted sharply with the straight concrete slab sides. They were close enough to allow a view of some of the lit suites — those that did not have their curtains drawn. "Must be over thirty stories high," he observed. "You said they were the jet set?"

"Well, maybe that's the wrong term, but you know, football players, hockey stars, business magnates, and politicians — those who have money."

Woodal's trained professional eyes focused on one lit square a few flights up, and although it was quite far away, he spied what was definitely a nude female form walking leisurely away from the window toward a sofa. The angle changed ever so slightly, and he let the image go. "Yes, I see."

Irene hadn't noticed and continued talking. "There — that dark triangle with the multicolored lights around it — that, I think is the municipal airport."

Woodal squinted into the watery veil carving rivers on the huge window. "Handy," he intoned.

"Also a nuisance if you need a quick connection to the International."

"They are a bit apart, aren't they?" He paused, obsequiously adding, "That is what amazes me about this country: space — pure, endless, unadulterated space."

Irene laughed. "Spoken like a true Englishman. You're stereotyping yourself. Our huge distances between point A and point B, I've heard said, are always noted by visitors from the UK."

He chuckled, at the same time thinking of the charade he was engaged in: a KGB agent with sinister motives playacting the role of an awed English gentleman. All quite rich, and he felt a pang of guilt. He was thoroughly enjoying her company under the umbrage of deceit. It was all a despicable business… "I suppose you're right," he remarked. "However, right now I'm for closing distances. I propose a toast — a toast that the distance between us becomes small indeed."

"A toast then," Irene chimed. "Oops, our glasses are empty."

"So they are."

"Another cocktail before dinner?"

"I'm not sure I can handle another stiff drink — at least not without some food."

"Do you suppose it's a plot by management to make us lushes?"

"They're sure taking their time in the kitchen. I forget what I ordered."

As if on cue, a courtly waiter arrived with the Chateaubriand Bouquetiere.

"Great! I'm famished!" proclaimed Irene.

As they whittled away at their mignons soaked in sauce béarnaise, they continued their small talk, each in their own way attempting to lay the foundation for a meaningful relationship. At one point, Woodal interrupted his meal to rip the front of a book of matches and stick it in the corner of the moving windowpane.

What are you doing?" Irene inquired.

"Indulging my curiosity," he replied. "I just wondered how long it will take to complete the full three hundred and sixty degrees. This will serve as my reference point. There…" He checked his wristwatch. "I was told it was about an hour and a half."

Irene shook her head. "Men. You're all the same. Little boys at heart. I bet that just about every male who has eaten here has performed the same trick."

Woodal poured Irene and himself a glass of wine from the bottle delivered to the table and raised his toward her. "I'd bet you are right. But here's to you, the mademoiselle who's got me going in circles, albeit slowly…"

The rich feast and wine, followed by coffee and liqueur, left them both suffused. The evening was proceeding grandly. Irene felt serene, warm, relaxed. Was it the booze or the company? Probably a little of each. Adam seemed so keenly interested in her, making flattering comments that appeared genuine. Why else would he have taken her here if that were not the case? He was a man of the world, who no doubt, Irene thought, could attract beautiful women. She suddenly became conscious of her limited experiences, her provincialism. While she talked about herself, she realized that she still knew next to nothing about him, his occupation, his likes, dislikes... Thus far, he had skillfully drawn her out but not himself; he engaged only in amusing but unrevealing chatter. "You know," she said, "to me, you're still a mystery man. You have coaxed and cajoled me into blabbering on — so now let's reverse roles. I want to know all about you."

Woodal was about to respond when the lights around them flickered then shut off. A few moments passed, and the rustle of restlessness that had settled over the room was becoming more pronounced. Finally, an officious young female with horn-rimmed glasses and pursed lips penetrated the subdued chatter. "Ladies and gentlemen," she announced in a thin, nasal voice, "please bear with us. Due to the storm we are experiencing a temporary power shortage. The elevators are not operational. We expect the resumption of power momentarily; meanwhile, the drinks are on the house."

"Keep them coming," someone chirped.

Shortly thereafter, hotel management broke out their emergency supply of candles and lit them in strategic locales, including the bar and washrooms.

"How romantic," said Irene.

"Quite." Woodal gazed out through the window, noting that the blackout affected a couple of blocks at least. He then took her hand into his and leaned forward across the table. "Darkness and a beautiful woman bring out passionate urges in me — any suggestions?"

"None that would be appropriate here," Irene mused coyly.

"Pity."

"I suggest," Irene continued, "that we order two more coffees while we discuss this unexpected failure of modern technology."

"As you wish, milady," Woodal droned in his exaggerated English accent.

By eleven o'clock, with the power still off and the air conditioning system inoperative, the restaurant was becoming uncomfortably warm. Some patrons became increasingly agitated. A number of couples, probably to the chagrin of management who were no doubt concerned about liability issues, procured candles and began their long descent to the lobby via the dark and narrow stairs.

Irene and Woodal hardly noticed the passage of time. For over an hour they gazed across the flickering light, bantering each other — from tastes in food to perspectives on music, society, even politics. For Irene, Adam remained shrouded, but she reasoned it was only a matter of patiently prying open his reserved personality. Possibly most proper Englishmen observed a certain protocol before exposing their male sensibilities to females. But she knew for certain that she was increasingly attracted to him, and she sensed that he was to her. She was about to raise the stakes a notch in this subtle (or perhaps not so subtle) game of seduction. "You have taken me out twice now; I'd like to reciprocate. Can you come to dinner Friday night — say six thirty? I am sure Dad would like to meet you. He's been something of a hermit lately."

"Thank you very much. I'd be delighted."

"Great!" Irene was happy that Adam seemed immensely pleased by the invite.

Almost in the same breath, he then casually slipped off the topic — a skill, Irene realized, he was very adept at — and said, "I propose that we leave this place, like some of the other more adventurous patrons. It does not appear that the electricity will be restored any time soon."

"Good idea," Irene agreed. She was getting a bit anxious, if not claustrophobic. "I've got to be at work early tomorrow."

Woodal scooped up the bill, gave it a quick glance, reached into his impeccable worsted suit, and pulled out his billfold; he laid a wad of bills on the table and set the tab on top. "Let us depart."

It was a long way down, guided only by the flickering candle carefully shielded by Woodal's cupped hand. After a couple of flights of stairs, Irene took off her shoes (the high heels made them uncomfortable); better ruined nylons and dirty soles than being crippled, although she knew that the backs of her legs would be stiff and sore for the next few days.

"My God," she puffed after a number of stairwells, "you have to be in shape to do this." She was hanging on to the back of his suit, one hand clutching the material above his belt, the other grasping the dangling shoes by the straps.

They were nearing the lobby, accompanied only by their increased breathing and the steady *click-clack* of Woodal's steps, when Irene let out a short, stifled gasp. Behind her, a door suddenly opened and a man entered. Woodal dropped the candle and whirled around, his hands in a poised, defensive position. The weak beam of a flashlight scanned their startled faces. Irene instinctively had one of her shoes above her head, toe in hand, the potentially lethal heel ready to strike any would-be assailant. She had dropped the other shoe.

"Excuse me, ma'am, sir," came the equally surprised voice, "no cause for alarm — hotel security."

Woodal was the first to recover. "No harm done."

The man shone his light away from their faces. "Sorry, didn't mean to startle you. It's been a hectic night."

He picked up Irene's shoe, gave it back to her, and with his flashlight, located the candle that had rolled against the wall. The hotel employee fumbled about in his trouser pockets momentarily before producing a booklet of matches, and in short order the candle was flickering once more. "Sorry again," he reiterated. "Did you want me to accompany you to the lobby?"

"Ah, that won't be necessary," replied Woodal.

"Have a pleasant evening then." He turned and quickly disappeared up the stairwell.

Irene sighed, relieved. "I think my heart sped up a hundred times."

"Mine skipped a beat or two," he agreed.

With his free hand, he embraced her by the waist, drawing her body closer to him. It was a compulsive gesture.

"Let's rest for a moment," he suggested.

Then, with only the slightest hesitation, he gently kissed her. This was followed by another more fully engaged kiss. Irene swayed slightly and backed into the wall. The candle went out again, but this time it didn't matter. He pressed against her; she responded. It had been some time since she'd experienced romantic excitement. He held her tighter, sticking the candle into his coat pocket; his strong fingers caressed the small of her back. Her shoes dangled like dead fish on a line, while she put her arms around his neck...

"I don't know," he whispered as they disengaged, "you have a certain appeal."

"I'm glad," she said.

"But as two mature adults" — he paused and placed a quick peck with his lips on her cheek — "the stairwell is not the proper place."

"You're right. So light the candle, and let's get out of here."

As they made their way through the lobby, both knew that a barrier had been broken between them, and they were on the threshold of a new relationship. He squeezed her hand gently as they avoided the array of strange, haggard, unshaven faces in the otherwise sedate and stately hotel. "Edmonton's street people have taken advantage of the blackout and have occupied the lobby," observed Irene. "Probably their only chance to frequent the Lacombe."

"You have your low-lifers, drunkards, castaways, and hooligans too," he responded, his eyes straining through the darkness, spying the host of "undesirables" who sought shelter from the storm in luxurious surroundings. His thought flashed to London and more vividly to Moscow with its own gutter people and where homelessness was not officially recognized; they lived in the shadows, often incorrigible and mostly battered, with cheap vodka providing the only solace against the cold night and their miserable existence. They, too, under similar circumstances, would have poured into the Hotel Ukraina or Rossiya (but with a decidedly more strident reaction from the authorities given the low tolerance level for hooligans in the Soviet state). Regardless, it was a worldwide urban phenomena, exhibited in every major city that he had visited.

In the pitch blackness, it took some time to locate Woodal's car. The underground parking lot, too, seemed a foreboding, eerie place. "Mugger's paradise," Irene noted as Woodal started the vehicle.

For most of their drive to Irene's home, they fell into a comfortable silence; each knew that at that moment, little needed to be said.

The air was cool and fresh, the storm sputtering out as Woodal escorted her to the front door. They embraced and kissed. Irene felt heady, thrilled like a teenager on her first date. It was uplifting, marvelous... "It's late," she whispered, finally gaining control. She didn't want him to go away. She wished to invite him in, but that was too brazen, too soon for her.

"Yes, it's late," he confirmed. "And we both have things to do early tomorrow." Reluctantly, he let go of her. "Till Friday?"

"Friday — around six thirty."

CHAPTER 21

That night in his hotel suite, Alexandr Lucovich, a.k.a. Adam Woodal, wrote a turgid, brief note to Drydenko stating that he had successfully made contact with Viktor Glinka's daughter and that he was proceeding to the next level. This coded communication he would place in the assigned P.O. box. Later, he knew, it would be picked up by courier, in due course delivered to the Soviet embassy in Ottawa, and ultimately transmitted to Drydenko personally. As for Bakinin, he would report to him only when he had the information.

At the moment, however, he was confused. Sprawled on the king-sized bed, his body felt limp, lethargic, while his thoughts nervously raced, attempting to make sense of his world and the reality he had discovered. The two didn't fit. It seemed that Drydenko wanted him to murder a helpless, sick old man. What possible threat could Glinka pose to Drydenko from here, halfway around the globe? It simply didn't make sense. How could he justify this mission that he was ordered to complete? Without answers or at least some sane reconciliation of these questions, how could he live with himself afterward?

It was beginning — the same agony, the torture he inflicted upon himself before he killed Rabiak. But this time, there was a difference. He was going to get much closer to his target and inflict collateral damage.

His thoughts turned to Irene. The jury was still out at this point, but she was a fine, earthy woman to whom he could, under different circumstances, be attracted to; perhaps he was already. He needed to further sort out his Adam Woodal persona with his unmasked self. Or did he much prefer to stay Woodal and forget about Lucovich? What would Woodal really evolve to, and could he live a normal life with a real home, a wife, and family? The answer was, of course, a big Russian *nyet*. He simply would not be allowed that freedom; too much had been invested in him, and it would be concluded that he was a liability; he knew too much. He would be "sanctioned" by someone like himself. Certainly, there was no shortage of such KGB foot soldiers. Still, lying on a fancy bed in a strange but engaging city, the Kremlin, his superiors, and their intrigues (which they seemed to be playing out as their own marionette puppet show) seemed remote and alien — even more so than from his flat in London. Distance and circumstances did make a difference and altered perspectives, he decided. It was Drydenko and his ilk who existed in isolation, indulging in old games with themselves, using others as cannon fodder. To what end? Power and political gain, he presumed, and his contribution entailed the death of an ailing old man in a far-off country for some *not to be known* crimes committed many years ago.

Lucovich lapsed into thinking about the unthinkable. Was there a way out of this insanity, or was he truly doomed, entangled in a web that would never let him go? Could he defect? Could he use this situation to disappear — to escape his past and begin anew? Was Irene the key? Could he seize that prodigal moment in time with her and … what?

The KGB agent finally succumbed to a restless, fitful sleep. In his dream, he saw Irene in a white tunic with a bright kerchief around her head, beckoning him to follow her through an open field toward a wide river … escape, across the Rubicon to sanctuary…

***

Toward the end of the week, Irene and Jane got together for lunch. Jane, with her usual aplomb, was relating her experience with an obscene phone caller the night before. "I was in bed, studying the inside of my eyelids and thinking about the trouble I was having with my cat that had made a mess of my neighbor's flowerbed, when the phone rang. This low, sexy voice, breathing hard, says, 'How's your pussy?' Well, I guess I wasn't quite with it, because I blurted out, 'If that goddamn cat is into the flowers again, it's going to the humane society.'"

Irene laughed. "So what did he say?"

"He hung up!"

"You really surprised him."

"Yeah — too bad. It might have been interesting."

"Aren't you afraid he'll call again?"

"Nope. I think I discouraged him... But so much for my exciting night. What about yours? Something is up."

"What makes you say that?"

"You look like you're on cloud nine."

Irene thought about Jane's comment. It was probably true. Since meeting Adam, she had felt unusually exuberant, a state she could not hide. She smiled more cheerfully, laughed more freely, and made those around her involuntarily respond to her infectious joy. "I am on cloud nine."

"Yeah, it shows — like a rose in a potato patch. And it doesn't take subtle female intuition to pinpoint the cause. Am I right?" Jane's eyes were twinkling.

"You could be."

"All right," Jane said as they were served the noon specials, spinach salad brunch for calorie counters. "Who is he? What does he look like? What does he do? Most importantly, is he married?"

Irene blushed slightly. "That obvious, is it? Well, I've been dying to tell someone."

"I'm all ears," said Jane as she popped a slice of hard-boiled egg into her mouth.

"He's a Brit. In Canada on business—"

"Where'd you meet him?"

"Pure coincidence — fate. I'll have to be nicer to Purry, wash her more often, change the oil—"

"Purry?"

"My Pinto. It was last Friday at Southgate. Purry wouldn't start, and out of the blue appears Adam. He fixed the problem, and presto" — Irene snapped her fingers — "disappeared before I could marshal enough words to say more than thanks. But then…" — she paused and ate some salad — "Monday, I was substituting for Lori, who had a filling fall out that morning, when again, from nowhere, he materialized in the office, asking for an appointment with Swartz… Then, he spills coffee on me—"

"He spills coffee on you?"

"A wonderful event… He was so apologetic, insisting on taking me out to lunch — the Crêperie, no less — and things sort of gathered momentum from there—"

"Okay, like what kind of momentum?"

Irene shoved her salad plate away and dunked her tea bag into the little tin pot. "Enough of this rabbit food… He asked me to dinner Tuesday night."

"And so what happened?"

Irene spooned out the tea bag and poured the liquid into a well-worn cup. "We went to the Chateau Lacombe — the La Ronde on top…" She proceeded to relate her evening's adventure with Adam, accurately but modestly, without embellishments. "Anyway, he's coming to dinner tomorrow."

"Sounds promising," said Jane. "You might have a live one."

Irene gave her a disgusted look. "I wouldn't put it that way, but I think, thus far, we're mutually agreeable. As a matter of fact — I was just thinking I'll invite him to be my escort to Nadia Mulchenko's wedding."

"That would be a good test, wouldn't it?"

"What'd you mean?"

"To see if he can hold his booze and not dance with two left feet…"

They both chuckled. "I suppose you have a point." Irene glanced at her watch. "Oops, we'd better be heading back."

As they merged onto Jasper Avenue from the greasy spoon they had just tried as a cheap change of pace, Jane was still plying Irene with questions. His age? Color of his eyes? Hair? His height? Other distinguishing features… She was one of those individuals who just had to know every detail — a chatterbox and notorious gossip but also a good-hearted soul who was genuinely happy for Irene, although she sometimes expressed it with a warped sense of humor.

As they hurried down the sidewalk toward the monolith square glass box they called their workplace, Jane, ceaselessly curious, asked, "What did — uh — Adam want to see Swartz about?"

"I don't know precisely."

"You should. Could be his divorce!"

"He's not married. I told you."

"Just joking…"

The two legal secretaries filed separately through the revolving glass door and fell in step on their way to the elevators. "Couldn't have been very important, though," Irene thought aloud.

"What?"

"Adam's seeing Swartz. His appointment was for this morning. I kept an eye out for him, but he didn't show. I asked Lori. She said he phoned yesterday afternoon to cancel." The elevator door slid open. Both entered. Jane pushed 7, Irene 5. "I must remember to ask him about that."

CHAPTER 22

If the way to a man's heart was through his stomach, then Irene had the battle won. At first, she toyed with the idea of going all out with a traditional Ukrainian meal — borscht with vushka, perogies, cabbage rolls with rice, baked corn meal, and chicken covered in a special mushroom sauce — but she was a working girl, after all, and did not have the time to prepare such an elaborate supper. Finally, she settled on something simple but palatable, she hoped: baked ham, scalloped potatoes with broccoli, and a Caesar salad. For dessert, apple custard torte. That, she thought, should be sufficiently impressive.

Woodal arrived fashionably late at 6:45 p.m. with a half a dozen roses in one hand and a bottle of Châteauneuf-du-Pape in the other. "I took a chance on the wine," he said. "Hope red is suitable."

"Absolutely. Oh! Thank you. What a lovely gesture, and I do appreciate the roses." Woodal handed over the paper-wrapped bouquet; womanizing or courting, flowers were always in vogue, he had learned.

"I'll just put them in water; meanwhile, meet my father."

Woodal smiled weakly — the moment of dread. When he killed Rabiak, he didn't have to shake his hand, talk to him, look into his eyes, discover that indeed this was a man and not a mere product of albumin and water. He understood well the thinking of those in Drydenko's position; one does not move up the KGB hierarchy (or any Russian hierarchy, for that matter) without covering one's arse, which included past vulnerabilities, indiscretions, failures; certainly, opponents would take ruthless advantage of whatever faint trail was left behind to follow. That, Woodal knew, was Drydenko's rationale and why he was there. Still, there was Bakinin to contend with — the rival who wanted to know why this man had to be silenced. That would prove more challenging, requiring deceit, patience and subtleness … asking the right questions. And he was curious. What *did* this man know, to be so feared by a Kremlin oligarch who would send an assassin halfway around the world to take care of the problem? In any case, he would have to fortify his resolve when the time came.

As Glinka limped toward him with the aid of his cane, the Soviet agent realized how easy it would be. A tiny pinprick would inject more than a lethal amount of toxin. A healthy man might fight it — the nausea, the paralyzed muscles, the lungs rapidly gaining fluid, the white blood-cell count accelerating — might resist the poison for a couple of days, perhaps a week, but a sick man… Glinka would be dead within a couple of hours. Woodal shook Glinka's weakly extended, limp hand. "How are you, sir?"

"I have seen better days, Mr.…."

"It's Woodal. Call me Adam."

"I am Viktor."

Viktor had a surprisingly strong voice, which appeared to belie his frail physical condition, thought Woodal as he assessed the slightly stooped man before him. "Well, I'm very pleased to meet you Viktor—"

"Any way … I have been sick … heart—"

"It was a stroke, Dad," interjected Irene from somewhere down the hall. "Not quite the same."

Glinka waved his hand in a gesture of dismissal. "Heart … stroke — no matter, terrible thing, you know — to be sick and old."

"Dad." Irene again interrupted in mock scorn as she entered the kitchen. "Are you going to be gloomy and pessimistic with our guest?"

"Not at all — just telling the truth."

"You're not that old, and you will recover — you *are* recovering," she affirmed.

The old man shrugged. "I s'pose, God willing."

"I'm sure you will," said Woodal, mustering a cheerful smile.

"Well … come and sit down, Adam. Make yourself at home." Glinka gestured to the kitchen table, angled himself to the nearest chair, and with a grunt deposited himself into it.

"Wouldn't Adam be more comfortable in the living room?" Irene asked, turning to her father.

"Oh, I'm good here. Doesn't matter where I sit," said Woodal, moving toward the table, which was adorned with an intricately embroidered white cloth, cutlery, four china plates, and three wine glasses.

"That's fine then," said Irene. "I guess we can forgo the predinner drinks. Dinner is almost ready anyway. I hope you're hungry."

"Starved," said Woodal.

"Good… Now, where's Carli?"

"I'm here, Mom." Carli entered the kitchen and shyly glanced at Woodal.

"You remember Adam?"

The child hesitated and in an unsure, small voice stated, "He fixed the car."

"Hi, Carli." Woodal smiled. "Nice to see you again."

"Mom likes you," Carli blurted out.

The blunt, unexpected, innocent comment threw everyone off balance, especially Irene, who blushed. Woodal quickly filled in the silence. "I like your mum and you too."

Irene recovered. "Sit over here, dear." She pointed to the chair that didn't have a wine glass in front of it.

Woodal undertook to uncork the wine; in the process, however, the cork crumbled and pieces fell into the bottle. "Well," he said, "made a hash of that!"

Worse yet, when he poured, some dribbled onto the tablecloth. "Good Lord, I'm exposing my clumsy traits again — first the coffee and now the wine. I'd make a bad garçon!"

"Oh, don't worry about that," Irene said.

"What's a gar-son?" chimed in Carli.

"You should know, Carli. Haven't you taken that in your French class?" asked Irene.

Carli thought momentarily, "I heard it before but I forgot."

"It means waiter," said Woodal. "I didn't know you took French."

"She's in the French immersion program," Irene responded. "The second official language in this country."

"Carli is also in the Ukrainian language program." Glinka joined the conversation. "Important for her to know that too," he added with elevated emphasis.

"Indeed."

"Sometimes, though," Irene interjected, "I think it's a little hard on Carli."

"It will not hurt her," her grandfather retorted. "She is young. The best time to learn different language is when you are young. Is that not so, Adam?"

Woodal thought of the number of languages forcefully, relentlessly drilled into him by the state instructors... He had to admit it did not hurt him and was certainly useful. "I see no harm in it."

"See, there you go. Carli will do just fine... It's good for her — to know her roots, her heritage."

"I'm curious. How do these language classes work?" inquired Woodal.

"Well," replied Irene, "let's see... It originated with the Ukrainian Bilingual Advisory Society — I think that's the official body — which draws its members from the city's Catholic school district, from parents who are members of the Ukrainian Catholic Parishes... At any rate, the program goes from kindergarten, where children develop oral skills in English and Ukrainian, through grades one to six. Carli is now in grade four, where reading and language arts are taught in Ukrainian for about fifty percent of the time. It continues thorough junior high — grades seven to nine."

"Impressive," said Woodal, "but where does French fit into the scheme?"

"In grades four to six, all students can take part in the regular oral French program," replied Irene. "That's where I'm a bit torn. I would like Carli to learn French — she enrolled this year — but it may all be a little too much to learn two languages."

"She will do good," reassured Glinka, "won't you?"

Carli nodded, adding, "I like French too."

"There you go," stated her grandfather. Turning to Woodal again, he continued, "Now that the English have joined the Common Market, learning more languages in schools will begin there—"

"It will probably take a while," Woodal replied, not really knowing. "We Brits are rather traditional… That sort of change will take time."

"Ah *tak*, yes, the stoic British." Glinka wore a serene expression, thinking back to the blissful time he spent there with Galina. "We lived in London before coming here. Yes — stiff upper lip and all of that…"

Woodal grinned. "It's not always like that."

Carli, who had been the object of this initial burst of grown-up talk, thrust herself again into the center of adult attention. "I know a joke about a waiter. Can I tell it?" She gave Woodal a mischievous glance and her mother a pleading look.

"As long as it's not rude," cautioned her mother.

Carli sat up pert in her seat, formulating her thoughts. "Um… What happened when the waiter dropped dinner?"

"We don't know, dear," said Irene. "What happened?"

Carli giggled, and in a rush of words, lest she stumble and get mixed up, pronounced, "Um… the break-up of China, the downfall of Turkey, and overflow of Greece!"

There was a hearty laugh from the adults. "Very good," proclaimed Woodal.

Carli felt self-satisfied until, in her excitement, reaching for her glass of milk, she spilled half on the already wine-stained tablecloth. After that, she retreated into model childhood, listening and obeying while grown-up talk whirled about her.

Overall, the dinner went amicably. Woodal ate a healthy portion, Irene and her father less so, while Carli only mildly protested that she didn't like broccoli. Amid the clattering dishes and squeaky chairs, the conversation remained at the level of general banality — cooking, the weather, travel, and music. This included getaways from winter blues and warm places to visit… All liked pizza, and the adults were partial to Beethoven, Mozart, and the Beatles but couldn't understand punk rock…

After dessert, Carli was informed that it was past her bedtime. She dutifully finished her second glass of milk and scampered off to wash up and put on her pajamas. She came back outfitted in a red sleeping garment and clutching a shaggy brown one-eyed teddy bear.

A classic Norman Rockwell, thought Woodal, having studied the works of the iconic American figure. Carli kissed her mother and grandfather and curtly said goodnight to Woodal. Irene escorted her child to the bedroom to tuck her in as was the usual practice. Grandpa had often done it, but now that he was less mobile, she undertook the honors.

After Irene returned, more coffee was served, spiced by the addition of Amaretto for the lady and two shots of Georgian brandy for the men, Woodal's being much more generous.

"What do you do, Adam?" Glinka asked, suddenly alert and focusing his attention squarely on him.

"I'm with a British investment firm, scouting out, as it were, your resource-rich province."

"Which reminds me," Irene said, "you did not meet with Mr. Swartz?"

"Oh … yes. No, I canceled my appointment. It appears that the company has no need to retain a solicitor after all… Viktor, Irene tells me that you have had an interesting life?"

Irene couldn't help but notice that Adam, like a seasoned courtroom lawyer, pivoted and redirected, turning off the inquiry into his own life and putting the onus on her father's.

From Lucovich's perspective, it was a tried-and-true technique — gain the person's confidence, let him talk, listen well, preferably over a drink or two, and eventually (sometimes it's surprisingly soon) ferret out whatever relevant information is needed.

Glinka rose to the bait. "I s'pose — not a pleasant time, for sure — which you two were lucky to escape. I saw much I did not wish to see and did things I did not want to do. And know things I should forget…" He shrugged.

"What did you do?" Woodal asked, leaning forward in his seat.

"I was a horse doctor for a short time in the old country, just before the war, then a laborer, soldier, and laborer again." Glinka said this with a faint smile.

"You came from the Ukraine?" Woodal prodded.

"No… Let me correct you." Glinka seemed to gather strength in his voice. "I come from *Ukraine*. There is a difference. I do not know my English grammar perfectly, but enough… When you say *the* Ukraine, it is not proper, no more proper than saying you come from *the* Britain, or I live in *the* Canada now. Ukraine is a nation, not a region of Russia like the Ural Mountains or Siberia. Someday it will throw off the tyrant's yoke—"

"Steady, Dad," Irene interjected. "Adam is not arguing with you."

"Indeed, not…" He had, though, plucked, quite inadvertently, a sensitive string that he could exploit. He sensed that the old man had something to say, and he wanted to talk.

"Why don't we go into the living room — make ourselves more comfortable," Irene suggested.

Irene excused herself for a few moments as soon as Viktor and Adam got comfortably settled in the small living room, glasses of brandy in hand.

"Doctor say not supposed to drink, but it is small glass and special occasion, eh." Viktor smiled.

Woodal returned a knowing smile. "So, you've had an interesting life in the old country?" he asked, hoping to restart a revealing conversation.

"Interesting? Perhaps not so much — terrible and dark, yes. I have seen too much death."

"You mean during the war?"

"War, yes, but before the war — the famine."

"Yes, there were bad crop failures in Ukraine—"

"Bad crop failures!" Glinka exclaimed incredulously. "Let me tell you — it was artificial famine — Stalin's famine. You do not read about it because Russians say it did not happen. The latest Soviet encyclopedia does not mention it, but it existed. How do I know? I was there! While Stalin sold 'surplus' grain at low prices on the world market, millions died, and those who survived were reduced to cannibalism — yes! Human flesh, packed, salted, and sold in barrels on the black market."

"Why? Why would a state — Stalin — do this?" Woodal asked, playing his role as an uninformed Englishman.

"War on the kulaks—"

"Kulaks?"

"Yes. You see, kulaks were those who had something — land, grain, animals — and they did not want to give it to the state for nothing. So it was taken away, but not without a fight! A man must try to protect his family and his property. That is natural. Anyone who resisted was labeled tight-fisted." Glinka raised his hand and clamped it into a fist. "Kulak — Russian for *fist*. We were supposed to be the wealthy farmers who were sabotaging the state's quota for the collection of grain — saboteurs, they called us! Wreckers, screamed the propaganda! Soldiers came, and we were disposed and deported to the terrible collective farms, and worse! Deported to work and die in what were called corrective labor camps. In Siberia, you know — like animals. No, worse than animals, because animals were considered valuable… I am talking about not hundreds or thousands but millions. Ten millions, perhaps, who knows? Of course, it was war on the kulak, and so crops were taken, then the land and livestock until there was nothing. Stalin sealed the borders and let us starve. My mother, father, sister, and brothers were his victims…"

Glinka stopped and cleared his throat, his eyes glistening. "Tell me, Adam, do you know of this? Have you read any of this in history books?"

"No, I can't say as I have."

"And why? Because officially it did not occur! Terrible events that one cannot imagine just disappeared like a pebble thrown into a stream, barely producing a few ripples." Glinka sighed. "There is no justice. Criminals, butchers, murderers are now statesmen in the

Soviet Union… Did you know I once met Stalin? A despicable creature who looked like an ordinary little man…"

Woodal's face remained placid, but this revelation more than piqued his interest. Could it hold the key to his mission? But how?

"When did you meet him?"

"A few days after the Germans invaded — June '41. I never told anybody about it. But it doesn't matter now." Glinka abruptly stopped, as if perhaps he had said enough. Taking a sip of his brandy, he passed over the event and continued. "Later, I joined a partisan group — surrendered to the Germans — had no choice, really." He shrugged. "After what we had been through, we believed the Nazis were the lesser evil. Imagine seeing the Nazis as liberators. Yes, liberators! We begged them to give us an opportunity to fight the Russians — the Red Army. Stupid Germans. Saw themselves as the superior race. Could have won the war if they treated the conquered correctly. They had Ukraine. But they were scarcely better than the Russians. Hitler's aim was to destroy the Slavs, whose territory the German nation could occupy. The Jews served as a kind of laboratory, experimentation on how to kill large numbers efficiently — no doubt the techniques learned to be applied to the Slavs… Of course, Stalin had already had a big start on this… After locking us up for most of the war, in desperation finally they said yes, you can now go fight the Russians. It was, as they say, too little, too late. Yes, we fought toward the end. Most of us died or were executed, but I had enough. I knew that I had to get out — escape, run away, get lost in the Western zone. Good fortune was with me, as I am here."

"Let us drink to that," said Woodal, raising his glass. He quickly added, "You should commit your experiences to paper. It would make for fascinating reading."

"You did, didn't you?" Irene interjected, suddenly appearing as if on cue. She remembered him working on his memoirs at various times before his stroke. In fact, she had mentioned it to Adam, she thought, at the Lacombe.

"I did not finish, and with my heart attack—"

"Well, now that you are recovering from your *stroke*," she emphasized, "perhaps you should get back to it — finish it."

"Maybe you are right — when I get better."

Woodal wanted to ply Glinka with further questions, especially about his meeting with Stalin, but decided against it for the moment. There had to be a sordid connection with Drydenko in all of this, and while Drydenko bluntly told him that it was better if he kept himself ignorant, that was not realistic. Bakinin's "request" could not be ignored. An impossible dilemma. For Drydenko, his intelligence-gathering was complete; Irene knew nothing of her father's secrets or past exploits; and the old man could be easily eliminated, and his memoirs, such that they were, disposed of. Such a course of action, however, was not advisable; he needed to know — not only because of Bakinin but for his own sake. He needed to change the rules of the game. He just didn't know how — yet…

"How much of the memoirs have you completed?" he asked.

"Why?" questioned the old man rather sharply.

Careful, don't push this, he cautioned himself.

"From what you have told me, it makes for a fascinating read."

"Would do you no good — it's written in Ukrainian."

Woodal almost let slip *but I can read Ukrainian* before collecting his wits. "Right, I see… So how much of it have you completed?"

"Through the war years — before going to England… Yes, I should work on it again — finish it."

"It would be good therapy, and I could help you," Irene volunteered, as if suddenly wondering why she hadn't offered before.

Glinka abruptly changed the topic. "I think I have taken enough of the talk this evening, and I am sure you two have something else to talk about. It is almost ten." He glanced at the old Westinghouse clock above the stove. "*The National* will begin. Think I will listen to Knowlton Nash give the troubles of the world, see what Trudeau is doing."

"Well, Dad, I'll leave you to it then." She turned on the tiny TV.

"In that case," Adam said, turning to her, "Why don't I help you clean up."

"It's not necessary."

"But I insist."

They cleared off the table. Irene neatly stacked the dirty dishes to one side, filled the sink with hot water, and pulled a drying rack from beneath the sink.

"Wash or dry?" he asked, taking off his blue sports jacket and rolling up his shirtsleeves.

"Why don't you just relax and have some more coffee. I can take care of this."

"Tut, tut. If you can't make up your mind, then I'll do it for you. I prefer to wash."

"Where's the soap?"

"Beneath the sink."

"Right." He found the yellow plastic bottle and squeezed a generous amount of liquid into the frothing water.

"Do the wine glasses first," she ordered.

"Right."

They settled into a steady rhythm of work, looking like a typical domestic couple. "Dad got a little wound up tonight. He rarely mentions his past."

"Probably did him good," said Adam. "You haven't read his memoirs, by any chance?"

"Heavens, no! He seemed quite secretive about that. Maybe I should."

"Can you read Ukrainian?"

"Yes, but painfully slow. I haven't progressed too far beyond kitchen Ukrainian. Besides, I'm out of practice. Carli will be much more competent than me — if she sticks with it…" Irene paused and fished out from a cupboard a dry dishtowel. "How would you like to go to a wedding?"

"A wedding… Are you inviting me?"

"Only if you want to come."

"As your escort?"

"That was the idea — it's next Saturday. A friend of mine is biting the bullet. Promises to be fun, if you're into eating vast amounts of fattening peasant food, drinking lots of Five Star whiskey, and jiggling it around dancing polkas."

"An offer I can't refuse, except, perhaps, for the dancing — 'fraid I'm rather rusty."

"Then we'll have to loosen the hinges."

They were interrupted by Glinka at the kitchen entrance. "Well, I am tired. So I will say goodnight. Nice to have met you, Adam. Hope I didn't bore you."

"Not in the slightest."

Irene gave her father a hug. "You should be exhausted. It's getting past your bedtime."

Adam stayed until almost midnight, feeling increasingly lethargic and content sitting on the sofa, his arm around Irene while the newscaster signed off and a movie feature was about to commence — *Splendor in the Grass*. With a sigh, he realized that it was time to go. He thanked her for supper; she thanked him for the wine and flowers. "And don't forget next Saturday — the wedding."

As he got into the car, all he could think of was that, with rose blooms come thorny stems.

CHAPTER 23

Woodal did not know exactly where they were, except that it was in the northern section of the city. "We're almost there," Irene informed him as he made another right turn, judiciously following her directions. To the left loomed the Byzantine dome of the Eastern Orthodox Church. "The hall is beside the church."

"Right."

Woodal had been in an indecisive mode for a week, and he knew he had to get on with it — ferret out what Glinka knew or did and finish the assignment. There was no denying that he was intrigued by the old man's mention of having met Stalin. Under what circumstances? Why? Was it significant? Had to be, since Drydenko and Bakinin were vitally interested, albeit for different reasons. Or was it something else entirely? At one point he drove by Glinka's abode, intending to speak with him, force the issue if necessary. Instead, he continued on downtown and dropped in on Irene at Swartz's office to take her for lunch.

She was the crux of his procrastination. He couldn't afford to get too intimately involved, but here he was still cultivating her and rationalizing it as a need to gather more information, even when it was obvious that there was no more to be had. The truth was, she was enjoyable company, and he decided for reasons that were at best ambiguous, if not outright muddled, to wait until after he accompanied Irene to the wedding before taking any decisive action.

Meanwhile, he had a few days to kill at Drydenko's expense (more likely and indirectly the Soviet state's discretionary fund). He explored the city, marveling at its diversity, richness, and available amenities. Capitalism may not have paved the streets with gold, but it seemed that not only the bourgeoisie but also the proletariat were doing well. Certainly, it didn't take a back seat to London in that regard. Nor did the surrounding countryside, he discovered. Of particular note was his road trip eastward on Highway 16. In the hotel lobby, he picked up a brochure on a Ukrainian Heritage Village and decided that it may be of interest. Why not? He had time on his hands while he worked out what was to be done.

Driving on a double-lane highway with wide shoulders into shimmering heat waves rising from a hazy, flat horizon, it seemed that the land was similar to the steppes back home. Good farming country, he deduced, appreciating the seas of purple and yellow interspersed with verdant fields and black summer-fallowed strips. In the distance, scattered throughout the checkerboard fields, stood stands of poplar, aspen, and spruce. Through the open window he inhaled the earthly fragrance. It reminded him of his own rural beginnings, even as he wondered why there were no agricultural workers to be seen...

In due course, after passing through some kind of wild preserve — far off he saw buffalo grazing — Woodal spotted his destination and made a right turn into an entrance, beyond which was a collection of old buildings. The sign read *Ukrainian Cultural Heritage Village*. Some kind of open-air museum — a reconstruction of a pioneer settlement.

For the next hour, he meandered with little clusters of people from artifact to artifact. Amid caragana hedges, gardens of potatoes, sunflowers, and poppies, the animal enclosures and thirty-odd structures, his mind went blank. He recognized many of the stylistic forms but had no real interest in a rebuilt 1920s Ukrainian settlement in Canada. At one point he edged close enough to catch a smattering of conversation between two older ladies, not quite babushkas but close (and overexposed in their shorts and sleeveless tops) as they observed a blacksmith demonstrating his skills at a forge. The women were chattering about some aluminum Easter egg in a place called Vegreville. "It's huge," he heard one exclaim. "Donated to the town to honor the hundredth anniversary of the Royal Canadian Mounted Police..." *Police?* He wondered what the police were doing constructing a large *pysanka*. He let the thought drop and walked away briskly to his car. He was going back to the city; the sun had given him a headache, the swirling dust irritated his eyes, and truth be known, the excursion was simply a sentimental distraction. Time to focus on his next course of action...

Following Irene's directions Woodal swung into the parking lot, which was rapidly filling up with vehicles; it took a little time to find a suitable space to back the rented car into. "There — perfect." He switched off the ignition and opened the door carefully until it tapped the plastic molding on a big Oldsmobile beside him. He then went around the front of the Chevy and ceremoniously opened the passenger door. "Milady," he intoned in his exaggerated English accent. "By the way, you look ravishing tonight."

Irene wore a cream-colored mandarin-style dress made of silky material with a matching jacket. The dress slid up as she got out of the seat, revealing plenty of smooth leg.

"Thank you. You look pretty dapper yourself..." He wore a newly purchased midnight-blue suit with straight-leg trousers, pleated at the waist. A starchy white shirt and dark-red tie enhanced his attire, even if it was a trifle wide, he thought, by Savile Row standards.

They entered the hall through heavy wooden doors that seemed to be the trademark of such all-purpose buildings; once in the foyer, there was another entrance into the auditorium proper. On one side of the archway stood the flower girls, ready to pin a carnation on his lapel and a corsage on her dress. On the other side, tuning up and laughing, was a five-piece dance band. "It's tradition," said Irene. "The girls provide the flowers and the band plays the Ukrainian wedding march as we enter."

"Right," he said, playing out his role as the uninformed Anglo-Saxon flummoxed by the unfamiliar environment.

As they proceeded, he pulled out a couple of bills, depositing each in the baskets provided. Meanwhile, the quintet struck up a vigorous rendition of the traditional melody. Irene recognized the violin player: an older man and obviously the group's leader.

"Boris!"

The man gave a wide smile. "Irene," he exclaimed after the music ended. "I haven't seen you in a long time."

"I didn't know you were the entertainment."

"No canned rock music tonight. Bride and groom wanted the good stuff so that the older crowd could enjoy too."

"That's great... Oh, Boris, this is Adam Woodal — Adam, Boris Dubs."

They shook hands.

"How's your dad these days?"

"Still recovering."

"He's not here tonight?"

"No. It'll be a while before he can kick his heels to your Kolomeka."

Their conversation was interrupted by another couple coming through the archway. "Well, back to work — talk to you later."

"Be sure to, Boris."

Irene and Woodal walked on, introducing themselves to the wedding party and the elderly parents of the bride and groom who formed part of the smiling queue that greeted the guests. "I hope you enjoy yourself," said Irene as they sat down near the end of a long table covered by an expanse of white cloth.

"I'm sure I will." Adam focused on the ever-increasing pockets of people filling the auditorium, reserving their places at the tables for the meal and festivities to come. "There's got to be over three hundred people here already," he observed.

"A typical Ukrainian wedding. The hall can accommodate over five hundred... Pulled out all the stops for this one, I bet," replied Irene.

Adam had a momentary sense of déjà vu as he heard the familiar litany of Ukrainian intermixed in creative ways with the "Queen's English" and mellowed by Boris and the other musicians in the background as they struck up the chorus again. These were really *his* countrymen, transplanted and modified to a new environment...

"Oh — here they come." Irene interrupted his reverie. The bride and groom had arrived. "Doesn't Nadia look lovely!"

"Quite."

Nadia wore a long, flowing white dress, and circling her careful coiffure was an embroidered coronet from which hung many multicolored ribbons flowing onto her back. The groom, in his light-blue suit with a frilled shirt and large bow tie, looked rather uncomfortable but resigned to the ritual about to begin.

"Not exactly spring chickens," Woodal ventured, noting that the happy couple were in their late thirties or early forties.

Irene poked him in the ribs. "I think it's Nadia's second and John's third. So ... they have been around the block," she whispered.

The wedding procession started to make its way up to the head table. The guests were on their feet, clapping in rhythm to yet another rendition of the wedding march from the tireless band. Adam leaned over to Irene while he clapped. "The groom must be someone of note for such an extravagant wedding."

"John Laska works for the city — engineering department. I image he can afford it. Nadia, too, has a good job, with the provincial government, I think..."

"I see," he said, thinking that the affair was extraordinarily extravagant for a couple who had been through multiple marriages. Certainly, an ordinary Soviet citizen would be hard pressed to put on such an extravagant event.

Finally, the entourage arrived at their destination below the stage; the newlyweds were seated at the center of the table, with three loaves of bread with a lighted candle on either side. The master of ceremonies, a plump little man, adjusted the microphone (which emitted the customary piercing squawk) and told the "cherished" guests to remain standing while the good father said grace. When that was duly performed, the rustle of moving chairs signaled that the eating and drinking were about to begin.

Irene glanced at her watch — ten to seven. "Excuse me for a few moments, Adam. Carli is at a sleepover tonight, so Pop's all alone.

Think I'll phone home before it gets too late — make sure he's all right. He didn't look that perky earlier today."

"Oh?"

"I'll be back in a jiffy."

While Irene was gone, Adam idly chatted with a couple seated across from him. Meanwhile, men appeared with bottles of white and red wine, which were strategically placed on the tables. They were followed by hustling women carrying bowls of potatoes, vegetables, meat, holubschi, and perogies. The wine was poured, plates filled, and the hall rang with clatter and laughter.

Irene returned, sliding into her chair and giving a playful squeeze to Adam's shoulder. "There — that's done."

"How is he?"

"Fine. Said he was going to bed early. Sometimes I feel badly about leaving him alone — but he didn't want to come."

Adam put his hand over hers. "Don't feel badly. He'll be refreshed and well rested tomorrow, which, I suspect, will be more than I can say for us…"

The supper was marvelous; the speeches from the head table were long, tedious, and often inaudible, but no one seemed to mind. Irene met more acquaintances, introducing Adam a half dozen more times. While far from an extrovert, Adam was enjoying himself as the evening wore on, his initial aloofness loosened by alcohol. He generally did not drink too much, knowing his limits, but in this case he could afford to indulge, since it would be absorbed by the healthy portions of rich food he consumed. He had to remind himself that he was a stranger in a strange land with a sinister purpose. It was not easy to sit benignly, soaking in Irene's congenial company without feeling a certain (albeit contained) disgust and loathing for himself, his occupation, and his motives. *A twinge of conscience I need to suppress*, he decided, especially since he was rapidly approaching a point where action was required. Meanwhile, he had to maintain discipline; there could be no slip in his persona in an unguarded or frivolous moment.

By nine, coffee and dessert had been served; Boris and his troupe had reassembled themselves on the well-trod stage above the head table, and people started lining up to pass by the bride and groom, wishing them well and depositing their envelopes containing a card and money in the box provided. That took another forty-five minutes. Finally, the lights were dimmed and the tables in the middle of the hall cleared, folded, and carted away to provide a larger dancing area. "I hope you've got your dancing shoes on," chimed Irene. "Boris is known for his polkas." As if to illustrate the point, the quintet furiously struck up "Helena Polka." In a trice the floor was packed with whirling bodies.

"Next dance. Let's sit this one out."

"Next dance then, Adam — but I'll hold you to it!"

The band didn't seem to want to stop. On and on flowed repetitious refrains. Finally, Boris sprang forward with increased energy, still madly sawing on his violin strings. He signaled that the tune was about to end. His eyes widened into a fierce bulge, reminding Adam of the portrait he once viewed of Ivan the Terrible just after he had, in a fit of rage, murdered his son. Accordingly, the sax man nodded to Boris; the accordion player nodded to the drummer; the drummer seemed oblivious to the gesture but banged all the harder on his skins and cymbals; the guitarist was completely forgotten.

Three sharp notes and they ground to a halt. Drunken men clapped and hugged their dance partners. Boris, his high Slavic cheekbones wrinkled by a proud smile, bowed graciously to his admirers. Adam clapped also, letting his eyes absorb the people on the dance floor. He found himself drawn to the primeval display of energy that seemed to fill the hall. It was as if the revelers were in a trance, gripped by a pagan ritual — as if the choreography was part of an amulet to drive away, at least temporarily, whatever evil spirits lurked. He felt a communion, a bonding with these anonymous people, most of whom could trace their relatives to his part of the world. He, too, needed to ward off pressing demons...

Irene tapped him lightly on the shoulder. "Our turn."

"Right."

She took him by the hand and led him to the milling swell of humanity. The band members had gathered their scattered notes and stopped quarreling just as Boris returned to the stage; he had hurriedly downed a healthy shot of vodka from behind the bar. Someone brought a tray with five bottles of Molson Ex and set it on the huge amplifier. They started playing again — a waltz.

"*Pytala sie Pani*," said Irene as they began to glide across the floor.

"What?"

"Name of the waltz — Polish, I think. Heard them play it on numerous occasions."

"Oh."

Irene, her eyes closed, swaying suggestively with every nuance and turn of Adam's body, momentarily broke away from his embrace. "You lied," she said. "You are a great dancer."

"I learn quickly." He smiled, gazing into her eyes and smelling her perfumed hair. There was a stirring within him. He sensed that she felt the same way — her remaining barriers were being dismantled by increasing familiarity and alcohol…

They danced through a couple more waltzes before returning to their seats. Adam was interrupted by an intoxicated fellow with a swarthy complexion who came over to him, a cigarette hanging from the corner of his mouth, the filter tightly clenched between his teeth. "Gottsha light?" he sputtered, unintentionally spraying saliva in all directions but miraculously still retaining hold of his cigarette.

"I don't smoke — sorry."

The man wandered off. Adam took out a handkerchief and wiped an eye. Irene, who had been at his side, also used the hanky. "At least he wasn't nose to nose when he asked."

"No harm done, and he didn't pick a fight!"

"You're right. Later, when everyone is sufficiently inebriated and feeling no pain — although in his case he's there already — they'll segregate into groups and start singing old traditional songs."

"Why not? It's another form of communication, of touching each other. The songs are a reminder of their origins and the past that links them," Woodal pronounced before he could stop himself.

"Very perceptive, Mr. Philosopher!"

Too perceptive, he thought, *I'm not playing my role of the stiff upper lip Englishman...* "Just an observation."

They sat in silence for a while. Adam sipped his wine and suddenly became aware that in the din of humanity, the music had stopped. Someone had gotten up on stage and was pursuing an animated conversation with Boris.

"Song request?" Adam asked.

"Oh, that's Mr. Muskas. He wants to contribute to the music — become one of the boys in the band. He usually gets his way at every *zabowa*."

"At what?"

Irene searched for the proper English translation. "You know — every time people get together for a good time ... a party."

Meanwhile, Muskas tripped over the microphone cord, causing the mike to fall with a loud thud in front of the guitar player, who, for the first time throughout the evening, exhibited obvious emotion: anger. He brusquely pushed past Muskas, who had been vainly searching for the fallen piece of equipment, scooped up the mike, examined it, and carefully slid it back into place on the stand. Muskas shortly thereafter was handed two maracas by Boris and ushered to the back, behind the drummer, where he could happily make his musical contribution. Boris then tested the strings on the violin and decided a tune-up was in order. He motioned to the accordionist, who hit a few notes in succession. While this was occurring, everyone on the dance floor impatiently waited.

"Adam — there's something I've been meaning to ask you for over a week now, but it always seems to slip my mind."

"Oh?"

"Remember when you showed up at the office that Monday and made an appointment to see Swartz?"

Adam nodded.

"I know you canceled it, but Swartz was curious about the company you worked for. I told him you never said, but he mentioned he would like to know. The firm caters to resource-based companies, and I think he keeps a contact file."

"Not a problem. I don't have any on me now, but I'll provide you with my business card with the particulars for Mr. Swartz's file."

"And I can tell him that you may get back to him in the future? Sorry, Mr. Swartz can become a bit anal when it comes to business matters."

"Right." Adam emitted a short laugh and cleared his throat. "The truth is that I was premature, and the company does not need, as yet, the services of Mr. Swartz. But the moment we do, you can tell Mr. Swartz that he'll be retained. Right now, though, the music has struck up, so let's dance."

Irene sighed. "Sometimes you're impossible—"

"'Tango of the Roses' — one of my favorites..."

Adam attempted to steer carefully, but it was futile — the floor was overcrowded with unsteady drivers. In the congestion, they moved as one, his right knee persistently aligned to an imaginary axis between her legs. The tango came to an unexpected halt. Almost immediately, the quintet erupted into a torrid polka. Adam tightened his hold around Irene's waist, and with a whoop they plunged into a quick two-step whirl, Irene beaming and her dress an airborne swoosh.

Later, the newlyweds, who had disappeared, reentered the hall. There were still a number of rituals to be performed, one of which was the throwing of the bride's bouquet to one of the unmarried females present, followed by the groom disposing of the garter in similar fashion, taken off the bride's leg to the beat of strip-tease music. *Old-world tradition to new-world music?* Woodal wondered.

The women grouped together in front of the stage. On the stage, Nadia, her back turned to them, accompanied by a drum roll, flung the bouquet over her head backward into outstretched hands. There was a loud shriek as the flowers bounced off a couple of hands directly into Irene's. Flushed, slightly embarrassed, she hurried off the dance floor with her prize amid applause. Adam gave her a kiss on the cheek. "It's an omen," he said. "Soon you will meet a dark, handsome stranger and—"

"Maybe I have already." They looked into each other's eyes. Adam shifted his away with difficulty.

"Now it's your turn…" she said.

Adam did not secure the garter belt that was thrown in similar fashion. He made a half-hearted attempt, but the toss fell short and two young bucks went sprawling forward in an attempt to wrestle the prize away from each other. "It just wasn't worth ruining my suit over," he explained to Irene.

After the wedding guests had settled down somewhat, Boris gave a loud shout into the mike. "It's time for the 'Kolomeka'!"

Mayhem broke out as the band began playing at a frenzied pace. The music was familiar to everyone — including Adam. It was the music of the warring Cossacks, of strength, skill, bravery, and cultural symbolism that was centuries deep. The people gathered around in a large circle, clapping, while individual performers, when the urge possessed them, flung themselves into the center: young women twirling in intricate steps and young men, their arms folded, squat-kicking out their legs after short vertical jumps in time to the beat. It was strenuous, requiring balance, strength, and practice. Then came the high leaps and splits. "Members of the local dance troupe," Irene remarked. "They're pretty good — dancercise class was never like this." She laughed, craning her neck to get a better view from outside the circle.

Adam looked on stoically. True, for a moment he thought of his birthplace; he was reminded of the deep black soil of the steppes, the sweet smell of the air, the laughter of his mother so long ago, and incense that filled the little church that he attended as a child. He had given that up — betrayed it. These people harkened back to a romantic past — a nebulous concept at best. His experience was born of harsh reality where totalitarianism ruled, demanding obedience and execution as an integral part of his survival. He needed to resolve this quickly before he succumbed to sentimentality and other dangerously soft notions.

⁎

There was no need to say anything; they had been building up to it all night. Once they were inside Adam's hotel suite, the dam burst. As soon as the door closed, he reached for Irene and guided her to the bedroom. In one swift motion he pulled her down onto him, giving her a long, thrusting kiss. She responded eagerly, then pulled away gently. "I need to use the bathroom…"

Irene walked into the bathroom, scooping up her purse along the way. She closed the door and stripped off her clothes, neatly piling the garments on the edge of the tub. She noticed the little TV set fastened to the end of the marble vanity, its blank screen angled toward the toilet seat. *God*, she thought, *what will they think of next! Whatever happened to reading while on the throne!* She let the thought drop. This was, after all, an executive suite. She had noticed, however fleetingly, the little fridge and bar, monstrous bed, wine-colored rugs, and the fancy writing table in a small sitting area. Adam traveled in style…

She brushed her teeth and stood in front of the mirror. "Pretty soon, old girl, you'll be in your midthirties," she muttered. *But still not bad.* Her breasts were generous, with a little droop, the nipples taut, hard, in anticipation.

All was not perfection, she knew. Her backside was a little plump, but not obnoxiously so — the classic features of a nude in a Renaissance painting. She gently slapped the left side of her bum; it quivered slightly but was still solid enough. She had kept in shape — *although a little more exercise wouldn't hurt. Oh well…*

She took out a little blue case from her purse. Popping it open, she hesitated for a fraction of a moment. Yes, she would use her diaphragm; it was much too soon to throw caution to the wind and risk pregnancy. She spread cream on the device and inserted it.

She hadn't gone through this ritual in over two years. *Two years!* It seemed like a long stretch of self-denial. Stephen had probably hopped into bed with more than a few women since… Even when their marriage was on the rocks, her emotions frayed, there was still the physical pleasure. An inner glow filled her — *sex, yes*, but part and parcel an emotional swell she felt for Adam. Was she falling in love again?

Irene emerged from the bathroom, conscious of her nakedness, her vulnerability. Adam lay on the bed, the sheet, blanket, and bedspread rolled half down. A muscular body, flat stomach, the build of an athlete.

"There you are... I thought you'd drowned!" he remarked.

Irene laughed, her initial shyness gone. They were simply two people with no clothes on. "Don't tell me you were getting impatient?" she teased.

Their lovemaking was unrestrained. They kissed and caressed. Then the moment came. Adam mounted her as she spread herself open, arching to meet his thrust. She let out a small gasp as he entered. At first, he was leisurely, tantalizing her with smooth, rhythmic jabs. Then he became determined, increasing the pace.

"Oh, Adam!" She dug her nails into the rippling muscles of his ribcage. The two bodies established a cadence; she pushed against him when he rose and sank deep into the springs when he bore down. She began to come, wave after wave, the intensity fierce. She could barely stifle a cry. "I'm almost ready," he said, "should I—"

"I've taken precautions," she exclaimed. "Do it!"

He released spasmodically, two, three volleys...

After, they cuddled, drawing the blanket and bedspread over them. Neither said anything for a long time, each lost in thought, savoring the ecstasy of their act. Irene spoke first. "You're the first man I've let into my life since Stephen."

"Oh? Separation ... can be very traumatic..." Adam was not sure what to say.

"I suppose. It's taken me much longer to recover," Irene replied, sounding bitter.

"I don't remind you of him, do I?"

"Not at all ... maybe the eyes, a little."

"How'd you meet?"

"The university here in town — gosh, I don't believe it — over twelve years ago. Seems like yesterday. He was a commerce student, full of schemes, determined to make a fortune, and he probably will..." She let the statement drop.

"Do you still love him?" *Odd question. Why am I prying?*

"No, but I did once very much… He just never grew up. I thought that he would — well, settle down after we got married, but I guess it just wasn't his nature. Women held a great fascination for him. He never quit sampling, even with a wife and child…" Her voice faded and became pensive. "Adam, I don't want to feel that kind of pain — or is it betrayal — again. I-I think I have feelings for you — at least the man that presents himself to me. Are you really that man?"

"What'd you mean?"

"I don't exactly know." She paused and gently ran her fingers down his hairless chest. "Look, Adam, with me, you get what you see. What I'm trying to say is that I am who I present myself to be. Are you really who you are? I still know nothing about you. I'm scared to take you at face value. There may be another man behind the mask of Adam Woodal."

He tensed slightly. "What makes you say that?"

"I'm not certain — woman's intuition."

"What is there about me that you cannot accept at face value?"

"You seem so … secretive. Why wouldn't you tell me about yourself?"

"There is little to tell."

"You said that before, and it's not true! What about your childhood, your family, your hobbies… What *do* you do?"

"Oh… I'll get around to it. I don't want to bore you just yet."

"You don't get off the hook that easy. I'm curious."

"Curiosity killed the cat."

"Now you're making fun of me."

"Sorry, I don't mean to. We'll have a long chat about me soon. I promise."

"Why not now?"

"Lovemaking and chatting don't mix."

"We're finished."

"Then let's do it again."

"You're exasperating! Do you know that? I just don't see why you can't talk to me about yourself."

"Why are you in such a hurry to compile my life's history?" His voice had a sharper edge than he intended.

Irene flushed a little, both with a dollop of anger and frustration. "Why do you always deflect a question with another question? That can be irritating, don't you see? I am trying to make some sense of my feelings for you, but it's difficult. You're elusive — a mystery man. I am sharing your bed but hardly know any more about you now than when you first appeared out of thin air in the parking lot."

He snuggled closer to her, wrapping an arm around her. "Try to understand, Irene. I have never been what one might call an extrovert. It takes a while to get to know me. Please, trust me, I will bare my soul to you—"

"Is that a commitment?" she whispered, moving closer to him.

"A promise. I have become smitten with you."

"Well, you're starting to grow on me." She giggled, thinking that perhaps she was oversensitive, attempting to extract too much, too quickly. "I'm sorry. I didn't mean to jump on you."

He hushed her with a kiss. He then raised himself up on his elbow. "Ready for round two?"

"As tempting as it is, I have to get home sometime tonight, and it's getting late."

"Right."

CHAPTER 24

Saint Basil Ukrainian Catholic Church was an imposing, modern brick-and-stone edifice adorned by nine pillared overhangs on all sides; it had massive wooden doors and was capped by a golden cathedral dome. Glinka labored up the concrete steps, pausing before the somber statute of Saint Basil the Great, his right hand raised as if he were delivering an inspired sermon before his flock. Woodal approached Glinka from behind, stopped, and read the Ukrainian inscription directly below the English, which the old man appeared to be studying intently.

St. Basil the Great
Father of Christian Monasticism
Founder of the Basilian Order
Commemorating the
1600th Anniversary of his saintly death &
5th Anniversary of Missionary work
Amongst Ukrainians in Canada by
The Basilian Order

The inscription meant very little to the KGB agent; he had no knowledge of Saint Basil (except of course, for St. Basil's Cathedral in Red Square) or the Basilian Order. But then, such matters were of little interest to him.

Casually stepping alongside the older man, he said, "Good morning, Viktor."

"Adam!" exclaimed the startled man. "What are you doing here? Irina's gone to work—"

"Yes, I know. I wanted to speak to you privately. Was on my way to your house when I saw you here."

"Out for my walk." Glinka, cane in hand, turned toward Woodal, wavering slightly. "I walk by this plaque and statue often, but only today I stop and read it."

"Ahh... Well, I do have a matter of importance to discuss. Perhaps you would like to sit for a moment..." Woodal gestured to a bench not far from the bottom of the steps.

"Okay," Glinka said as they slowly descended the steps toward the bench. "You wish to talk to me about Irina and you?"

"Not directly — let's sit here," Woodal said with a sigh as Glinka eased himself onto the bench. The rubber was about to hit the road, and Woodal wasn't sure if this was the proper locale, given how the old man might react. "It involves you, or more precisely, your activities during the war in the old country. That was a fascinating story you told last week, and I wanted to know more details."

Glinka's eyes narrowed in suspicion. "I do not want to talk about—"

Woodal interrupted him and said in Ukrainian, "Viktor, you were involved in, shall we say, intriguing activities that are of great interest to my superiors and ... the Soviet State," he added.

Glinka's eyes widened. All these years. It couldn't be. Not here — not in Canada. He was safe. He could feel his heart start pumping faster; he sucked in more air.

"Please, Viktor." Woodal noted the man's quickening breathing and stricken pallor. "I do not want to alarm you. And I mean no harm." He sat beside Glinka.

In a feeble voice, the Ukrainian asked in this native language, "What is this all about? Why are you here?"

"I'm not sure, to be truthful. I want your cooperation in ... my inquiry."

"Who are you?" Glinka asked, seemingly to steady himself.

"I think you know who I represent, but to repeat, there is nothing to be alarmed about — just provide the information I seek."

"And my daughter? That was all ... all a trick to—"

"No, not entirely," Woodal said quite honestly. "I am getting ... fond of Irene ... Irina."

Glinka made a move as if to get up and flee from this suddenly disagreeable encounter, but a discreet restraining hand alit on his arm. "Please, Viktor, let us talk."

"I know nothing. Let me go."

Woodal took his hand away but sallied forth. "Much is known about you. Your partisan activities, which you mentioned to me, your connection to Vlasov; your work with British intelligence. Yes, a large file has been built up."

"Most of it lies! I am an old man on a pension, living peacefully."

"And it can remain so if you tell me what I need to know."

"Bastards!" Glinka raised his voice, his face becoming flushed. Anger had gripped him — anger and fear. How dare they! He could barely control his trembling.

"Please do not upset yourself. Your activities are a thing of the past. Water under the bridge. I accept this. My superiors do not seek redress or revenge." *Not exactly true.* "I simply want to know what you did in the war to arouse the notice of certain officials in the Kremlin."

"What kind of information? I don't understand."

Khorosho. Now we can get to the heart of the matter, thought Woodal. "I just—" The roar of a diesel engine cut Woodal off. Below the steps, a bus pulled into the curb.

Two people exited and walked by. Woodal waited until the noise subsided, watching the purplish fumes of the diesel fuel dissipate. "Why don't we go to your home to discuss this further in comfort over a cup of tea..."

***

They were seated in the tiny living room, Glinka on the sofa, Woodal on the old lounge chair opposite.

"So tell me," Woodal said brightly in Ukrainian, "have you had any contact with the motherland in the last few years?"

"No."

"Have you followed events in the Kremlin?"

"No, I am not interested anymore. I am Canadian now. This is my country." Glinka said this with defiance.

Woodal nodded. "Perhaps that is the proper attitude. However, it is your past that is of interest — at least to my bosses. Does the name Andrei Drydenko mean anything to you?"

"No."

"Think back, Viktor. Perhaps during the war—"

"No. The name is not familiar. What is this about?"

By way of an answer, the KGB agent produced from his breast pocket a brown envelope. "In here, there are two photographs — supplied courtesy of Deputy Director Bakinin — one from a recent *Pravda* clipping and the other taken in the late forties. They are of Andrei Drydenko. They will serve to refresh your memory." He took the photos out and laid them on the cushion of the couch beside Glinka's cane. "Again, I am only after information. There will be no reprisals against you, no matter how serious your crimes or distasteful to the Politburo they may be… But you and this man" — he tapped the photos lightly — "are connected, perhaps in passing, perhaps quite innocently, but you know him by face, if not name. And I want to know what you know about him… I understand that you are an ailing man whose memory has faltered, but look closely, take your time. I can make some tea or coffee if you want—"

Glinka waved him off and reached for the pictures. "Why is this man so important?"

Woodal shrugged. "As I said, I am only a field agent. This is — how shall I put it — an internal matter. Provide me with what you know and forget we had this talk—"

"And my daughter — you used her to get to me?"

"I am sorry for such deceit. I can only say that I will disappear with a saddened heart. But it is best that she not know of our discussion here. So please study the photo."

Even with the scarred face and drooping right eye, Glinka recognized Timoshenko's attaché. His reaction gave him away.

"So you do know him." Woodal made it more of an exclamation than question.

Glinka said nothing but continued to stare at the photos. "Yes," he finally acknowledged in a low, hoarse voice. "I was there when he acquired his injury."

"Please explain."

"So Drydenko is his name. He was General Timoshenko's attaché in '41. I gather he is alive and well and has sent you."

"He is now a deputy director of the KGB... I need you to explain."

"It was all because of my notable face, so he said — or should I say Dr. Bodrev's face."

"Who?"

"A face that got me close to Stalin — alas, not close enough. It is all in my memoirs — at least that part of it."

"And your memoirs are in your study?"

"Yes — in the file drawers. I can—"

"Never mind about that now; just tell me what happened. What did you do for Drydenko, and where does this Dr. Bodrev fit in? Start at the beginning."

"I need to go to the toilet," Glinka announced. "Old men sometimes can't stand the pressure..." He gave a crooked smile.

As Glinka made his way down the hall to the tiny lavatory, he thought of the man he had met so many years ago in Gorky Park... A cold fish, he was even then... *Am I a loose end? Is that it?* Or was it something different — some sort of investigation was taking place. After all, Drydenko had killed Dr. Bodrev — he had practically admitted it at the dacha... *Maybe they haven't pieced it together yet — the plot, the elimination of the doctor — or why would the agent, Woodal, or whatever his real name is, be asking questions?* How much was known? Nothing? Everything? Then how did they find him? He had no idea, but a KGB agent was here, halfway across the globe...

Glinka made a mental note to look up Deputy Director Drydenko in the Soviet Who's Who. He'd go to the university library tomorrow. Questions continued to intrude in rapid succession, all revolving around how to interpret the Soviet agent's request for information.

Did they find out what happened to Doctor Bodrev? Was a trial being prepared? How many were involved in the conspiracy? Were they still alive? But that was so long ago... Why pursue it now? Did they want him to corroborate that, in fact, there had been an assassination plot against Stalin? He had told no one — *let sleeping dogs lie.* It would have served no purpose and might have gotten him killed (*still might!*). Besides, who would have believed him? Was it part of a power struggle in the Kremlin? If he told Woodal what he knew, would he be left alone? Most of all, was there any threat to Irina and Carli?

Glinka tried to dismiss such a possibility, but it wouldn't go away. *Stupid old man ... talked too much the other night...* The more he thought about it, the more agitated and troubled he became. He suddenly felt like a rat in a maze: many passages to scurry down, but no way out...

Glinka really did not feel well and he did not look well. The bathroom mirror reflected a very pale, drawn face. He bent his head over the sink, splashing his cheeks with cold water. *Slow down, old boy*, he thought. *All this stress is not good... Try to calm yourself...* He took a step toward the door and almost collapsed, a sharp wedge of pain searing across his chest. Both hands were needed to stay propped up against the sink... The pills: He had to get his pills. He reached up to the white medicine cabinet, but the effort was too great; he felt himself falling, tumbling into a dark abyss. On the way down, for a fraction of time he saw it all: his homeland, mother, father, sister, and Irina and Carli...

CHAPTER 25

Woodal tried to save the old man — he really did. But CPR did no good. "It must have been a massive stroke," he muttered to himself, finally stopping his ministrations.

After that, he sat back in momentary panic. His first instinct was to leave — flee the scene. However, he calmed himself and thought through the situation. Nothing could be done for Glinka except move his crumpled body from the bathroom floor to the sofa in the living room in order, he hoped, to ease the shock when Irene got home — make it look like Viktor lay down and never woke up; that he died peacefully in his sleep.

Glinka was not a heavy-set man; still, Woodal struggled with the dead weight, angling the body out through the bathroom door and dragging it, hands and arms around his shoulders, the head loosely lopped downward on his chest, down the hall into the living room. The easiest part was to lift him onto to the low, well-worn sofa.

Woodal was fairly sure that no one had seen him go into the house with Glinka. Nevertheless, he instinctively peered from behind the drawn curtains to check the street and make sure there were no visitors coming up the walkway or unusual activities. Monday morning, the neighbors had gone to work and all was quiet.

His second order of business, now that his breathing had returned to normal, was to find Glinka's memoirs. He needed to know Glinka's secret. He was sure that the old man would have told him but ... alas. The KGB agent made his way to Glinka's little study.

The manuscript entitled *My Life* was not hard to find. It rested at the bottom of a gray metal three-drawer filing cabinet. The neatly stacked pile of loose sheets was placed in a box that once contained typing paper. He took it out and set it on the old writing desk where the typewriter sat. Just to be thorough, he then opened the other two drawers. The first had nothing of note: numerous files of household bills and tax statements. The second appeared empty except for an aged wooden Dutch Masters cigar box. In it, Woodal discovered Glinka's immigration documents and identity card, under which, curiously enough, was another card for one Dr. Bodrev. Glinka had mentioned his name, Woodal remembered. More intriguing was the grainy photo attached, for it could have been mistaken for a considerably younger Glinka. *Strange*, he thought as he took the cigar box and placed it on the desk beside the manuscript box. *Was Dr. Bodrev an alias Glinka used? And for what purpose?*

Not entirely satisfied that he had secured all pertinent items, Woodal continued his search (albeit hastily); for what, he wasn't sure. The one large desk drawer yielded a stack of notepads, a stapler, an eraser, a pair of scissors, and numerous pens scattered about, but nothing of value. He also did a quick review of the small bookshelf that he had first noted when he came by to take Irene to dinner. Again, nothing of a personal nature — no notebooks or diaries, just historical and literary tomes, from Hrushevsky to Shevchenko.

As Woodal made his surreptitious exit from Glinka's house with two boxes in hand, he felt a sense of remorse knowing that he probably contributed to the old man's death. Still, he reassured himself, it was inadvertent. He had no intention of "sanctioning" Glinka, or so he had convinced himself. Most of all, he felt concern for Irene, or more precisely the shock she would experience (and perhaps Carli too) when the corpse was discovered... It just couldn't he helped.

***

Cloistered in his hotel room, sipping his third cup of coffee, Lucovich, alias Woodal, was slowly working his way through Glinka's autobiography. Glinka was the son of a relatively prosperous farmer in southern Ukraine. He had a normal boyhood (to a point) that Glinka described quite vividly. Indeed, Woodal thought the old man had a flair for descriptive prose, going on for pages describing the rich Ukrainian land, the white-washed peasant cottages, the cherry orchards, the domes of churches, and the folk that he had encountered: mustached, sun-burnt men and smiling, bronzed women with bright bead necklaces. It was, Woodal believed, rather idealistic, rustic, and impressionistic — the reminiscence of a man in his twilight years recollecting scenes that in his mind's eye brought him emotional fulfillment. A recapturing of what once was, but perhaps in a more distorted and favorable light. Woodal smiled, realizing that at the moment, he did not have the luxury of being a literary critic. He continued reading…

Glinka launched into a long tirade on Stalinism and collectivization. For Stalin, Ukraine was the most difficult country to deal with because of its large population. Yet it was critically important to subjugate it, not only because of its raw materials, agricultural potential, and developed heavy industry but also because of its strategic geographic position to the Black Sea and Eastern Central Europe. Lenin had allowed the policy of encouraging the minorities in their languages and traditions in the hopes of appeasing and harnessing ethnic aspiration to communism. He had little choice, since his attempts at collectivization had failed with the peasants resisting and, in the process, threatening to topple the war-weary, weak regime. Thus, throughout the 1920s, Ukrainian intellectuals took advantage of this official relaxation to promote and expand the use of Ukrainian in schools and in government and to place their own in positions of authority. They articulated nationalistic ideals and at the same time criticized the Soviet system.

After ruthlessly consolidating his own power, Stalin decided in 1930 that the time had come to suppress this "Ukrainianization" movement, which had been flourishing throughout the twenties, and to get rid of the intellectuals and cut down a notch the individualist peasantry… Glinka had evidently done some research to supplement his eyewitness account; the text was replete with statistics... *He should have been a historian,* mused Woodal as he glossed over these pages, becoming increasingly impatient, wondering if there was anything pertinent about Drydenko to be learned... He skipped ahead.

Most of the Glinka clan did not survive the famine. Glinka saw his mother and father wither away; the grain requisition detachment took every morsel of food in the household — not only the grain but also the livestock and workhorses. They were left to starve... Then came the news that the land many Glinkas had worked with loving care for generations was theirs no longer. They were branded as kulaks and were to be deported to Siberia and the labor camps...

Father died before they came... Mother died shortly thereafter of malnutrition, but also, we suspected, of a broken heart... Bohdan, broad-shouldered and black-bearded, the oldest of my brothers and the strongest, along with shy Ihor and silent Nil, were hauled away in the middle of the night, never to be seen again — at least not by me... Anna and I remained behind, hidden away. As the youngest, a few days before they came, it was decided that we should make our way to Ivan Gordesky, a friend of our father who lived in a nearby village. There was no point in staying... Besides, all the food was gone, with even the cats, dogs, and birds eaten. By now, no animal was alive in the countryside.

Even the rats were being stalked by human predators. We surely would have perished if Ivan and his wife had not taken pity on us at considerable risk to themselves. It was a crime against the state to harbor kulak fugitives... Miraculously, Gordesky was left relatively unscathed, but then he owned no land; he was a boot maker... He couldn't shelter everyone, it was presumed: as it was, he could barely feed us, although under the circumstances it was remarkable that he could provide for us at all... The Gordeskys were kind-hearted souls — childless. Nadia Gordesky fussed so over us, adopting us as her own... In retrospect, I think Ivan had connections. And he was, after all, a fine boot maker, and local party officials needed boots. Perhaps his talent saved him — and us... Little Anna, bewildered, frightened, cried and cried... She did not survive the winter. I think she caught pneumonia... Mrs. Gordesky took Anna's passing very hard...

Woodal paused, took a sip of his cold coffee, and briefly reflected on his childhood and adolescence. His dream of ever becoming a teacher (or anything else for that matter) ended abruptly with that one unauthorized train ride. He could still recall the dank, dark room, permeated with the faint smell of urine; they interrogated him for hours, working in shifts, allowing no rest, no food, no reprieve of any sort until they broke him down ... down into a whimpering, terrified wretch ready to do their bidding. It occurred to him that he was still doing their bidding; that he was still part of the system that had spawned a relentless, incestuous, obscene bestiality. Woodal shook off his wandering thoughts and concentrated on the yellowing pages before him.

Over the next few years, young Viktor managed to survive with his benefactors; the Gordeskys treated him like their son, and Ivan endeavored to teach him his trade. He also read vociferously anything he could get his hands on. That was Nadia's doing; she insisted that he have schooling... One day, he told Ivan that he wished to become an animal doctor; it was something he and his father had talked about. It was a noble, worthwhile profession for a Glinka with the family's roots deep in the soil. Gordesky, after some argument, relented; he had no right to constrain the boy. Let him follow his father's wishes and his own inclination... Glinka acquired the necessary books, studied hard, and passed his qualifying examinations. He was off to Kiev to enroll in veterinary college...

Yes, Irene mentioned that, Woodal remembered. He skimmed over the next few pages, which dealt with the year spent in Kiev, some of the people Glinka met, and the generosity of Gordesky, who supported him financially.

Glinka also made references to the purges, which terrorized Kiev, pointing out that in 1937 Stalin declared war on the leadership of Ukraine, arresting and eliminating three successive prime ministers and ultimately the entire Ukrainian Politburo because they were not subservient enough to Moscow. In 1938, Nikita Khrushchev, Stalin's new hatchet man, was appointed in charge of the Ukrainian Communist Party. He eradicated any lingering remnants of "Ukrainianization" and began a campaign to enforce the compulsory teaching of Russian in schools...

Glinka's veterinary training came to an abrupt end after a year; Gordesky died, and the money to support his studies stopped coming. Glinka was in need of employment.

Thanks to Gordesky, however, the young Ukrainian did have a trade — as a boot maker. With that he managed to obtain permission to move to Moscow. Why not? He supposed that the many hundreds of people flooding into Moscow needed boots and shoes, although when he got there, he realized that one's priorities above all were food and shelter. Thanks to Stalin's five-year plans, which emphasized heavy industry, the cities became focal points for a massive influx of workers — the industrial proletariat — many of them from the rural areas where collectivization had made them redundant peasants. The result was chaos. Moscow's facilities could not absorb such an input of humanity. Not that it mattered to Stalin or his henchmen. This represented Stalin's version of the Industrial Revolution in England during the late eighteenth and nineteenth centuries, when English farmers were forced (by enclosure laws) into the newly developing cities and transformed into an urban proletariat destined to eke out their lives in squalor and poverty amid the deafening drones of heavy machines and the overcrowded, unsanitary shacks of the ghettos. In England this transformation was relatively gradual, but in the USSR it came swiftly, brutally, with a human casualty figure that far outstripped the English example.

Glinka found work in a shoe and boot factory, not as a skilled craftsman but as another faceless robot chained to a bench, tacking on soles. Woodal read on: more pages of historical and personal accounts. In this factory, materials were scarce and the end product was poor in quality, limited in amount, and dear in price. Aside from securing work necessary to eat and afford a tiny room (shared with two other workers) in a dilapidated building, Glinka was intent on discovering the whereabouts of his three brothers. There had been no messages, no letters, and no clues. It was as if they were feces flushed down the toilet and gobbled up by the sewer system. But Glinka believed Moscow was a good starting point for his search — the entrance to the sewer system. That's why he stayed...

Glinka had begun to despair of ever learning the fate of his brothers when he met Yuri Bristov, a youthful Red Army officer. Woodal rubbed his eyes, stretched, and continued on. Glinka devoted a number of pages to this tall "Cossack" with the deep, sparkling blue eyes. The Ukrainian helped Bristov out; indeed, probably saved his life. On a cold December night, he found Bristov sprawled in an alley covered in his own vomit, a victim of too much bad vodka. Glinka had just finished his shift at the Markov Boot Works and was on his way home. He couldn't leave the man there; he'd surely freeze to death. So he half coaxed, half dragged him to his hovel. Fortunately, there was no one else there to argue over bringing yet another body to share accommodations, and Glinka let the intoxicated man sleep it off in his cot.

The men became friends and shared confidences, and even a woman briefly... Yuri, it turned out, like Viktor, was bitter; his father, a high-ranking army officer, had become a victim of the purges, summarily tried and shot as a spy. "My father," he told Glinka, "could no more be a spy than my mother could grow a beard."

Although Bristov had not been molested by the secret police, he became an untouchable. No one in his right mind would associate, at least publicly, with a man whose father had allegedly committed a crime against the state. "Stalin is a butcher," hissed Bristov to Glinka one night over a bottle of vodka. "And I wish I would be in a position someday to cut out his heart."

It was a remarkable statement, uttered in an atmosphere where even thinking such a thought would bring, at the very least, ten years of hard labor and at worst, an unpleasant termination in the Lubyanka. Having spoken so frankly of his feelings, Bristov inspired Glinka to talk about his life and of his deep, unrelenting hatred for Stalin as well. The men had a bond and objective in common and could trust each other.

"Perhaps I can help you locating your brothers," Yuri offered after Viktor related his despair that he would never be able to find them.

"How?"

"Despite my non grata standing, I have just been elevated to personal attaché to an important officer who knew my father. It's still a fairly inconsequential position, but I do have access to records. I can make discreet enquiries, although I must be careful — few comrades would openly wish to acknowledge me. It's a long shot. I make no promises, but I owe you one…"

For three months, nothing was said of the matter. Then one day, a haggard-looking Bristov intercepted Glinka at the factory gates as the latter was on his way home. "I am terribly sorry, my friend," he finally said after walking with him some distance, "but your brothers are dead…"

For a few moments Glinka could not grasp the finality of Yuri's blunt statement. "Are you sure?"

"Yes."

"How? Where?"

"At Yakutsk, Siberia… The details are sketchy. Their names appeared on an official list. I did not want to be the bearer of such news, but as your friend, I thought it best you know; otherwise, you may spend the rest of your life in a futile search."

Glinka was consumed by grief, self-pity, and finally rage. He was all alone in the world now with nothing to live for — except revenge. Bristov was his only true friend, and they continued to commiserate. He never did discover how his brothers died.

Meanwhile, unbeknownst to Glinka at the time, Stalin and Hitler had reached an accord. On the surface, the Nazi-Soviet Pact was an agreement of nonaggression and neutrality. What wasn't divulged was the secret protocol that in effect partitioned not only Poland but also much of Eastern Europe between the two regimes. With the agreement, it looked like Stalin had averted his nation's involvement in a pending general war. At least it appeared that the motherland had obtained immunity from attack by Hitler…

June 22, 1941: Woodal noted that Glinka had underlined the date. Bristov told him that day that the Germans had invaded the Soviet Union and that he, in all probability, would be transferred to the front. Glinka was stunned; he didn't know what to think, suddenly having ambiguous feelings. He argued with Yuri; maybe it wouldn't be so bad for the Germans to eliminate the communist regime. Why should he feel otherwise toward the regime that murdered his family? Life for the populace would surely be no worse under the Nazis…

Bristov chided him for his attitude. "I will fight," he declared, "for my country. The regime is another matter — a lower priority for the moment. There will come a time when we can strike a blow at it as well…"

June 25: Again the date was underlined. Yuri paid Viktor his last visit, as it turned out. The young soldier was in an agitated, excited state. As they walked through an alley Glinka often used as a shortcut home, Yuri pronounced, "I came to say goodbye. I am leaving Moscow tomorrow… I also have a proposition for you — one that may cost your life. Remember the last time we met, I told you that there may be an opportunity to strike a blow at Stalin and his regime even as we fight the war?"

Glinka nodded, although that wasn't exactly how Bristov had expressed it. At the moment, he was more concerned about losing a friend, possibly forever.

"Well — it's here! There is a chance…" Bristov hesitated, as though debating whether to go on.

"What are you saying?" asked Glinka, puzzled.

"I-I would have volunteered, but I didn't have the right physical characteristics or skills — but you do! I told him about you and that you had medical training. It can work if — if you are willing." Bristov suddenly became nervous, breathing shallowly.

"I don't understand—" Glinka began.

"Stalin! Stalin has gone mad. He has become … unstable. He is to be … eliminated — assassinated for the good of the country."

"What — by whom?" Glinka asked disbelievingly.

Bristov stopped and furtively glanced around to make sure no one was within fifty feet. "The generals, but it's best you not know."

"Obviously your superior—"

"Please, Viktor, don't ask questions, and listen..." His voice trailed off, then seemed to gather strength: "I suggested you because — well, you are the only person that fit the plan — the perfect person to kill him."

"What!" Glinka could hardly believe his ears. "What are you talking about?"

"There was no one else on such short notice. They are desperate. It must be done soon ... and I convinced them that you — well, I-I assured them that you could be trusted and that you could do it."

"Yuri, you're mad... I — how?"

"Don't say anything to me. I agreed to approach you. If you were — are — ready for such a task, go to Gorky Park tomorrow afternoon. Here are the instructions." Bristov fumbled around in his uniform pocket before handing Glinka a folded sheet of paper. "Read this and get rid of it. Hear them out and give them your answer. It has to be soon."

"Yuri, I—"

"Forgive me. If anything goes wrong, I have put you in extreme danger, b-but if this is to be done, you would be the only one with a chance of succeeding. You will see tomorrow. Now, I better go." He gave Glinka a farewell hug. "Whatever happens, I will always be your friend — even if you do not go to Gorky Park, I had no right, I know, but..." He did not finish the sentence.

"And I yours..." replied Glinka numbly.

"See you after the war," Bristov said as he briskly walked away, leaving Glinka standing like a solitary statue in the shadows of the alley. It was the last time he ever saw Yuri. Later he learned that his friend had been killed by a stray shell.

Woodal turned the page, his pulse quickening. Suddenly, Glinka's memoirs had the trappings of an unbelievable thriller. An assassination plot against Stalin!

Glinka described his meeting with a tall young officer. At no point did he mention his name or the names of his accomplices, except, of course, Bristov. The plan was simple but ingenious. Glinka was to pose as a Doctor Bodrev (name underlined in the manuscript) and administer to Stalin the poison either through a syringe or tablets. Glinka correctly deduced that the plot would have had to originate in the upper echelons of the Soviet military. Only a select few would have known that Bodrev had been summoned from Leningrad; complicated arrangements would have been necessary to intercept Bodrev and substitute the Ukrainian.

Glinka was in turmoil when he met the conspirator. Stalin was the enemy, yes, but so was the attaché he met in Gorky Park. Yuri notwithstanding, he loathed the military — the men who followed Stalin's orders. The red brigades plundered his family's home, stole their food and land and hauled away his brothers to be disposed of. He silently cursed Bristov for entangling him in an impossible situation. Yet his hatred needed an outlet, and what better one than Stalin, the architect of the horrors he witnessed. The attaché represented the lesser of two evils. The stranger in the park gave him no quarter, no guarantees, just the opportunity for revenge — take it or leave it. Strike down Stalin and see what follows; it could be no worse. Glinka seized it like a starving man would seize rancid meat.

When the assassination plan was outlined to him, Glinka thought it impossible. But the attaché produced a photograph of Bodrev. Glinka stared at it incredulously; he indeed bore a remarkable resemblance to the doctor, except that Bodrev was older, five to seven years, possibly ten. It was difficult to tell. Bristov must have seen the photograph, and knowing of Glinka's background in medicine, of sorts, he became the godsend to these desperate conspirators. The chance for success was slim, but without Glinka, none at all.

A second meeting was arranged in the same place in the dead of night. At this one Glinka was provided with the necessary tools for the task. "Here is Bodrev's medical bag," said the attaché coldly. "In it you will find a makeup kit, hair dye, and a file on Bodrev — very incomplete, but read it, memorize it, and destroy it. Also a layout of Stalin's dacha and further instructions for after ... and this." He produced a key and gave it to Glinka. "It is to Bodrev's hotel room, the Metropol, room 323. His clothes are there; wear something suitable as becomes a prominent doctor when they come for you."

"What of Bodrev?"

"That is no concern of yours; he has disappeared." The attaché ignored Glinka's shudder.

"Yes, but—"

"One more thing." He gave the Ukrainian an icy stare. "You may not succeed — take these." He handed Glinka a small container with two capsules.

"What are these?"

"Cyanide. If you are found out, better you should die quickly — for all of us."

Woodal was fully engaged, sitting on the edge of his seat. *Absurd*, he thought. Was this fiction?

After arriving at Bodrev's hotel suite, Glinka described in some detail how he altered his facial features to add years and spread the dye through his hair to produce a touch of gray. His only guide was the tiny identification photo he stuck into the corner of the grand mirror while he nervously applied the cosmetics. As he turned the pages, Woodal marveled at the man's audacity. In fact, the audacity of it all...

June 28: Oh how I wished I could have killed him. With all my being I wished ... I had gotten in — I still can't believe it. I knew I was on a suicide mission, but to actually come that close, to be facing him within arm's reach of plunging the needle into him... Then, he abruptly dismissed me, stating the examination was over. Before I could collect my thoughts, react, the guard came in and escorted me out... The man who would rid Ukraine and Russia of Stalin had failed... In retrospect, I would pray in thanks that I came out alive, for now I realize I had much to live for...

Woodal continued reading, but he knew Glinka's secret — or at least his part of the secret. The events afterward — attempts to do away with Glinka, the attaché's offhanded confession that he murdered Bodrev and that the body was (presumed) buried somewhere near that cottage. Of course, Bodrev's assassin pointed directly to Drydenko, Timoshenko's attaché.

The memoirs abruptly ended with Glinka's arrival in London. There was some further wartime information and contacts but nothing of particular interest in regard to his mission. Woodal now knew Glinka's secret and why Drydenko was so desperate.

The KGB operative sat motionless for a long time, attempting to digest what he had learned. Suddenly, this whole mission, while still quite bizarre, made sense. Drydenko was on the verge of attaining a high plateau of power — or failing in disgrace or worse — depending on what his opponent knew... So, Glinka was a loose end; for no matter how remote, how improbable, there would always be a nagging doubt, the possibility that Drydenko would be exposed. The danger would be even more if he became the head of the KGB. The increased profile would be international news and result in a manifold increase in attention. He would no longer be just another faceless Soviet bureaucrat, but a media personality, noted and scrutinized. The temptation for an alluring and potentially very high-profile story would be too great to ignore. It was, after all, quite insidious — a hitherto buried generals' plot to assassinate Stalin coming to light. No doubt it would be compared to the attempted putsch against Hitler, except in this case the intended victim hadn't found out. If Bakinin and other Drydenko detractors did, though, Drydenko would be crucified...

So what was to be done? What good to him was this information? First, he'd appease Drydenko. A short, coded message informing him (complete with an obit) that Glinka was deceased (leaving out the details), that his daughter knew nothing of her father's past activities that would prove harmful to persons in the Soviet Union or to the fatherland's national interests, and that no damaging personal materials existed.

As for Bakinin, the path of least resistance was simply to supply him with what he learned and let politics take its course. Of course, that was predicated on a number of assumptions: that Drydenko would lose in the power struggle; that he would never discover the source of this information leak; and that Bakinin could be trusted. All three were dubious assumptions. No matter how this played out, Woodal needed some sort of leverage or safety valve that would assure his survival.

He put the scattered pages of the memoirs back in order, slipped them into the original box, and tucked it into an oversized briefcase. He would make copies and open a safety deposit box in one of Canada's five leading banks that Irene told him about while he thought out his next series of moves.

CHAPTER 26

Viktor Glinka was buried in a small Ukrainian cemetery on the outskirts of the city. The weather reflected the mood: a dull, overcast day with the sky threatening to burst into tears but managing only the odd sprinkle or two. There were about thirty people huddled around the casket and freshly dug hole. The same old wrinkled priest who earlier that day gave the mournful mass in old Slavonic at the church was now droning on with some well-practiced verse: "...and forgive them every sin committed in life; for no one is without sin, only You, who can give repose to the departed..."

Woodal's mind wandered again as his ears tuned out what was being said by this shaman dressed in burial black, focusing once more on Irene, who was clutching Carli, valiantly fighting for control, her lips quivering slightly. Sorrow, intermingled, no doubt, with guilt — for not being there. The mitigating factor — he died peacefully in his sleep.

Of course, Irene found the old man where Woodal had placed him. Thank God, Carli had gone to her friend's house after school, giving Irene time to collect herself and call the ambulance. "Poor Dad, he must have had a seizure in his sleep," she told him. "Must have been fairly early in the day — heard the attendants say that rigor mortis had set in..."

Woodal cast a sideways glance at Carli. Did the eight-year-old understand death? Carli seemed inscrutable and to be coping as well as her mother. Grandpa had gone to Heaven, she was told, forever... She would, no doubt, miss him, he surmised, and only later analyze what she was witnessing. By then, time would have made the event only a snapshot, a blurred memory. What she truly felt at the moment he could not begin to comprehend. His ruminations were again interrupted by the priest's pontificating on the afterlife: "…to souls of Your servants where there is neither sickness, nor sorrow, nor sighing, but life everlasting…"

Right!

Actually, the turnout wasn't bad, Woodal noted, surveying the gathering, most of whom were getting on in age. Glinka had friends, at least those who cared enough to come and pay their last respects. And that was something. He knew that should he die in the near future, there would be far fewer at his final resting place to bid him adieu. It could not be otherwise for a man of multiple identities who had long ago forsaken and severed relations with relatives and friends. But that was a morose way of looking at it, because in the final analysis, it didn't matter if there was one or thousands at the grave site. Why should it? Everyone still died alone. The earth still reclaimed its own individually. It was natural to return to the soil, to be ultimately biodegraded — ashes to ashes, dust to dust… His thoughts flashed to Kremlin Square and the sight of Lenin's diseased corpse lying in state, preserved, enshrined, and as potent as when the man had been alive. They would never let him rest. Even in death Lenin upheld, albeit symbolically, the edifice that he had created in which so many were ensnared, including Glinka and himself!

Woodal became aware that Irene's friend, Jane, cast him quick but frequent peeks. He had met her at the funeral parlor. Since, she had been periodically observing him, curious, no doubt, about Irene's new man. He wondered what Irene had told her about him. It was a relationship that he would have to deal with… The priest's voice intruded on his scattered thoughts again. "…and the Lord himself will come down from Heaven; those who have died in Christ will be the first to rise and those of us who are still alive will be taken up in the clouds, together with them, to meet the Lord in the heavens. So we shall stay with the Lord forever…"

Right!

But what now? For all intents and purposes, his assignment was over. Glinka was dead and Drydenko would be satisfied, thinking his secret was safe. Bakinin would receive his leverage and hopefully Woodal would not be a casualty as that political game played out. There was only Irene to deal with. She had asked him to return home with her. Or he could just as easily be off to the airport on a flight back to London. Or Moscow. Was it as simple as that? He didn't wish to leave Irene in limbo. Yet there it was; he had broken a cardinal rule of his profession: Never get too involved emotionally. Was he? Or was it that he just wasn't eager to go back?

Finally, the funeral service was over. Glinka's body had been lowered into the ground, and the priest had crossed himself for the last time. The bereaved were quietly dispersing. Irene exchanged a few words with Jane, who gave her a huge hug and departed; others, too, offered their condolences.

After everyone had paid their last respects, a man about Woodal's age, somewhat taller, with rich, curly brown hair, a well-formed jaw line, and a sharp nose, approached Irene. Woodal hadn't noticed him before (he seemed to just materialize) but instinctively knew who he was. Curious, he edged closer within earshot and listened.

"Irene — I am terribly sorry…"

"I know, Stephen. Thank you for coming."

There was an awkward pause. Irene's former husband fidgeted, uncertain. They were strangers now. "It must be an ordeal for you… How's Carli holding up?"

"We're fine."

"Your dad was a good man."

"Yes, yes he was."

"If there is anything I can do … for you — for Carli, please call."

"I will."

"I'm truly sorry — for everything."

To Woodal, it appeared that Stephen had run out of things to say. They both had. He realized that he was witnessing a painful situation between two people who at one time meant a great deal to each other.

Stephen looked around and spotted Carli, who had been delayed by Mrs. Holenski giving her a pep talk and hug. He turned to her as she came to him, leaned down and gave her a hug as well. The puffy-eyed child seemed dazed.

"Are you okay, sweets?"

"Yes, Dad."

"That's good... You come and visit me soon."

Carli glanced at her mother, who gave a slight nod and ran her hand through Carli's hair. "Yes, Dad, I will."

Stephen cleared his throat. "With your grandpa gone ... you'll have to help your mother take care of things from now on... You'll do that, won't you?"

Carli nodded.

"That's my girl."

"Will you be coming back — to live with Mom and me?"

It was a question neither parent was prepared for. They gave each other a furtive look.

"No, Carli... I don't think so," Stephen said quietly.

"Why not?"

"Someday, Carli, you'll understand," Irene interjected, giving her daughter a gentle squeeze.

Carli said nothing, sensing the tension and hurt.

"Well, I better be going," said Stephen, straightening himself out. He turned to Irene. "You'll keep in touch?"

"Yes."

He then pressed his hand tenderly into hers, his face slightly contorted. He whispered, "God, Irene, I'm sorry it worked out this way."

"So am I, Stephen."

"For us — but especially for Carli."

Irene let out a sigh. "We'll manage."

As he departed, Stephen's eyes momentarily met Adam's; there was a hint of acknowledgment. It was as if the two men knew their respective status in Irene's life and accepted it.

As Woodal moved to Irene, she gripped his arm, her face down, colorless. "Take me home, Adam," she said. As he, Irene, and Carli made their way to his car, he could only reflect on how complicated his life had become in a couple of weeks.

***

Irene turned to Adam, her eyes red, close to tears. They were in her father's study. "Th-this place has so much of Dad in it — I can't believe he's gone." She hesitated, produced a Kleenex from her sleeve, and blew her nose. "I came early this morning — couldn't sleep — to tidy up... It's silly, I know. It helped me, though — keep his presence alive — but ... well, I can't seem to find his memoirs. I'm sure he had it in the filing cabinet—"

"It's missing?" Woodal asked, surprised, both feigning and not. He didn't think that Irene was overly interested in her father's memoirs or that she'd get into them so quickly. "Maybe Carli?" he heard himself say, frowning.

"Carli hardly goes into the study." Her voice cracked. As if to reassure herself, Irene called her daughter, who had been in the bathroom. "Carli, honey — are you all right?" The child appeared, looking deflated and bewildered. She had been crying.

"Yes, Mom."

"Oh, Carli." Instinctively, Irene walked over and hugged her.

"I'm okay, Mom. Really, I am... Grandpa's gone forever, I know that. He went to Heaven, didn't he?"

"Yes, Carli, he did," replied Irene.

"Did it hurt — going to Heaven?"

"No, honey, it didn't. It's a real nice place."

"The angels will take care of him?"

"Yes they will—"

"Carli." Woodal gently broke into the conversation. "Did you go into Grandpa's study and touch anything?"

"No," replied the child hesitantly. "I never go in there."

"Never?"

Carli shook her head.

"Then that's fine," he concluded lamely.

Irene stroked Carli's hair and gave her a smile. "Are you hungry?" Supper won't be ready for a little while."

"No, Mom. Can I go to my room? I'm tired."

"Of course, and I'll be up in a little while…" When Carli was gone, Irene said, "Adam, I just don't know what to think!"

"When Carli is rested, why don't I take you and her out for supper."

"That would be great, thank you."

"And don't worry about the manuscript. There has to be a logical explanation. Maybe your father put it elsewhere?"

"I can't imagine where. The only other place I can think of is his old trunk in the basement near the fruit cellar. He's stored some memorabilia, old photo albums, and other personal knick-knacks in there, but I can't imagine…"

"Well, you can have a look there later." Woodal tried to sound reassuring and nonchalant at the same time. "Right now take a deep breath, relax — don't let this add to your stress. You'll have plenty of time to sort things out."

She sighed. "You're right."

"Umm…" He cleared his throat. "There's another matter I would like to talk to you about… I didn't want to catch you completely off guard."

"Oh?"

"I need to go to London."

"Oh?" He could read the disappointment in her face.

"That's the bad news… The good news is that it will only be for three weeks — a month at most."

"This is sudden… I thought—"

"I know it's horribly bad timing, but it can't be helped — company emergency, and just as I was getting to know you… I hate to spring this on you, given the circumstances."

"When are you leaving?"

"Tomorrow, I'm afraid. There are business issues that demand my attention, but I have some unfinished business here… I want to come back," he emphasized.

"I…" She faltered.

"Do you want me to come back? For the brief time that I have known you — well you are, as the English would say, my cup of tea."

"I don't know what to say or think…" It was as if she had overdosed on a combination of good and bad stimulants. The logical half of her brain advised her to be cautious, prudent — to analyze her feelings and take the time to find out what made this man tick. After all, he had not exactly been forthcoming with her. In truth, she knew practically nothing about him. Her emotional side suggested otherwise — encourage him; he was making a commitment, was he not? Which to trust? "Yes, I'd like you to… You can't postpone your trip for another few days or so?"

"I truly would if I could, but the matter is too pressing. I promise, after my business is concluded, I will come back to … our business."

PART FOUR

CHAPTER 27

It was already mid-July, but London remained unseasonably cool, with unusually strong winds. *Add rain to the mix*, lamented Woodal as he stepped from the cab and wearily took his suitcases out onto the sidewalk.

"Been unsettled in Blighty since the beginning of the month," said the old cabbie, tipping his cap after receiving the fare. "Thank you kindly, guv."

Woodal turned, grabbed his baggage, and made his way to a four-story brick building. His accommodation was rather modest; the Komitet was not overly lavish when it came to their agents living abroad, particularly in high-priced "capitalist" markets, like London. As well, the idea was to not get too comfortable, he supposed. Still, it suited him fine, a slightly seedy abode in the East End, close to where Brick Lane met Bethnal Green Road, to be more precise, and away from the Savile Row district. The seedier sides of London had much in common with the less well-off proletarian sections of Moscow.

When he'd left for Canada, there were all sorts of domestic troubles that Londoners were contending with, including a three-day workweek thanks to the widespread strikes in the coal industry and the resulting energy shortages. On his return, he could add terrorism to the list. Newspapers headlines screamed that the Provisional Irish Republican Army had just exploded a bomb in the White Tower at the Tower of London. Only one person was killed, but over forty were injured, some very seriously. Understandably, the city was on high alert.

He trudged up the dark and dank stairs (there were no windows in the stairwells) and down the hallway to his door. When he inserted the key and shoved, the door did not immediately open. *Right!* A significant pile of mail had accumulated on the other side. Utility bills and other such pieces were mixed mostly with junk mail and flyers shoved through the letter slot. Communications of importance from his superiors had their own special drop sites. He'd sort through the pile later.

The flat was quite small; the entrance had a closet and boot rack; to the right was a bedroom and bathroom and a tiny kitchen through an arch; the hall opened up straight ahead into a living room. Woodal lived sparsely, but then he was rarely home.

It was cold, musty, and alien, he thought, as he bent down in front of the gas fireplace and pushed the knob several times before it flared. *Good, the place needs warmth — and some cheering.*

Time to take stock. He had let Drydenko know that his mission was successfully completed: Glinka was dead (obit and funeral photo provided) and there were no incriminating entrails left behind. That would please Drydenko, but he knew that the deputy chief of the KGB would still want to be debriefed in person. Bakinin was a different story; Lucovich needed to plot out his options.

Thus, London was a necessary forty-eight-hour stopover where he could make arrangements for self-preservation. Thereafter, he'd embark on another "business" trip that would take him to Berlin and onward to Moscow. He had to make the sinister assumption that he could suddenly become expendable for both Drydenko and Bakinin. Indeed, in due course, when the time came, he could reasonably surmise that he'd be targeted — if he wasn't already. He was not dealing with naïve youths from the Komsomol, but experienced, deadly, power-hungry men. How he navigated their intrigues was the key to his survival.

***

As Lucovich descended the narrow steps of the Aeroflot IL–62M, he was exhausted. He suspected that it wasn't so much from travel fatigue as from nervous exhaustion. Still, there was the flight from

Heathrow to Frankfurt and on to Berlin, the elaborate arrangements necessary to cross into the eastern sector, and finally the jaunt to Moscow and Vnukovo 11, a special airport for Kremlin VIPs. No sooner was he off the plane and had collected his luggage when two ruddy-faced men in blue serge suits approached him.

"Alexandr Lucovich?" asked one.

"*Da.*"

The man produced the familiar KGB identification card. "Come with us."

They escorted him to a fat black Chaika. Obviously, he was to be kept under tight security — at least until his meeting with Bakinin was over.

The automobile idled in front of the terminal just long enough for one of the stone-faced men to retrieve his two large brown Samsonite luggage bags. He ruefully heaved them into the trunk, slammed the lid, got in the back seat beside him, and the car sped off.

It was 2:00 a.m. Lucovich felt very uncomfortable; his stomach was protesting loudly (too much kvass on the flight), and his eyes burned like he had stared into a bright light bulb for far too long. *Must keep alert*, he thought as his heavy head slumped against the back seat and window. The driver turned off the dual highway and drove with dispatch on an undulating blacktop road. Lucovich glanced back periodically and noticed a black Volga following close behind. *Escort?* The limousine kept switching from one road to another, moving in an evasive, seemingly erratic pattern. Was it his imagination, or was Bakinin taking no chances with his guest?

One more turn and he could hear the crunching of gravel; they were ascending a winding, narrow road lined with tall pines, the tops of which were bathed in the eerie glow of the moon's light. Finally, they arrived at a large dacha nestled among the trees.

Lucovich and his luggage were brought inside. As he entered he glanced at his Gruen — it had been forty-five minutes since he got off the plane. The place was expansive, like a cavern, filled with resplendent and no doubt expensive objects, mostly art and statuettes. *Perhaps it was once used as a dance hall*, thought Lucovich. *Now it's probably Bakinin's private, out-of-the-way bailiwick.* He was led into a large suite, the luggage set inside the door.

"You will spend the night here," informed one of the escorts. "Breakfast is at nine. Be ready. You will be called."

With that, both men left the room. The heavy oak door closed with a thud, followed by a click. He had been locked in.

Plush, thought Lucovich as he inspected his surroundings. Very plush, more so than the executive suite he had occupied in downtown Edmonton. He was glad to be left alone for a few hours. His only thought at the moment was a satisfying shit to empty his cramped, kvass-filled bowels, a hot shower, and sleep...

CHAPTER 28

"Ah, Comrade Lucovich, just in time for breakfast," said Bakinin. The notorious KGB deputy director was seated at a medium-sized oak table, cracking a hard-boiled egg. He was fastidiously dressed in a red tie and gray wool suit that puckered slightly at the shoulders. Lucovich, still somewhat estranged from his surroundings, curtly nodded and sat down on the only other chair at the table. He had been rather rudely awakened at eight thirty by one of Bakinin's foot soldiers who marched in and roughly shook him, stating that he was not to be late for breakfast, scheduled at nine. And then, on his way into the dining room, he had been searched as a precaution. Lucovich now wondered what other surprises awaited him. They were three or so feet apart — an ideal distance from which to have a frank, if not intimate, conversation.

"*Pozhalusta.*" Bakinin motioned to a bowl of eggs and a plate of toast and croissants and preserves as he salted and spooned out his egg. He was enjoying it with obvious relish.

"Coffee, just coffee will be fine, for now," Lucovich said.

Instantly, a manservant appeared with a Pyrex pot of coffee, which he gracefully poured into a delicate white china cup set in front of the Komitet agent. Lucovich noted a large Bunn coffee maker stationed strategically on the right-hand side as one entered the ornate dining room. It was the type he'd seen in Swartz's office, halfway around the world. Irene momentarily flashed across his mind. He brutally suppressed the thought. He could ill afford distractions; quite possibly his well-being was on the line — depending on what he said to Bakinin.

He took measure of the diminutive human with creeping unease and revulsion. *This could go terribly wrong*, Lucovich thought. *I've walked into the predator's den with only one trump card to play, which could be wrenched away.* Tactical error? But what better choices did he have? He tried to pull himself together…

"Comrade Lucovich, I am so glad you saw fit to come. Did you have a pleasant flight?"

"It was rather long," said Lucovich. *And possibly ill-advised.* "Nevertheless, pleasant enough."

"Good … good. Tell me, how was Canada? Although I have read and studied it, in all my years of service to the state, I have never had the opportunity to visit North America…" He sounded almost wistful, as if the fact that he never visited North America somehow left a deep and indelible hole in his life.

"Decadent to be sure, in some ways … decent and wondrous in others." The KGB agent didn't know why he said that, but if Bakinin wanted to engage him in small talk, then so be it.

Bakinin gave a hollow, humorless laugh. "Decadent, decent, and wondrous — Comrade, what an interesting choice of words… I take it you have found something or someone who intrigues you over there?"

Lucovich knew he was being baited, and rather crudely at that. *The dwarf probably knows about Irene — she is mentioned in the dossier…* Nevertheless, Lucovich was not about to let anything slip of his own volition or volunteer any extraneous information. "There are many, ah … things … in Canada to appreciate, as there are here or anywhere else in the world. Each country has its own unique characteristics."

"Well put, Comrade, well put. And you plan to return to Canada, yes?"

"I have completed my assignment."

"Ah yes, the assignment…" Bakinin stopped abruptly and changed the topic. Perhaps he didn't like to talk business over breakfast. "What do you think of my retreat? Is it up to standard, considering your recent trip to a decadent country?" He vaguely gestured with his hands, inviting his guest to inspect the spacious surroundings.

Lucovich was impressed — Italian-tile flooring, a chandelier over their table, Persian rugs, large, luxurious potted plants at each corner of the dining room, carved wood paneling, and a huge fireplace made of enormous field stones, roughly cut... "Yes, a notch above. Very grand. Was it a private club or dance hall by any chance?"

"No, I believe it once belonged to a landlord, built by peasant labor in the nineteenth century. It now belongs to the Soviet people, but I occasionally occupy it during my tenure in office as their ... ah, servant. It's very useful for meetings such as these." Bakinin let out a thin, nasal laugh. "Of course, it has been updated somewhat — modernized."

"It's not your private dacha?"

"In a manner of speaking, I suppose it is. Some of my predecessors found solace here, and no doubt, so will my successors..."

"Do all individuals in your esteemed position receive such retreats?"

"I suspect not, my facetious friend," answered Bakinin with a smile that did not extend to the eyes. "Some of us are more fortunate than others." He paused and added, "But then some of us are more deserving than others."

Bakinin had devoured his egg and now focused his attention fully on him. "Comrade Lucovich" — he leaned forward intently — "we parted last in the belief that we can be of great service to each other. You agree, yes?" Apparently, the small talk was over.

Lucovich cleared his throat. "Yes, that was the general understanding. And I do have something that is of value to you. I do, however, have a couple of requests in exchange—"

Bakinin raised his hand like a gendarme directing Paris traffic, a smile scarring his face. "I understand, Comrade. We are here to trade, perhaps, even to barter a little, since each side has something of value to offer. You have information for me — I can be of service to you. Am I not correct? Otherwise you would not have come, yes?"

"It was a matter of — options." *I really had none*, thought Lucovich. "But you are quite correct."

"Good, as long as we understand each other." Bakinin took a slurp of his coffee. "Now" — he paused and wiped the corners of his mouth with a napkin — "shall we proceed?"

Lucovich nodded. "My terms—"

"Terms? Ah ... how capitalistic of you! It's a sale then ... like a commodity — not a gentlemen's agreement — service in lieu of. There is a distinction, is there not?"

Lucovich was a little taken aback over Bakinin's sudden semantics. "I-I suppose it is, in a manner of speaking — a little of both."

Bakinin gave him a hooded stare, a man not used to such language as *terms*, which quickly translated to *demands*. "So then ... what are your *terms*?" He said the word with evident distaste, as if swallowing a bitter pill.

"Very well," said Lucovich, fully aware that Bakinin had been put off. He had rehearsed this in his mind ever since he left the UK. "First, I wish to leave the Soviet Union — safely and permanently. I have another identity, as you are well aware, and the appropriate documents. I require the official authorization to—"

"To disappear? To become a nonperson as far as the state is concerned?" Bakinin cut in, peering at the younger man as if he were a misguided, wayward son. "Drastic, Alexandr — very drastic. Has the motherland treated you so badly that you wish to *fly the coop* — is that how you say it... Ah, maybe Canada has been too good to you; maybe you have found a sweetheart, yes? Are not the Russian girls good enough for you?"

"I've made no plans to return to Canada—"

"So you want to disappear?" Bakinin repeated, again, interrupting Lucovich. This time he said it in a bemused way, as if he couldn't quite believe it. "Well, the state has invested a considerable amount of resources in you, yes? Including an English man's identity, which now apparently you want to become. How can the state trust you? You have specialized knowledge of a compromising nature to the Komitet, yes? You know what we do with traitors, do you not?"

"Yes, I was sent halfway around the world to do just that."

"So you were…"

"Nevertheless, I would need assurances," Lucovich continued, "that no retribution will be — ordered later."

"Assurances?" Bakinin seemed genuinely puzzled, raising an eyebrow.

"Yes, it has to be made to show officially that Alexandr Lucovich no longer exists as far as the state is concerned. Nor will Adam Woodal be called upon in the future—"

"And how am I supposed to do that?"

"Undisclosed agreement signed by you, presumably as the head of the Komitet—"

"You trust Soviet documents to protect you." Again, a snatch of bemusement crossed Bakinin's lips.

In for a penny, in for a pound. "I trust that our agreement — which also includes $5,000 American dollars, funds to get me started on a new life once Adam Woodal becomes unemployed, will never come to light … become public. Those are my — is my request."

There was a prolonged silence while Bakinin digested Lucovich's *request.*

"I must say, Comrade, you are quite audacious… As for assurances…" He shrugged and then smiled shrewdly. "In the end, you will have to trust me. Legal niceties aside, in these kinds of transactions one's word is one's bond. There can be no other real guarantees."

"Still, in exchange for information vital to the state *and your advancement to the head of the KGB,* I would like a formal document signed by you — a consummation and detailing, if you will, of our agreement to the effect that I have ceased to exist as a Soviet citizen and that my services will no longer be required — as Adam Woodal or anyone else for that matter. In other words, I am no longer of interest to the state… Of course I will, in turn, sign a confidentiality agreement."

"I see — clearly you want out."

"Yes, I do," Lucovich replied quite truthfully.

"And with a little change in your pocket as well." Bakinin smiled harshly.

"For my troubles and my due pension … to help me on my way."

Bakinin noisily shoved his chair away from the table as if to distance himself from Lucovich and groped around in the inside pockets of his dapper suit. He fished out a Dunhill pipe from one side and a pouch of Sail tobacco from the other. "Why American currency? Why not British pounds or Canadian dollars?"

"It is the world's most stable currency now," Lucovich replied bluntly.

"You *have* become a real capitalist, haven't you? No doubt you wish it paid to your Swiss account…"

It wouldn't come close to yours, thought Lucovich, remaining stoically silent. He awaited the Komitet deputy's answer.

Bakinin unhurriedly proceeded to stuff long strands of tobacco into a charred little hole. He lit up and briskly blew away the aromatic cloud that had settled about his face. "Your requests are problematic, even with the best intentions on my part. But … surmountable. The money can be taken care off with a judicious redeployment of resources. However, your total disappearance is a much greater challenge. The Soviet state likes to keep track of its citizens. I'm afraid you would still be Adam Woodal, our man in London — at least until I became the head of the Komitet and able to affect such a change without repercussions. As I said earlier, in the end it's still a matter of trust."

"And the documentation of our … agreement?"

"That, too, can be done. And exactly what would I receive from you, again?"

"The means to enable you to become the next KGB chairman."
There it is, thought Lucovich, *the prize and what lies beyond.*

"Hmm…" Bakinin took a couple of furious puffs from his discolored briar. "Let us go into the adjoining study, where we can be more comfortable…"

Bakinin led Lucovich to a palatial sitting room, two sides of which were lined with bookshelves containing thick volumes. Of what,

Lucovich could not ascertain from his vantage point. They sat down on either end of a small curved red velvet couch. "Would you care for more coffee, or something stronger perhaps?" Bakinin inquired solicitously.

"No, no thank you."

"Then let us continue. What have you to tell me about Comrade Drydenko's past activities that may have compromised him?" The dwarf's eyes bore into Lucovich.

Before Lucovich could answer, a manservant suddenly appeared carrying a silver tray and a carefully folded note. Bakinin caught the man's eye and stood up. "Excuse me," he said. Taking the note, unfolding and giving it a cursory glance, he nodded to the man, who hurriedly departed. Turning to the seated KGB agent, he said with a trace of annoyance, "I'll only be a moment. Duty calls…" With that he departed back toward the dining room.

Lucovich collected his thoughts. *The crunch has come. What I am about to say will either save me or sign my death warrant!* It was an enormous but necessary gamble. He was almost tempted to cross himself and silently pray — in case there really was a God. He needed all the help he could get…

True to his word, Bakinin slithered in sooner than Lucovich would have preferred. "Now," he said, seating himself again, "you were about to tell me some things of interest, yes? Start with your trip to Canada — Viktor Glinka is no longer with us."

"You are well informed."

"My source is most reliable." Bakinin smiled thinly. "I saw the obit. Says he died of a heart attack?"

"Viktor was a sick man."

"So you solved Drydenko's problem, yes?"

"As far as he is concerned."

Bakinin nodded. "And the connection between Deputy Director Drydenko and war criminal Glinka?"

This is it, thought Lucovich. *I have to choose my words carefully — to say enough but not too much.* "Drydenko and Glinka collaborated in a criminal conspiracy during the war."

If Bakinin was surprised, he hid it well. "A criminal conspiracy?"

"Correct, one that would severely diminish his prospects of advancing his career should it ever come to light." More superfluous dangling bait, but Lucovich couldn't help himself.

"Well, I am most intrigued. And you have details — Drydenko's role, how Glinka fits, others involved, where, when — clear evidence?"

"At this point that is all I am prepared to reveal," Lucovich said while shifting his weight slightly, reaching into his right trouser pocket and pulling out a long, slender key. A bit dramatic, perhaps, but it served as his prop. "This unlocks a safety deposit box in one of London's prestigious banks, wherein is contained the answers that you seek. The documents there will collaborate in detail what I have just revealed."

There was a long intense pause as Bakinin eyed the key and the younger man. Then he spoke slowly and deliberately. "Comrade Lucovich" — *No more Alexandr* — "I am a patient man, but you are straining it, and time is pressing. You have been brought here because you possess certain knowledge. I want the whole story, not just be tantalized by a tiny piece from a large puzzle... Our understanding was that I am willing to scratch your back if you scratch mine—"

"That is what I am afraid of," Lucovich stated evenly. "Once you have all the information from me" — he shrugged — "you may scratch harder than I wish."

Bakinin unexpectedly chortled, loud and good-naturedly. "You mean I might scratch you out!"

"Correct."

"So we come back to your ... *terms*, yes?"

"When I return safely back to England, I will await your official document with *your* signature, as discussed. As soon as it arrives, I will send the full story — Glinka's story — through secure channels directly to you. If the funds arrive, then you shall take delivery of additional evidence damaging to Deputy Director Drydenko. I shall have to trust that my status will change when you become head of the Komitet." *With your signed document as leverage, hopefully...*

"So those are your terms," acknowledged the humpbacked man, "and the official *document* outlining our agreement evens out the odds a little, yes?"

"Yes, that about sums it up."

"Why come back to Moscow at all?"

"You insisted — at least that is what was conveyed to me — we meet face to face."

"True." Bakinin waved his hand dismissively. "I thought we'd have an informal personal chat where ... information was exchanged for 'future considerations.' I underestimated your cleverness and the formality of your plan."

"I came voluntarily" — *never mind there would be repercussions if I didn't* — "to illustrate good faith on my part."

Bakinin expelled an exasperated sigh. "I could acquire the key and extract the necessary information from you involuntarily."

"Perhaps." Lucovich bluffed; he knew all too well the veracity of this threat so calmly delivered. It was a gamble he had to take. "However, my sudden disappearance will not be lost on Deputy Director Drydenko. You have maneuvered behind the back of an equal — a man as powerful as yourself. It ... it may take time to obtain the information from me, and that would allow your adversary the opportunity to take countermeasures..." Lucovich trailed off, having made his case.

"You are playing a dangerous game, Comrade."

"I am well aware of that. But you see my point. If I provide you with the information and the means to obtain the necessary proof now, you may change your mind about any bargain or worse. I may become ... expendable."

"So... I should accept what you are offering, yes?"

"As you have pointed out, each of us has to trust the other to a degree in this matter. There is no other way. Otherwise, we both lose."

Bakinin rose from the couch with a grunt, moved to the small coffee table, and tapped his pipe on a large marble ashtray. "Hmm..." He scratched his ear. "Drydenko was involved in a criminal conspiracy," he repeated once again. "That is all I am to know. You refuse absolutely to give any more of the details contained in this deposit box…" He seemed to be thinking out loud.

"I cannot say more — but we both know that if I deceive you or renege, I can be dealt with anywhere in the world. I have every intention of living up to my part of the proposed agreement."

"I see. So that is it?"

"Yes. We meet halfway."

"Very well, I suppose I must accept. But the sooner, the better. I would need to study this information and set into motion the proper investigations."

"How long?"

"Within two weeks. You will receive what you want and you give me what I want. For now, you are my asset and guest. So stay at the dacha until we can make discreet arrangements to get you back to London in the next couple of days."

Lucovich hesitated; he didn't particularly like this suggestion. "I would like to attend to some matters in Moscow—"

"That would not be wise," snapped Bakinin. "You shouldn't be seen in Moscow."

"I will be discreet—" began Lucovich.

Bakinin cut him off. "Understand my position. I have acted — shall we say, somewhat imprudently by bringing you here secretly. If word should leak back to Drydenko, it would compromise both of us. If you stay here until we can get the appropriate transport out…"

"I have a meeting scheduled with Drydenko." Lucovich was hoping to avoid any mention of this, which was just another complication. "It was at his request. Like you, he wanted a report from me in person — to assure him that Glinka is deceased and that no harmful information has survived. It would be most suspicious if I did not show up to get … debriefed."

Bakinin sighed. "We better take you to Moscow then."

***

Later in the day, on his way to the Kremlin in the black polished ZiL, Bakinin mulled over his encounter with the brash KGB agent who left earlier for Moscow in the company of his guards. Leaning forward, he told his driver to turn off the air conditioning; the steady hum was interfering with his concentration. Yes, Lucovich was clever and believed he had his exit strategy worked out. And to a point he did, but it was more survival than exit in nature. Lucovich was inexperienced and a trifle naïve, he decided, when it came to the art of politics. A field operative all his life, he simply did not know how the system really operated. But Bakinin did; he spent the greater part of his career manipulating it. A half sneer, half smile crossed his lips as he leaned forward again from his soft vinyl armchair seat and picked up the radio phone.

CHAPTER 29

Lucovich told his escorts to drop him off at the National Hotel at the corner of Tverskaya and Mokhovaya Streets near Red Square and Alexandrovsky Garden. He did not, however, enter the posh hotel; instead, with his luggage in hand, he hailed a cab, an older, beat-up Volga. He told the driver, a swarthy fellow with a Lenin cap, that he wished to go to the Red October, the two-star accommodations he had visited previously.

This time around, his room was a slight improvement with brighter decor and relatively new furniture. Still, the lock was flimsy and the halls dim. He suspected that on more than one occasion Petrovka 38 had been dialed and that the Criminal Investigation Department of the Moscow Militsiya was familiar with the establishment. It was just that kind of place. He didn't mind...

Later that night, he ventured into the bar and sat for a while on a corner stool, nursing a couple of ounces of cheap Ukrainian vodka. He was hoping to spot the prostitute he had encountered the last time. He had forgotten her name — if he ever got it in the first place. After a couple of hours, no luck. Just as well, he concluded; his meeting with Drydenko was early the next morning.

In truth, Lucovich was more than a little anxious about his appointment with Drydenko. He really didn't know what to expect.

As it turned out, he needn't have worried. Drydenko was benign and well satisfied with his report. And why not? His account was simple and had an authoritative ring — mainly because it was largely true. Glinka was a frail man, recovering from a stroke, he recounted to the deputy director. "His memory was scattered ... faulty ... I engaged his daughter" — he did not mention Carli — "and she knew nothing of her father's war activities, criminal or otherwise... Moreover, Glinka did not appear to have been a man of letters and as a consequence did not leave any memoirs or other materials of interest... The past has been buried with him," he assured Drydenko.

For his part, the deputy director listened intently, nodded sagely, and asked very few questions. Lucovich even managed to avoid answering the one key point he debated: whether he explicitly eliminated Glinka (although that, no doubt, was the impression Drydenko received). He did not ask directly, and Lucovich saw no advantage in providing an answer, truthful or otherwise. He vaguely alluded to his being a "contributing factor," and it was left at that.

Drydenko was pleased, indicating that Lucovich's career path was promising and that in a few months (presumably when Drydenko was put in charge of the Komitet), Lucovich could look forward to rapid promotion, along with other benefits. In the meantime, if there were more immediate needs...

Lucovich thanked Drydenko for his confidence and intimated that he was, for the time being, content and would wait until the proper occasion arose. For now, his plan was to return to the UK and continue with business as usual.

***

Two days later, Lucovich resumed his life as Adam Woodal. He did not relax until he was back in his London flat, where, absolutely exhausted, he simply slept for twelve straight hours. Once he acclimatized himself again, he found that he indeed was free — or at least not tethered to any task or individual. His handler had been informed that he was on special assignment and would be unavailable for a while. Thus, there were no standing orders or directives, no drop-offs, surveillance duties, or clandestine trysts. Aside from his clerk's job at Harrods (part time at that) he had little to do and was unfettered to idle away his time enjoying London in late summer.

This state of affairs lasted for about a week, until Bakinin's package arrived at the designated P.O. box site. Contained therein was a document with the "official" terms of agreement that, alas, as it turned out, was rather skewed. The letter forthrightly stated that during the course of his work, Lucovich had unearthed a disturbing criminal conspiracy involving the war criminal Viktor Glinka and (now) Deputy Director Drydenko. This was communicated to Bakinin (no mention that Bakinin had approached him) and appropriate action was taken — mainly that Lucovich would investigate further and report to Bakinin with the evidence in hand. Bakinin's signature appeared at the bottom. There was no mention of the $5,000 US Bakinin had agreed to supply or the context of their discussions.

The deputy director was covering his ass nicely, thought Lucovich, and this document, as it stood, was not sufficient, he suspected, to cover him or damage Bakinin should Lucovich need it as a bargaining chip. But there it was, and he had to live with it. So it really did come down to trust...

Nevertheless, there was a more pleasant surprise: a separate package that contained $2,500 US in crisp $100 bills. The note attached stated that the remainder would be forthcoming on delivery of his information. Bakinin, then, was moving expeditiously and wanted not only Glinka's memoirs but also supporting evidence — in this case Dr. Bodrev's identity card and travel papers.

Lucovich had done his homework. He knew all about Bodrev, the famous physician who, after visiting Stalin's dacha, vanished from the face of the earth. Glinka connected the various dots and quite clearly indicated that Drydenko — as attaché — was responsible for the good doctor's death. There was even a good description, if not approximation, of the grounds where the body was buried. Presumably, the remains could be found and excavated if the property could be located, which, perhaps, wouldn't be too much of a stretch. Moreover, there would be a great deal of consternation. Bodrev's younger brother, Georgi, was currently a powerful candidate of the Politburo. More than anything, that would prove Drydenko's Achilles' heel.

Of course, once Bakinin received the material (to be placed in the same P.O. box), he would also connect the dots. It would not turn out well for Drydenko. That, though, was hardly his problem; he just had to make sure that he didn't get in the crosshairs of Drydenko before Bakinin pulled the plug…

CHAPTER 30

They met in a nondescript office a few blocks from 2 Dzerzhinsky Square, one of those neutral locales that the KGB had at its disposal for confidential meetings. Everything about it was standard issue: a dull-green felt-top desk, two pine armchairs, and one letter-sized filing cabinet. While Arkady Zhutoff stationed himself outside the entrance, below the weather-worn sign indicating that the building was the home of the Georgian Export Company, Bakinin shuffled in. He was a few minutes late and thus found Drydenko behind the desk, which presumably would give him a psychological advantage in any negotiations. *Except this time,* mused Bakinin. Drydenko could not imagine what his nemesis had up his sleeve.

They exchanged pleasantries tersely, like two swordsmen before their duel. Bakinin settled into one of the armchairs in the shabby room, directly in front of Drydenko. Earlier, the office had been electronically swept for listening devices (standard procedure in any high-level off-the-record talks for officials who needed to talk frankly).

It was Bakinin's meeting, and he launched into a rambling monologue that did nothing but irritate Drydenko. "We are both old warhorses, Comrade — yes, old warhorses who have witnessed much, know much, and, I dare say, have done some unpleasant things. Am I not correct?"

"True," acknowledged Drydenko, "but you have not come here to reminisce about old times. *Your old times.* Your note requested an urgent meeting. I—"

"That is the trouble nowadays," Bakinin broke in. "We are always in such a hurry to get on with business. We rarely reflect on life and how good it's been to us — especially in our senior years."

Drydenko was becoming more annoyed with each passing minute. He had canceled a couple of important appointments to accommodate his rival, and now the sleazy *muzhik* was blathering without coming to the point! What the hell did he want? They had not spoken to each other, except in the most perfunctory official way, in over four months. There had developed a cold war between them that had dipped well below the freezing point as each gathered support for the KGB chairmanship due to be decided possibly before the new year. The jostling and shuffling about of personnel was evident from Leningrad to Odessa, and many local bosses and their underlings had their careers in the noose, depending on which of these two men they supported. "Comrade Bakinin, I would be delighted to converse with you well into the night over a bottle of vodka at my villa or a health spa, but at some other more opportune time. Today I am pressed."

"Yes, yes of course, I understand. I appreciate your sparing the time to see me." There was a hint of sarcasm in his voice. "I wish to discuss with you our future plans."

"*Our* future plans?" Drydenko was clearly puzzled.

"We seem to be heading for a collision course over the chairmanship of the Komitet once Yanev retires. I thought perhaps we should discuss it to see if ways could be found to avoid unpleasantness between you and me — for the sake of the morale within the ranks and a smooth transition."

Drydenko could not resist a smile. An outrageous understatement, blandly delivered!

Bakinin continued, "I am reliably informed that, privately, Comrade Yanev favors your candidacy. His recommendation — when he chooses to make it — no doubt carries much weight in the Politburo. Nevertheless, I also have allies in the Politburo and Central Committee, and that is where the struggle shall occur. I wish to minimize the rancor and bad feelings that may come to pass. We are, after all, still on the same team."

Drydenko leaned forward and rested his elbows on the desk. "What are you suggesting, Comrade Bakinin?"

"One of us, in the interests of ... of the state and its security, shall have to withdraw and endorse the other."

Drydenko straightened, instantly alert. Was Bakinin about to concede? Did he know he was beaten? Was he offering an olive branch? Was he indicating that he would be willing to continue in his present post as Drydenko's subordinate? All this was totally unlike the crafty lizard...

"I am suggesting, Comrade Drydenko, that you withdraw your name and endorse me in an appropriate speech to the Politburo—"

"What?" the big man exclaimed incredulously. "Why would I do that? I have always thought you a little mad but — but this! It is you who should withdraw. You will be outvoted. The chairmanship will be mine ... when Yanev retires!"

Bakinin remained unruffled by Drydenko's indignation. "Under normal circumstances, perhaps, but not after your colleagues learn of some of your ... ah, trespasses. I only want to spare you the embarrassment of—"

"What are you babbling about?"

Bakinin decided to plunge the knife into Drydenko slowly and methodically, working his way up to the final twist. "Let us start with your unhealthy private life, yes? Most unhealthy... It seems bourgeois moral decadence has overwhelmed you—"

Affronted, his face turning red, Drydenko half rose from his seat before calming himself. "What are you suggesting with your slanderous innuendos?"

Bakinin couldn't resist, although he promised himself that he would not reveal this aspect of his intelligence-gathering. But now it seemed an appropriate prelude — throw Drydenko off balance. "Klara."

"Klara!"

"Yes, I know about Klara and your private adventures..."

"You know what, precisely?" the chagrined would-be KGB chief managed to blurt out, giving himself time to think.

Bakinin crossed his legs and smiled. "The Saturday visits to your villa and what goes on. Do you want the details?"

"How would you know what goes on in my villa unless... Is she your spy?" He could hardly believe it!

Bakinin frowned. Perhaps he had been indiscreet in mentioning Klara, but he did want to misdirect Drydenko while he set up his shot at the jugular. "You engaged her yourself," he said, meekly spreading his arms.

"The slut... Was she a plant — to spy on me?" Drydenko repeated.

"I am sure that she has been well paid for her services ... by you," Bakinin replied, deflecting the question. "As I said, you engaged her."

And you took advantage of her entrepreneurial spirit, thought Drydenko. *What else does she know and has passed on to Bakinin?* He would deal with the matter later. "Bakinin, you are a despicable little bug... You will only seal your fate if you circulate the debasing lies of a — a whore. How many others have you spied on? There will be those in the Politburo who will ask that question and will not take kindly to your snooping into private lives, especially if it is suggested that it could be their private lives."

Bakinin shrugged and uncrossed his legs. "You may be quite correct, but such perverted escapades..."

Drydenko glared menacingly at the shriveled humpback in front of him. He outweighed the bastard by forty pounds and could break him like a twig. He could barely stifle the urge, and it was almost worth facing the consequences... He forced himself to relax. If Bakinin wanted to make an issue of him and Klara, then he could counter with accusations of his own — point a bony finger right back. "You know, Bakinin, members of the Politburo were not happy with your butchery of the Ivasnik case. It was ... disgusting."

Bakinin seemed unperturbed. "Messy, yes — with some unfortunate spinoffs — but necessary. It taught others a lesson."

Drydenko did not respond. He recalled the consternation expressed when the well-known Ukrainian-nationalist musician was found dead near Lviv. It was not that he died; that part had been sanctioned, but rather the method. Volodymyr Ivasnik's body was discovered hanging from a tree near a military base; his fingers had been broken, his eyes plucked out, and a number of cranberry tree branches were embedded in his ribs. The official Soviet press stated that he had committed suicide. His funeral resulted in mass demonstrations of over ten thousand, and Lviv University students boycotted classes. It took several uneasy weeks for the frightened authorities to restore order. Aghast, some high-ranking party officials suggested that such barbaric executions were intolerable and that the KGB officers involved should be severely reprimanded. Of course, nothing was done and the case was hastily closed.

Drydenko fired another volley at his rival. "Was Olga Rak's death also necessary?"

"Comrade Drydenko, I see you are well versed in the affairs of my section. A section which often must deal with threats to the state in an indelicate way. Of late, no doubt, you have been instrumental in pointing out some of the deficiencies of my work to colleagues… About Rak, I know nothing. In any event, both the Ivasnik and the Rak incidents were closed."

"Then I suggest you forget about Klara and me. You will find no advantage in dragging my personal life—"

"Of course, your private affairs with Klara or anyone else for that matter can be overlooked but…" Bakinin paused, studying his opponent for a few seconds. "There is also the Glinka affair."

Drydenko visibly paled.

"I see I have struck a nerve, yes?"

"What do you know about Glinka?" he hissed.

"Enough to destroy your career."

Drydenko said nothing, his mind racing. Was this a bluff? He didn't say anything to Klara, but then again, she had access to his files… Or had he been betrayed by Lucovich, who told him that Glinka died with nothing left behind… Was this a bluff? Bakinin may be snooping again, attempting to unnerve him by mere mention of a name…

Bakinin plunged the knife deeper. "I know about your man, Lucovich, and why he was sent to eliminate Glinka."

"Just what do you know?"

"Everything. Your information security safeguards," Bakinin prattled on calmly, "are riddled with holes ... but no matter. Your unofficial 'sanctioning' of Glinka, while suggestive, can be rationalized innocently enough if necessary... Certainly, your particular interest in Glinka drew my notice..."

Drydenko felt a wave of nausea and panic engulfing him; he sat riveted in his seat, staring at the hated man. Finally, he weakly countered, "I don't know what you are talking about."

"Dear Comrade, most assuredly you do — nasty business, but then you were young, naïve, and under orders, yes? However, your colleagues in the Politburo and particularly in the Central Committee may not take such a charitable view. An investigation would have to be launched—"

"You know nothing," Drydenko said hoarsely.

Now for the twist of the knife. "The assassination plot on Comrade Stalin? Audacious, I must say. Doctor Dimitri Bodrev? And most intriguing how Glinka fit in. I wouldn't have believed it if I hadn't seen the photo — a close likeness, to be sure. Need I go on?"

Drydenko opened his mouth, but nothing came out. There was nothing to say.

Bakinin filled in the silence. "Of course, I do not know every detail..." In fact, he knew only what Glinka's memoirs spilled out, but it was more than enough. Drydenko was a defeated man. "Once an investigation is begun," he said again, "well, Comrade, I am sure all the sordid details will come out... And it is quite personal, actually. Did you know I was charged with finding out what happened to Dr. Dimitri Bodrev, my one and only unsolved case — until now. The case cost me a few years in Norilsk's corrective labor camp, and yes, my health! No matter... I am sure it will come as a great relief to Georgi Bodrev; he always wondered what happened to his beloved brother. I can most assuredly guarantee that it would not go well for you if Georgi knew of the Glinka Affair. He can be ... formidable, particularly in his role as chairman of the disciplinary committee on the Central Committee. If I choose to reveal your crimes, that is..." Bakinin stopped and let his words sink in.

"Comrade Bakinin," Drydenko began and faltered. He saw his career — nay, his life, crumbling — ruined for sure, if he was lucky; executed for treason and murder, if not...

"I understand your position. What you did you did a long time ago ... Well, you have performed valuable work for the party and state since..."

"I..." Drydenko began again and stopped.

Bakinin continued talking, redundantly, it seemed to Drydenko, just to hear himself relish his fate. "Your colleagues in the Politburo and Central Committee will not be forgiving. At the very least, it's treason, a harsh charge with fatal consequences, usually... Yanev is an old Stalinist; he will certainly turn on you, never mind Bodrev."

Drydenko found his voice. "Have you informed anyone of these — these allegations?"

"Andrei," Bakinin said in a placating tone. "We are cut from the same cloth. And although we have differed on policy matters and in tactics, I do not wish to destroy a man who has performed such diligent service. In some instances, I have admired your work! No, no... I suggest that between us we can settle this unfortunate affair without others intervening, yes? What we both know need not go any further than this room."

Drydenko sagged. He knew what was coming, but he had no defense. If a breath of this leaked out, he would be crucified; that was the harsh reality within the system. In as firm a voice as he could muster, he asked, "What is it that you want, Comrade Bakinin?"

Bakinin smiled patronizingly. He was tempted to prolong his adversary's agony, to make him grovel at his feet, but that would be pushing it too far. The man was beaten. It was time to claim the prize that went with victory. "Within forty-eight hours," he said solemnly, "you will compose a letter indicating that you have withdrawn your candidacy for the post of chairman of the KGB, citing health reasons and whatever other appropriate justifications you deem necessary. In that letter, you will endorse my candidacy in the strongest terms possible — be nice, yes?" Bakinin smiled. "A copy of the letter will appear in *Pravda* and *Izvestia*. Furthermore, you will personally telephone the party secretary and inform him of your decision to withdraw. You will then telephone every member of the Politburo, conveying the same message. At this point, I do not ask you to resign your current position, nor will I ask it of you when I become chairman. I leave that decision entirely to you. That is the price to be paid for my silence on this matter — our little secret, yes? A small price indeed to cover treason and murder... You will, of course, have all your privileges intact — including Klara." Bakinin couldn't resist snorting out a nasal chuckle. "Are we agreed?"

"I-I need to think—"

"There is, my dear Comrade, nothing to think about. You have no choice. If you persist in opposing me, then by the end of this week your dreaded secret will be out."

Drydenko felt drained. His throat was dry; he suddenly needed a drink — something to steady his nerves. He nodded. "Yes, yes, I agree to your terms."

"Good, Comrade, good. Wise decision. I shall expect to receive a copy of your resignation letter by the end of the upcoming weekend. Now that this piece of nasty business is over with" — Bakinin literally sprang up from his chair — "just like you, there are other matters I must attend to today!" With that he vigorously shuffled out of the office, closing the door softly behind him, leaving Drydenko staring into space.

CHAPTER 31

For another thirty minutes Drydenko remained rooted to his chair. His mind was like a scratched record stuck on one refrain: *What to do? What to do?* It was the historic lament of the Slavic soul. At one point, he reached for his small attaché case inconspicuously propped against the leg of the desk, pulled out a single sheet of paper, and in a shaky hand began to write: *It is with deepest regrets...* He could not continue. He crumpled his attempt into a ball, squeezed hard until his knuckles whitened, and dropped the stationery back into his case. *Zina, Zina, how I wish you were here...*

On his way back to his office, he ordered his chauffeur to stop; he needed to walk a little. Vasilevich deposited his boss at the corner of Hotel Moskva on Karl Marx Prospekt and idled the ZiL along slowly at a discreet distance.

It was a warm, sunny day and the boulevard teemed with Muscovites. Usually sullen and preoccupied, the crowds today seemed depressingly cheerful with flushed, shining faces. *Must be the weather*, Drydenko thought as he crossed the wide thoroughfare and headed toward the thick red-brick walls of the Kremlin. He paused at the Sobakina Tower; near the huge wrought-iron gate, he bought a piroski from a bloated babushka. The street vendor gave him a toothless smile as he counted out the kopeks. Passing through the gate, he entered Alexandrovsky Garden and there beside the gray obelisk erected as a memorial to the revolutionaries, he ate the piroski and charted his future course.

As he studied for a few moments the granite slabs marking the grave of the unknown soldier, representing those nameless patriots who died defending Moscow against the Nazis, Drydenko realized that his time had just about run out. Once Bakinin consolidated his position as Komitet chairman, he would be dealt with swiftly and harshly. Most likely an accusation would be made, a secret trial held and, if he was lucky, a demotion to an administrative post far from Moscow, deep into the bowels of the hinterland. If not, then he would suffer the fate of Beria — a speedy execution. That was the usual practice when cleaning house in the inner circles... He cast his eyes to the six urns on his right; these urns held the soil from the six "heroic cities" that withstood the German onslaught during the war. Was he not a hero? Did he not serve his country well? Was this what he had earned? He read them off: Leningrad, Brest, Kiev, Volgograd, Sevastopol, Odessa. His mind wandered back to Volgograd (then named Stalingrad) and Zina... Perhaps he should visit her for old time's sake, say goodbye; her apartment was not far... He decided that that was not necessary and would in all likelihood not be appreciated.

An hour later, Drydenko was back in his office on 2 Dzerzhinsky Square. His mind was clear; his resolve firm. It was a dangerous gambit, the very last resort as desperate as the assassination attempt on Stalin so many years ago. It could go terribly wrong. But what choice did he have? It was the only way to deal with his circumstances — a contingency plan that he had hoped never to use. He poured himself a stiff shot of his best cognac and gulped it down before lifting the phone receiver and dialing a private number. *Option Z* was about to be put into play.

"Yes?" came a gruff voice at the other end.

"I said I would not ask, but only as a last resort," Drydenko explained in a low, hoarse voice. "Time has run out on me... I am terribly sorry."

"So am I, but I understand, and a debt needs to be paid."

"I have been pressed into a corner," continued the deputy director by way of justification. "A corner I cannot escape from without your help So ... time for extreme countermeasures."

"When?"

"It needs to be done very soon, before the weekend — by Friday night."

"I understand."

"Is that possible?"

There was a prolonged pause. "Yes, I have access and the means."

"Again, I only ask this as my final option."

"It will be done."

Drydenko put the receiver down and buzzed Klara in the outer office.

She whisked in, looking radiant as ever in the new dress she bought the week before; it was of modest length, as befitted her secretarial role, except for the rather revealing V-cut in the front.

"Klara, please cancel all my appointments for the rest of the day — and I will not be taking any telephone calls, no matter who is on the other end. Is that understood?"

"Yes, Andrei."

"I would like your company Friday night at the dacha."

"Friday?" She frowned slightly and in a lower voice said, "Andrei, you know it's always Saturday."

"Yes, of course, but this is a special occasion."

"A special occasion?"

"It is important that you come Friday night."

"I…" Klara thought of the evening she had planned elsewhere.

"Vasilevich will pick you up at the usual time."

Klara nodded uncertainly and said, "Very well." She would have to break her other appointment for the evening. There was no use arguing with Drydenko when he made up his mind about something. She just hoped that his sudden deviation from the established pattern would not become routine for the future.

CHAPTER 32

The apartment building was on a quiet, unassuming street. Arkady Zhutoff drove him to the alley around back in a black GAZ saloon, not the limo, which was too conspicuous. After a quick reconnoiter to make sure nobody was around, he parked, got out, and opened the rear door. Bakinin emerged and limped a few steps to a nondescript side door. He produced a key from his coat pocket, inserted it, and made his way in. He slowly ascended a flight of modest stairs to the second floor. There he proceeded down the corridor to room 207.

Zhutoff waited until his boss was inside, then he moved the car to the front of the street and entered the building through the main doors via the key provided. He also went to the second floor, where he remained stationed at the end of the hall like a watchful baba, except he didn't knit. Thankfully, there was a threadbare sofa he could plop on and patiently wait for the next three or so hours.

Bakinin was extremely careful to lead what appeared to be a dull, monastic private life. After all, there was no such thing as social deviancy in the Soviet Union (that was regarded as mental illness requiring treatment in a psychiatric ward). And if one didn't have a wife or mistress or both, then one better have an irreproachable existence. The odd rumor notwithstanding, he escaped scrutiny — at least officially.

Still, Bakinin knew he was … different, and that this was his Achilles' heel, which he judiciously sought to keep secret. It was the result of his childhood experience, he fervently believed. When he was seven or eight, he couldn't be sure, it started. Not his fault really but that of his parents and the church, or rather, the sweaty, bearded priest who proved anything but orthodox when it came to his altar boy. Aside from performing his duties in that incense-permeated little church, Bakinin was obliged to help his "holiness" tidy up after service. The problem was his "holiness" could resist neither the sacramental wine nor Bakinin.

In retrospect, he had to admit that he had been, if not physically damaged, at least traumatized. No matter, he found ways to cope. His "holiness," along with his mother and father were suddenly gone, decreed enemies of the people, arrested, interrogated, and in the case of his parents, sent away. He wasn't sure where their journey ended; they were simply taken from their home in a quiet village about a hundred kilometers northeast of Moscow, eventually herded into a northbound cattle car, and along with thousands of others, disappeared. He never saw them again. He considered it their penance for turning a blind eye while his "holiness" had his way. As for his "holiness," he was summarily executed — a frequent occurrence for priests. "God will know his own," was the joke Bakinin heard repeated by the officials who signed the death warrants. Still, he believed the priest imparted to him a transference that left a troubled yearning. Ultimately, it needed to be satisfied.

Meanwhile, Bakinin and his two other siblings began a new chapter as wards of the state and as Komsomol youth. Unlike his younger brother and sister, who were submerged into the proletarian masses, he stood out despite his diminutive size and physical weakness (later to learn that he had an irregular heartbeat with complications that in his fifties led to a stroke). He survived well enough, mentally intact and with only a slightly lame right leg and arm to indicate his serious condition.

An astute, diligent student, he was noticed by instructors as potential NKVD material. (After all, he had turned in the priest and snitched on his parents for their "antistate" activities). And he did seem to have a talent for intelligence work, which was useful for NKVD agents who were too physically deficient for the military.

There was the unfortunate three-year hiatus in Norilsk after he failed to find Bodrev. It was in this purgatory that his "need" was awakened. One particularly shy young comrade guard was amenable, but the conditions were primitive and opportunities limited. After a brief dalliance during his second year, Lev fell sick and died of an undetermined illness.

Bakinin remained self-constrained until he returned to civilization and resumed his rise up the NKVD ranks. But the needs persisted, and he finally found a way to fulfill them discreetly every other Friday with Sasha.

By happy circumstance Bakinin was able to "save" Sasha from the clutches of a psychiatric ward or worse when he was caught in a compromising position with another "deviant" during an NKVD raid on suspected dissidents. Bakinin read the file, saw the photo, and interrogated the nervous young man, taking his full measure. Mysteriously, thereafter, Sasha got lost in the justice system and then disappeared completely without any records.

The flat was quite large, with a tastefully furnished living area complete with a burgundy leather sofa, two ornate, brocaded chairs, and two small tables on either side of the sofa. The walls were a faded green, with only one large painting hung on the longest portion, a pastoral scene of peasants happily working in a field. The most prominent object was a grandfather clock occupying one corner. A bookshelf with a few scattered volumes and a heavy velvet curtain drawn across a small window completed the living-quarters decor. A short hallway led to a tiny kitchen, while to the right was a modestly sized bedroom with a toilet off to the side. Bakinin had never ventured into the bedroom; his business with Sasha was always consummated in the living quarters.

"Ah, Sasha, you are looking well," Bakinin remarked in his most cheerful voice. He was happy to see Sasha but particularly pleased about his recent meeting with Drydenko. Tonight was his private night to really celebrate. Indeed, he ordered Arkady to procure an additional dose of his "usual" stuff plus a large bottle of Ukrainian plum brandy.

Sasha had a narrow face with delicate features that included a small purposeful chin, slender nose, taut cheekbones, and rather opaque hazel eyes that peered out from behind round rimless glasses. His head was capped with short well-groomed black hair. He was dressed in an olive-green tunic, somewhat reminiscent (or mocking) of the old Soviet-style dress code, and wide blue trousers.

"As are you," he replied. "Here, let me." He took the deputy director's overcoat and brandy bottle. He draped the coat over one of the chairs and set the brandy on a table with the two crystal glasses beside the sofa. The mosaic wooden floor creaked as Bakinin made his way to the sofa.

"Shall I?" Sasha started to unseal the brandy bottle, deftly producing a cork opener.

"Please do," Bakinin said as he sank with a sigh into the bosom of the sofa.

Sasha poured two generous shots into the crystals. "*Nazdarovya*."

"*Nazdarovya*, Sasha." Like the young man, Bakinin raised his glass.

They both took a sip. There were formalities...

"You have behaved these last couple of weeks, yes?" asked Bakinin. "Don't want my Sasha to get into mischief."

"I have — always do."

Bakinin nodded. "Good, good. You know how important that is. It would not do to get noticed, yes?'

"I do understand," Sasha said, his lips forming a crooked smile. His material wealth in general and well-being in particular depended on him not coming under any suspicion or official notice, let alone trouble.

"Anything to report?" Bakinin asked, taking another tepid sip of brandy. He went through this "official report" phase mostly as a ritual to justify their trysts — just in case. Sasha's secondary occupation (besides pleasing Bakinin) was to be the deputy director's eyes and ears at the prestigious hotel in which he worked as an attendant as part of the hotel's guest service. He was to report on foreign visitors who might be of interest — no particular reason was needed. Sasha rarely had anything to relate, but that wasn't the purpose of Bakinin's visit.

The only time Sasha said anything of remotely mild interest was his observation of a tourist smuggling a local resident into the hotel (citizens were not allowed to intermix with foreigners). Bakinin listened to the details and made a note to check on it after the weekend, but his mind was on other business with Sasha.

"No, there is nothing of note," replied Sasha.

"Good!" Bakinin seemed in an especially good mood. Sometimes he wasn't...

"Before we go too much further, I mustn't forget the stimulant that Arkady acquired for me." From his pocket he produced two packets of what was euphemistically labeled as "recreational narcotics." He never asked directly where Arkady acquired these packets of white crystal power, but the methamphetamine mixture worked wonderfully well when mixed with alcohol, providing what he could only describe as a euphoric experience.

Bakinin carefully opened them and dumped one into Sasha's glass and the other into his own. He knew the inherent danger that ingesting these crystals could be habit-forming but he believed himself to be extremely disciplined. *To be used only on occasions such as this with Sasha to heighten the senses*, he rationalized as he watched the crystals dissolve in the brandy.

"Drink up. Sasha... Arkady has provided a couple of extra packets to remove any lingering melancholy."

Sasha smiled his crooked smile again. Why not? He'd just as soon start his pantomime routine of removing his tunic, trousers etc., but forced himself to relax. He learned that he couldn't be too rushed. Bakinin did not appreciate haste; he needed time to savor his laced brandy and let the drugs take effect. Normally, it took at least two glasses. "Not too quickly," he had admonished. "It feels cheap then... Take your time and strip your uniform with dignity. Let me anticipate the cheeky parts, yes?"

So Sasha and Bakinin drank at a leisurely pace until by some unspoken command it was time. For Sasha it was all part of a seduction game with Bakinin more an onlooker than participant until the end, when he couldn't help himself...

Tonight, however, Bakinin did not react in his usual manner. As the evening wore on, his eyes dulled, his speech slurred, and he now slumped into the cushions of the sofa.

"Are you all right?" Sasha asked as he viewed Bakinin's contracting form. There was no answer, but suddenly Bakinin jerked as if prodded by an electrical charge. The deputy director moaned, tried to say some words, but all that came out was spittle. Bakinin's face was a contorted sheen of sweat; he started gasping for air with his breathing increasingly ragged.

"Shit!" exclaimed Sasha.

His erection softened as he moved closer to the shrunken little man in obvious medical distress. Perhaps he should get his bodyguard to help, but as he moved, he realized that his feet felt like they were encased in cement and his face and hands were succumbing to numbness. Moreover, his breath, too, had become labored. He fell to the floor, surprised and puzzled at the same time.

***

Arkady Zhutoff knocked softly on the door of room 207. It was the hour to depart; Bakinin never stayed past three o'clock. When there was no answer, he took the extra key from his coat pocket and unlocked the door, quietly closing it on entry. He glanced around in the subdued lighting of the flat.

He was not surprised at what he saw. Bakinin, partly undressed, lay curled, almost knotted on the sofa. His body appeared to have convulsed violently before he died. And surely he was dead, from the stare of his vacant eyes and the release of his bodily fluids. Certainly, there was enough warfarin and strychnine in the crystals to kill a horse. Zhutoff wrinkled his nose at the stench.

Sasha was sprawled on the floor, evidently trying to reach the door. His slim, naked body was inert. Just in case, Zhutoff leaned down, put his hand on the big vein in the neck, and took a pulse. It beat faintly. Once that was confirmed, he went to the sofa, liberated a cushion, and with considerable force placed it over the face of the prostrate figure. There was a feeble twitch of arms and legs in protest before relaxation.

Zhutoff had no quarrel with Bakinin, although he was disapproving of his private activities. Overall, the deputy director had treated him well enough. Still, a debt was a debt, and he owed Drydenko a big one. Drydenko assured him that it would be collected only under the most dire circumstance, and only once. Now the debt was paid!

CHAPTER 33

By 6:00 p.m., Drydenko was ready. He had finished his meal, dismissed the charwoman, although it was not her night off, took a long, hot shower, slipped into his customary kimono, and picked out his favorite video cassette. He had viewed it many times before, finding it intensely erotic, satisfying in a sadomasochistic sort of way. The fantasy evolved around a male who was kidnapped and sexually abused by three women.

At precisely 7:30 p.m., Klara arrived, and Vasilevich hastily retired to his own small cottage nestled in the pines of the property. Drydenko had previously informed his chauffeur/personal valet that his services would not be needed for the rest of the evening.

The KGB deputy director studied his mistress for a long, reflective moment when she entered his chamber. She was wearing a tight-fitting white blouse and a flowing blue skirt, which he noted she had never worn before. "I'm glad that you came," he said, moving toward her, extending his arms in greeting.

Klara embraced him more tentatively than usual. "Andrei, you knew I would come."

He gave her an odd look. "I wasn't entirely sure."

"You said this was a special occasion?"

"Yes, very much so."

"Is it some kind of celebration? A victory of some sort for you?"

The old man pursed his lips but didn't answer.

"Andrei — what is it?" There was a trace of anxiety in her voice.

"Would you like a drink? My special cognac perhaps?"

"No — no thank you, Andrei — later... Tell me what has happened?"

He took her by the hand and led her to his bedroom. They sat down his massive waterbed, feeling the gentle rippling of the surface through the sheets and brightly colored quilt on top. Drydenko turned to Klara and without a word found the gap in her white blouse and caressed her breasts. Finally, he said in hushed tones, "Klara, you know I am very fond of you."

She smiled and pressed closer to him; he tilted her head toward his and kissed her. Then he undid the blouse as far as it would go and slid the material aside on either side so that it fell from her shoulders. He unclipped the bra, exposing her pert breasts.

"Now step out of that skirt," he ordered.

Frowning slightly, Klara did what she was told, getting up, unbuttoning the fluffy garment, and pushing it aside. She was in front of him, fully vulnerable. He didn't move from his sitting position for a moment, as if in deep thought. Then he grasped both of her arms and brought her to her knees in front of him.

The woman from Smolensk hesitated and resisted for a fraction before acquiescing. Drydenko was acting a little more brazen than usual, but he was a lustful old goat — and she had been compromised before.

Drydenko's kimono parted as he slipped the cord from his waist. Placing his hand firmly on her shoulders, he said in a disturbingly quiet voice, "I am very disappointed in you."

Klara looked up at him and attempted to rise, but he firmly held her down, one hand on her shoulder, the other stroking her thick black hair.

"Andrei? Is something wrong?" There was a note of escalating alarm in her voice.

"You betrayed me," he said, shaking his head.

"Please, Andrei. I don't understand—"

"Then I will explain." With that he shoved her back. She sprawled awkwardly onto the floor.

He sighed. "You really are an enchanting little fuck!"

Klara's eyes widened and started to water. This was the first time that he ever addressed her in an abusive, derogatory way. "Andrei—" she began.

He cut her off. "Why did you do it? Didn't I treat you well? Don't you live well? What am I not seeing?"

Taken aback, her lips trembled. "I-I don't know what you are talking about."

Drydenko's eyes flashed in anger; he raised his hand as if to hit her and then thought better of it. She shrank farther into the rug.

"Don't bother lying to me. I know. Just answer me — why?"

"Andrei … please."

"Andrei, please, is it?" he mimicked. "No! No, my dove — there will be no *Andrei, please* tonight. You spied on me for… I don't know for how long, but long enough! Bakinin knew about every important piece of information I entrusted to you — didn't he? Well, there will be no more reports on affairs of state or Comrade Drydenko's lusty evenings with his secretary — bitch!"

Ears reddening and her cheeks ablaze, Klara could only think of escape. Her tear-filled eyes darted toward the drawn curtain and the huge sliding glass door that led out onto the terrace. It was the closest route. She tried to get up, but he pushed her down again, hard. "No, Klara — there is no place to go."

"Wh-what do you want from me?"

"First, an admission — the truth. You sold out to Bakinin, didn't you?"

"It wasn't like that."

"He promised you what? A more luxurious apartment? More clothes? A rich bank account in Zurich, perhaps?"

Yes, and more, Klara wanted to say defiantly but faltered. How could she tell him that she did not want to continue to be an old man's chattel; that she had her pick of young, important men who were only too eager to help her up the ladder of success?

Drydenko with his obsessions was beginning to clip her wings, stifle her advancement. Word got around quickly. She was considered Drydenko's property. And who in their right mind would encroach on personal property belonging (potentially) to the KGB's next chairman? Bakinin offered her a way out.

"I'm sorry," she whispered instead.

"Your treachery might sign my death warrant, Klara — bury me … but," he added chillingly, "it doesn't matter anymore."

"Wh-what are you going to do?" Klara asked in a cracking voice, thoroughly frightened now.

Drydenko did not answer but picked up the discarded cord from his kimono, which lay on the bed.

"No! Andrei — please. I'm sorry. I can make it up to you—" Again she tried to rise from her prone position. He slapped her across the face. The force of the blow sent her sideways. While Klara lay dazed, he hunched over her, planting his feet on either side of her lithe form. He wound the cord around her neck and slowly began to pull outward on either end, cutting off the air supply.

"My lovely dove," he said quietly. "I've only killed one human being. That was a long time ago, in the line of duty. I was sorry that it had to be done but … it was exhilarating to have such control, such power over life." His thoughts flew back to the night he killed Bodrev.

In desperation, Klara started to thrash about, clawing at his exposed groin, which only seemed to urge him on further. His face seemed juxtaposed between pain and pleasure.

The telephone rang jarringly. He hesitated then relaxed his pressure. He stepped over to the night table and picked up the receiver, leaving Klara gasping for air, the cord askew around her neck.

"Yes?"

"It is done."

"No complication?"

"No."

"Good." With that, Drydenko put the receiver back into the cradle.

After an indifferent glance at Klara, he picked up the kimono cord, which now lay on the floor, and tied it around his waist. He then went out of the room, only to come back in short order with two glasses of brandy. He indicated for Klara to sit on the bed, and when she warily obeyed, he handed her a glass.

"Here's to Comrade Bakinin, who will no longer come between us. And here's to us!" He smiled at her imploringly and quickly downed his drink. "Please do not let this unfortunate episode spoil our arrangement. You are forgiven!"

Klara sat frozen, her drink in hand, not sure of her next course of action.

"You can go now," he said in an even, mild tone. "I expect you next week — at the usual time." He smiled again, the right side of his face crinkling into folds ever so slightly.

CHAPTER 34

Arkady Alexandrovich Zhutoff was a squat, heavily muscled man who at first glance could not be readily marked as a Kremlin foot soldier. Dressed casually, he could be mistaken for a swarthy laborer who drank lots of vodka, joked with the guys, watched sports, and ruled over a fat, sedentary wife with many kids. However, in the proper light, adorned in a dark suit or, more likely, a long topcoat and hat, he became a much more sinister figure — the kind who showed up unexpectedly at your door in the middle of the night.

Zhutoff thought briefly about Bakinin as he prepared to leave Moscow, at least temporarily, to complete the last portion of his debt. No regrets, really; he did what he was obliged to do. *Still, it is a bit unsettling*, he decided as he cleaned his apartment, part of his ritual before sojourning abroad on a mission. Later, he'd pay his bills and spend a couple of hours with his mother. Indeed, he'd take her to the ballet. She'd be pleased; he'd be bored, but it somewhat mollified his sense of guilt at leaving her for a prolonged period of time in her tiny flat. It was the only thing he ever truly felt guilty about in his life. His mother said nothing about his disappearing on the odd occasion. She knew that he was an important man engaged in affairs of state.

***

Zhutoff's first assignment for Bakinin almost a decade ago had been ideal as far as he was concerned. It involved a rather unfortunate dissident who, it seemed, was destined to spend most of his adult life incarcerated. This particular fellow had first seen the inside of a jail in Poland, in 1933, when at the tender age of sixteen he was arrested because of his activities in the Communist Party of Western Ukraine. Born and raised in the Volyn province of Ukraine, which at the time was under Polish domination, he apparently ran afoul of the Polish authorities. It was a common enough occurrence; Warsaw in the interwar period was forever suppressing rebellious Ukrainian groups. He was released in 1939, shortly before the outbreak of war, only to be rearrested by the Soviets when they invaded Poland. He found himself in a penal labor colony. Why? The dossier never stated, and Zhutoff didn't really care. At any rate, when Soviet-German hostilities erupted in 1941, he was pressed into a "punishment" battalion and sent to the front. The unit was promptly surrounded by German troops, and he ended up in a German death camp in Ukraine. After two months, he managed to escape and on foot made his way back to his native province, some six hundred miles away. By this time he had become thoroughly disillusioned with Stalin's brand of communism. In 1943, he joined the Ukrainian Insurgent Army but was captured within a year by the NKVD. Although initially sentenced to death, a lenient prosecutor commuted it to twenty years of hard labor in a gulag. He was released in the mid-1950s and allowed to return home. The KGB kept tabs on him; he had, after all, all the traits of a social deviant. He was again arrested in the late 1960s and charged under Article 62 of the criminal code: Anti-Soviet Agitation and Propaganda.

To this point, Zhutoff had nothing to do with the case. However, when the dissident was released, the newly appointed deputy director of his section gave him a thick file and said, "Find out where he goes and what he is up to."

Zhutoff followed the man to a small town just outside of Moscow. There the man settled into a small cottage to live out what remained of his twilight years. After a couple of months of sporadic surveillance and two or three clandestine searches of the cottage, Zhutoff concluded that this particular fellow had learned his lesson and was now a "reformed" Soviet citizen. He was about to ask permission to terminate the assignment when a copy of the man's memoirs fell into his hands en route to an Italian publisher. A vigilant postal employee (and state informer) had intercepted the suspicious envelope. The manuscript was delivered to Zhutoff, who duly passed it on to Bakinin for evaluation by the appropriate authorities. The result: arrest and conviction of the unfortunate fellow, again for anti-Soviet agitation and propaganda.

It seemed to Zhutoff that these deviants never learned, and as sad as it was, the state was obliged to root out such presumed slanderous writing (he did not bother reading it) and miscreant behavior. It couldn't be allowed to fester and spread, like black mold in a damp basement, lest it affect other, healthy parts of the Soviet edifice.

An example had to be set, and it was ten years in a labor camp, this time to be followed by a further five years of internal exile — if he lived that long.

Zhutoff was commended for his diligence. Although feeling a tinge of pity for the dissident, who didn't appear a bad sort, he nevertheless took satisfaction in his work and the fact that he did his duty. This case was not too difficult because it involved little risk to himself (indeed, none at all) and allowed him ample time to drink strong coffee and kvass with his old comrades and keep a periodic eye on his aging mother.

In most respects, Zhutoff remained the ideal NKVD agent, dedicated, diligent, careful, and not overly imaginative or intellectual. Above all, he knew who buttered his bread and consequently how to follow orders. He was aware that Bakinin trusted and relied on him. "Stay close," Bakinin informed him a few years earlier, "and you will survive your profession — perhaps even prosper." Zhutoff took Bakinin at his word and had never deviated, even if some assignments were "off" somehow and his boss bent the rules.

So what he did was not personal; there was no grudge or score to settle — not at all. In fact, Bakinin was more than fair to him on most occasions. No, his betrayal was all about family and a debt that needed to be paid. More explicitly, it was for his brother Lev.

During the Great Patriotic War, Zhutoff found himself assigned (for reasons that remained unclear to him, since he had not shown any particular intelligence-gathering attributes or skills in military training) to the SPETSNAZ battalion of the Red Army, responsible for keeping the political leadership abreast of what went on in the military. This "intelligence battalion," quite independent of the other branches, was the eyes and ears of Stalin and his Politburo cronies who were especially interested in knowing what the generals and the headquarters staff were not only planning but also thinking.

At the end of the war, Zhutoff discovered that his brother Lev, who was with motor-rifle troops, had been arrested for unspecified reasons. Of course, this was common enough as Stalin retightened his grip on the homeland. Hundreds of thousands coming back from the Western Front were suddenly deemed "unreliable" and accused of being a "threat to national security." Zhutoff received no details of Lev's alleged crimes against the state. Perhaps he got too close to the enemy and was judged contaminated or he spoke to the wrong person or was in the wrong place or there was a bureaucratic error or he simply became part of a gulag quota that needed to be filled. It didn't much matter the reason, only that Zhutoff had to do something if his brother was to survive.

Thus, it was with a great deal of trepidation that he went up the chain to his next in command and explained that Lev was not a traitor and had in fact done, nay, was doing his duty to the motherland before this calamity befell him. Andrei Drydenko listened, nodded gravely, and said he'd look into it.

As it turned out, Lev was scheduled for deportation to one of those distant and mysterious gulags that seemed to swallow up great legions of peasants and intellectuals, as well as soldiers and priests. However, chances were that Lev would be shot before he could be marched onto a boxcar for the long train ride north — over fifty percent of those arrested were.

Drydenko could have ignored or dismissed Zhutoff's plea, but for whatever reason, he didn't. Instead, he interceded on Lev's behalf with General Timoshenko, who quietly made sure that Lev was not summarily executed. Lev still ended up in a corrective labor camp (not even a great general and war hero could prevent that) near Omsk to do five years of hard labor. But he survived and was quietly living with his wife and daughter in that city.

Zhutoff was eternally grateful, and although he was loyal to Bakinin, almost to a fault, he agreed that he would repay Drydenko, who took a great risk in intervening. After two decades of silence, Drydenko was calling in his favor, and he had to reciprocate.

Favor for favor; risk for risk. The debt had to be paid.

***

To fully complete this debt to Drydenko, Zhutoff abandoned his beloved Moscow for London. He had been there only once before on a minor mission and found the city too frenetic, alien. He had never encountered such ostentatious wealth. Because of his imperfect English, in the past his assignments had been limited to the predictable confines of Eastern Europe. Here, he was overwhelmed and chagrined. So many stores, the variety of commodities for sale, the expensive motorcars — capitalism run rampant. And Comrade Lucovich seemed to be enjoying himself. *His expense account must be astronomical*, brooded Zhutoff with a touch of envy, *and so will mine be if I am not careful.* But there was no doubt about it, the Soviet state's resources were being generously applied to rich food, fancy clothing, and possibly "other" unnecessary luxuries. *A very wasteful agent*, Zhutoff decided.

By habit, Zhutoff was much more frugal. He checked himself into a more modest hotel, ate simple meals, and eschewed the idea of partaking of London's glittering nightlife. From other agents he had heard of the pleasures of Western women, but the fancy, painted, scantily dressed females he encountered here just made him nervous, although he couldn't pinpoint why. Besides, he had a strict rule: Never mix business with frivolous pleasure. It was not healthy in his profession. His only large expense, outside his accommodations, was going to buy something nice for his mother, although he hadn't decided what as yet.

In fact, he was thinking about it as he sat in Alexandr Lucovich a.k.a. Adam Woodal's flat, waiting for him to arrive.

CHAPTER 35

Woodal was idle and thus restless. He had become a man of leisure with his handler suddenly gone dark, unavailable. Given this reprieve from the mundane mechanics of spying — no contacts to meet or dead letter drops to pursue for over a week — he dreaded his growing boredom and mounting anxiety. He had presumed that it would be business as usual in London until Bakinin sorted out his plans in Moscow. Apparently, this was not the case, and it had just become a little too quiet for his liking.

Still, he was finding diversions. Today it was a number of pleasant hours in Hyde Park, which, like Gorky Park, fulfilled a similar function, an escape from the walls of his flat and refuge from the frenetic chaos of the city. He really hadn't been overly interested in museums and cultural events that tourists found so fascinating (besides, he wasn't a tourist). He thought them stuffily English with a relentless stream of historical snobbery attached — at least from the descriptions he perused. Thus, he hadn't visited the Tower of London or the British Museum; nor had he taken in a play at the Globe Theatre. Indeed, the extent of his sightseeing was an outing to Madame Tussaud's (out of morbid curiosity) and to Greenwich, where he viewed the *Cutty Sark*, Britain's last "tea clipper." He found both mildly interesting, a bit like the Ukrainian Village outside of Edmonton, which in truth was intrinsically slightly more germane, if not interesting.

He had gone to the park for a jog, taking his time circumnavigating the grounds and ending up at Serpentine Lake.

Here, he sat on a bench, soaked up the late-afternoon sun, and watched people out on the lake pedaling boats. His excursion ended with a stop at a pub in Kensington Gardens. He was becoming fond of somewhat warm British bitter.

As he returned to his apartment and took the well-worn steps to his flat, he had a momentary thought of Irene — a tranquil, gentle thought. He recalled his dream of Irene beckoning him from a misty shore to follow across a wide river — to cross the Rubicon. It quickly slipped away. Truth be known, he wasn't tempted. The sentiments expressed in his subconscious were not real; they did not have the kind of bittersweet unction required to make him act. It just wasn't him; nor did he want it to be.

He inserted the key and with a twist unlocked and opened the door in one motion. Three steps in he stopped, suddenly alert, the hairs on his neck prickling. There in the shadows sitting on his living room recliner was the dark form of a man.

"Don't worry, I am not here to kill you," said Zhutoff in a low, gravelly voice. "If that were the case, you'd be dead already."

Lucovich took a moment to recover, consciously settling his heart rate and cautiously taking the key out of the lock.

"Please close the door," Zhutoff ordered. "We have some private matters to discuss, and it keeps out the draft." He smiled from the shadows.

Lucovich recognized Bakinin's favorite goon as much by his shape as his voice. What was he doing in his London apartment?

"You have me at a disadvantage, Mr...." Lucovich either couldn't remember his name or was never properly introduced.

"Zhutoff — Comrade Zhutoff."

"Comrade Zhutoff," Lucovich repeated. "To break and enter into one's dwelling is against the law in this country."

"True, but I did not break anything — merely let myself in. And you won't be calling the police, so..."

"Deputy Director Bakinin and I had an arrangement."

"Ah... I guess you haven't heard."

"Heard what?"

"That he is no longer with us. He had a massive stroke and unfortunately did not survive. The 'official' news undoubtedly will be out shortly."

"I see…" said Lucovich, caught totally off guard and wondering what this unexpected development meant. His deal with Bakinin was no longer viable? Had he been found out? But if that was so, it would have been one of Drydenko's agents on his recliner. Indeed, why was Zhutoff in London? What did he want, and what did he know?

"I am sorry for your loss," Lucovich said in a hollow voice, not knowing what the game was.

Zhutoff shrugged. "Yes, it was most unfortunate."

"I don't understand… Why are you here?" *More precisely, why did you break into my flat?*

"Oh, that part is simple. Deputy Director Drydenko sent me."

Alarm bells went off in Lucovich's head. He thought about exiting his apartment quickly; instead, in an even voice, he said, "If I am a target, the deputy director should know that I have taken precautions to protect myself. I have certain documents safely stored that—"

Zhutoff raised a hand to cut him off. "As I said, if Deputy Director Drydenko wanted you … eliminated, it would have already occurred."

"I see," said Lucovich, not really understanding. In fact, he was totally flummoxed.

"I doubt that you do," Zhutoff sighed, "but then I am not sure that I do. What do you have to drink, by the way?"

"What?"

"To be sociable — while we talk."

Lucovich stood dumbfounded, assessing the bull of a man calmly seated in his living room, probably with a Makarov nine-millimeter holstered to his torso. He then proceeded to the kitchen and opened a cupboard door, where on the second shelf sat a half bottle of Stolichnaya. While Zhutoff warily looked on, he took the bottle, twisted off the cap, and poured a generous amount into two round glasses; he walked into the tiny living room and handed one to Zhutoff. He sank into the rustic couch opposite and waited for Bakinin's ex-goon (he presumed) to clarify.

"Do you know why I let myself into your flat?" Zhutoff asked, accepting the glass.

"I couldn't hazard a guess."

"I was curious — how agents live in the decadent West."

"And?"

Zhutoff looked around. "Not that much differently. A little more space, a few more conveniences, but modestly." His tone was one of approval.

"On my compensation, this is what I can afford."

"Ah yes, true." Zhutoff nodded. "Our employer is not noted for overt generosity."

"Then we will drink to that!"

"Why not? *Nazdarovya.*" Zhutoff raised his glass.

"*Nazdarovya,*" echoed Lucovich. And they downed the burning liquid.

"Well, Comrade Lucovich, I will be blunt," said Zhutoff, wetting his lips as if to savor the burn. "You are to come to Moscow. Deputy Director Drydenko has matters to discuss with you."

"And if I refuse?"

"That is not an option, as you well know."

Lucovich did not argue the point. "Do you know what this is about?"

"It is not my business to know. I have been given my instructions, and I will carry them out."

"How is it that you work for Deputy Director Drydenko... You were with Bakinin?"

"This is true... However, circumstances have changed." Zhutoff smiled thinly.

"Well... I would need a few days."

"That is not possible. We will be leaving later tonight in fact."

"That urgent, is it?" *And I am not to be trusted.*

"Those were my orders, to escort you personally to Deputy Director Drydenko. Whatever else there is to discuss ... it will be between him and you. Now..." — Zhutoff slapped his thigh with his hand — "how about one more glass for the road?"

CHAPTER 36

"So we meet again," Drydenko said with an affable smile, which did not extend to his eyes. "I am glad that Comrade Zhutoff was able to persuade you to come back with him. I trust he was an amicable traveling colleague."

"He was delightful," Lucovich retorted stonily.

For the most part, Zhutoff was a silent and sullen companion. From London to Frankfurt and on to Berlin and Moscow, his words were few and far between. And when he did speak, his interests seemed to revolve around "Western decadence" and his mother, or more precisely what he should buy for her. Lucovich suggested, half in jest, a purse or scarf that he could help him select and get a discount at Harrods on the way to Heathrow. Zhutoff apparently did not discern the attempt at levity; he muttered an intelligible comment and seemed to consider the offer before informing him that he could pick up those items just as well in the GUM store in Moscow.

Drydenko laughed, appreciating Lucovich's implied sarcasm. "Quite so… Please have a seat. We have many important things to talk about." He gestured to a high-back chair directly in front of his large, neat desk. He leaned back into his plush chair as if to truly settle in. "This time, perhaps, we can be more frank with each other."

Lucovich nodded, his face passive, and sat where indicated, folding his arms across his lap. He had no idea what to expect.

"Tell me," Drydenko continued, "how did you come to meet the late Deputy Director Bakinin?"

Lucovich explained the circumstances. There was no point in denying or subverting what occurred. After all, Zhutoff was there and could bear witness.

"Deputy Director Bakinin was a sly one." Drydenko nodded with a small smile. "But setting that and his recent departure aside, what did you find out? More than you told me already, that is?"

"The version I gave you is essentially correct — except for my dealings with Bakinin," Lucovich replied.

"I think not. What you left out is what you know of the nature of Glinka's activities in the war and why it was necessary to eliminate him. He told you?"

"No — there is a memoir and other documents that narrated most of it." Lucovich saw no advantage in keeping secrets. In fact, this revelation might save his life or at least provide him with some leverage.

"I see... And where is this memoir and documents?"

"I've made arrangements to keep the original and copies in various safe places only to be released in case of my sudden, unforeseen demise—"

"Released to the newspapers?"

"And a certain Politburo member who would be vitally interested."

"I see... You know," Drydenko said with a thin, twisted smile, "you are sounding like a character from a bad American movie... Is this a 'shakedown'? No, wait! You have created a 'dead man switch'!"

Lucovich straightened in his chair. "I prefer leverage — for my survival."

"I could call your bluff."

Lucovich did not respond.

Drydenko pursed his lips and leaned forward. "So that I am clear — what was your arrangement with Bakinin? I know what he wanted, but what did you hope to gain in return?"

Lucovich told him. Drydenko shook his head in mock disbelief.

"Money — perhaps a modest sum, but to disavow one's country and the Komitet, to retain your Mr. Woodal alias or disappear altogether? Not possible. You have been led badly astray. We couldn't have that; we'd open the floodgates — lose too many assets. Bakinin was 'pulling your leg,' as the Americans would say. He couldn't let you get away even if he wanted to, and of course, neither can I..." Drydenko threw up his arms as a gesture of futility. "Not possible," he reiterated.

A long pause ensued while Drydenko seemingly pondered his options. "No, Comrade Lucovich, I can't just let you go — whoosh ... vanish. There would be too many questions asked and unpleasant consequences for me and you. I am inclined to 'call your bluff'!"

"We are at an impasse, then? No arrangement?" *Might as well know where I stand*, he thought.

"On the other hand," Drydenko raised his hand in placating fashion, "perhaps we can compromise, come to some agreeable accommodation before deciding to 'cash in our chips.'"

Lucovich waited. Drydenko sighed and continued. "It is not necessary to be so drastic ... a standoff, yes, but not a shootout at the O.K. Corral..." He smiled at his American analogy.

Lucovich shifted in his seat. His backside was becoming uncomfortable. "I am listening."

The deputy director picked up a letter opener from the desk and toyed with it. "First, and this must be absolutely clear, you cannot escape your duties to the motherland — that, I can assure you, was never in the cards. It would effectively make you a traitor, and we know what happens to traitors. Mr. Woodal could never become your reality, but remain an alias — if that... However, your position could improve materially with a substantial promotion both in stature and authority. It has occurred to me lately that I may have need of a general polovnik, a chief inspector, so to speak, of field personnel — one who could probe the activities of Komitet agents when their investigations go awry or they die under mysterious or suspicious circumstances. I, of course, would expect regular reports and have you close at hand, but not Moscow — that's Comrade Zhukoff's domain now. So ... you would no longer be Mr. Woodal or live abroad, but you would be alive and have a substantial improvement in your net worth..."

***

Later, Drydenko assessed his meeting with Lucovich. He really couldn't blame him for his actions, not totally, either for his arrangement with Bakinin or his threat. He did what he had to do to protect himself — what options did he have? Still, he was a loose thread who potentially could unravel the delicately woven fabric. Whether he was bluffing or not, he simply knew too much.

In the end, he would need to be dealt with. Drydenko could proceed in two ways: forthwith call his bluff and eliminate the wayward agent or, for now, wait until Yanev retired. Let him survive, albeit within lethal reach.

And how would Zhukoff feel about finishing off this bad business with Lucovich, even if his debt was paid in full? Certainly, his pot could be suitably sweetened...

CHAPTER 37

February 1975

Drydenko was exceedingly pleased. Finally, the word had come down: He was on the cusp of becoming the head of the KGB! There were still some formalities to go through, but privately he was assured that his star had risen and that a sufficient number of comrades had attached themselves (and their careers) to it. *And so they should*, thought Drydenko, *given the number of "favors" I bestowed on them*. It was in the bag; Yanev said as much, albeit discreetly, at a reception the night before. A formal vote in the Politburo was just days away. The unexpected death of his chief rival (hastily hushed up publicly, given the circumstances) over six months ago certainly helped his cause, and while there were capable challengers in the wings, the die was cast.

To be sure, Yanev's retirement had moved at a glacial pace. No matter, though; it just gave him more time to get his ducks in a row and resolve outstanding issues — issues that really could not be left unattended without serious consequences. First and foremost was what to do with Lucovich. He could not allow the agent to resume his double life in London. That was abundantly clear. No, to go back as Mr. Woodal was problematic at best and more likely a disaster, he concluded. Suppose the agent truly wanted out? It was much easier to defect from London than Moscow. And what stories he could tell? Aside from the little secret between them that would threaten his newly obtained position, Lucovich had other tidbits of information, from various covert operations and drop points to assassinations, which would be of interest to MI6 and make him a high-value turncoat.

Of course, he had conveyed as much to Lucovich, informing him that his assignment in the UK was terminated. After posting the appropriate letters of notice to his employer and landlord, Adam Woodal quietly disappeared with no forwarding address. But that could not be the end of it. What Lucovich could never know was that Drydenko had begun the elaborate process of undermining and condemning the agent: Drydenko's "research" section, Ivan and Yuri Orilov, were combing through his activities, his interactions, and painstakingly preparing documents exposing him as a double agent. The brothers were his most trusted and discreet researchers; they could fabricate a document as well as a great forger could copy a master's painting. They had been instrumental not only in locating Glinka but also preparing his files, and now they were onto Lucovich.

It wasn't too difficult to create subterfuge to discredit an opponent or agent. Innuendo here, a cryptic note there, doctored selected memos on sensitive matters coming to light and all attributable to Lucovich. Suspicion would build and cast doubt on his loyalty and reliability until the dossier grew thick enough to ensure his demise. The kind of work the Orilov brothers performed emerged with the creation of CHEKA but hit its high-water mark in the Stalinist purges. *They carry on a venerable tradition*, mused Drydenko, one that was indispensable to him. He always made sure that they were treated well.

However, while this was in the works, Lucovich needed to be handled.

Drydenko had begun his cover story on the day the agent was summoned back from the UK, even before he knew the full circumstances and details of the threat Lucovich posed. It was a good scenario. Lucovich was to be elevated a number of notches; in fact, named to a newly proposed position: Special Adjunct Overseer in charge of KGB investigations, Kiev District. He would be reporting directly to Drydenko as the head of the KGB in Moscow. While the terms and jurisdictional parameters were being refined, Lucovich would remain in Moscow, with an upgraded apartment and substantial increase in salary. Technically, he was under assignment for Drydenko — but in a nebulous capacity until his new position could be officially unveiled. This information was kept under wraps because, as Drydenko explained, "some noses would be out of joint."

"Be patient," Drydenko advised. "In the meantime, enjoy what our fair city has to offer!" Lucovich did not object. *Why would he?* reasoned Drydenko. *The Ukrainian capital is a civilized enough place and his position constitutes a quantum leap upward.*

For the hundredth time, Drydenko evaluated his decision and decided that it was the only logical one — or as logical as it got if he was to be his own master and in control. He had to call Lucovich's bluff. He couldn't just have him hanging out there. Lucovich had to be neutralized, no less so than Glinka. The risk was an acceptable one, and if it resulted in any potential fallout, that, too, would be neutralized. By that time Lucovich's credibility would be nil and he would be dead. And who would be foolish enough to stick their neck out and demand an investigation?

Perhaps the trickier part of Drydenko's scheme was to get Zhutoff on board. The fellow had a strange sense of loyalty and had fulfilled his solemnly declared debt *to the fullest*, Drydenko assured him. There was, however, a certain inflexible, old-believer morality to him that made Drydenko uneasy. True enough, Zhutoff was now "reassigned" to Drydenko's section and as such would follow orders. Still, Drydenko wanted to appeal to the man's rather anachronistic Soviet motherland's sense of legality and justice. He called in the large, wily agent and stated in hushed confidentiality that there was growing evidence that Lucovich had been turned, that he had committed treason.

The problematic aspect, despite the thick dossier compiled by the Orilov brothers of Lucovich's transgressions, was that Zhutoff was not stupid. He probably figured out that this was not the whole or even the real story, that it was more personal than that. After all, he knew of Lucovich's meetings with Bakinin and that it had to do with Lucovich's mission to Canada on his behalf (although, evidently, not any of the details, as far as Drydenko could tell). And of course, Zhutoff was sent to London to fetch Lucovich, which Drydenko spun as his becoming suspicious of the agent's *unauthorized activities…* Nevertheless, Drydenko reasoned, Zhutoff might remain a little curious, if not skeptical. But then Arkady was a foot soldier and obeyed the chain of command, especially when presented with an impressive file detailing Lucovich's crimes against the state.

At the meeting, Zhutoff was as stoic as ever, saying little but nodding. He frowned slightly when Drydenko gave him the time frame and suggested that the sanction be "above suspicion," as it was in the case of Bakinin. A date was set, but with a fleeting smile, Drydenko allowed the agent discretion on the timing and the means…

***

For the moment, Drydenko put affairs of state on hold. It was Saturday, and Klara would be at his dacha soon enough. In fact, Vasilevich was about to go and pick her up. But not before he delivered his other package, however, which Drydenko looked forward to receiving as well…

Ah, Klara, Drydenko ruminated as his thoughts wandered into a darkened corner. All things considered, their relationship remained satisfactory. Klara was dutiful enough, acted and said the right words both at the office and, of course, in his bed, but there was no denying their relationship had changed. There was an underlying emptiness that he couldn't quite put his finger on — ever since that night when he showed his wrath at her betrayal. It was close; he barely controlled his rage. *Regrettable on both sides,* he rationalized. But it was over; he forgave her. He had told her so…

Nevertheless, and quite understandably, Klara was shaken and inevitably it was taking time to readjust their relationship to a more trusting level — not to have her stiffen at rougher play or suggestion of certain "indulgences," no matter how banal they turned out to be. She wasn't the loose, confident, free-flowing woman he originally enticed to his dacha. It seemed now like a fee-for-service arrangement, which, he supposed, had always been the case but which he felt had grown over the months to something more substantial. He sighed. Only a matter of time, he hoped, before trust on both sides would be fully restored and normalized as before.

There was a discreet knock on the door. "Yes?"

Dimitri Vasilevich, his bodyguard and valet, opened the heavy oak door with a creak and stood in the entrance with an embroidered cloth bag in hand. "Your special order—"

"Ah ... good. No trouble getting it then — I wasn't sure."

"No trouble, but it was the last bottle in the shipment apparently. There won't be another batch for about three weeks."

Drydenko nodded. Even at the special outlets for high-ranking party members, certain products, like a very fine cognac, were not always readily available.

Vasilevich took a couple of military strides from the doorway and handed Drydenko the bag. He gingerly took out the Baccarat crystal decanter and read the label: Richard Hennessy.

Bottled the same year Stalin died — wonderful! He carefully set it on the large dining-room table. A rare cognac indeed, which he could hardly wait to sample.

Vasilevich stepped back. "I shall be off to pick up your guest," he informed his boss.

"Very good," responded Drydenko, somewhat distractedly, his good eye wandering to the cognac.

With that the tall, clean-shaven man gave a curt nod, abruptly turned, and exited the room.

A rather pedestrian, if not dull young man, mused Drydenko, albeit with a solid military pedigree if his father was any measure. In truth, Drydenko didn't know what to make of Dimitri. The man kept to himself, was always there when needed, and unobtrusively so, which Drydenko appreciated. More to the point, he did what he was told and was discreet in what he saw — the perfect manservant. Drydenko had known Dimitri's father, who served in the same unit during the war. He (like his son, in all probability) was not officer material and thus never rose through the ranks like Drydenko. On the other hand, Vasilevich Sr. was capable enough and, more importantly, loyal. After the war, Drydenko offered him a position as an undersecretary in his section. It was a fairly low, paper-pushing job but secure. Drydenko met his son fresh from finishing his training at one of the twelve military colleges in Moscow. He was far from one of the top students and quite at a loss in terms of his future. In fact, Vasilevich Sr. worried that Dimitri's prospects would be settled by others and that he might well end up in hinterland somewhere or worse — in a place like Afghanistan. Drydenko, always attuned to creating people grateful to him, offered to see if there was a place for him closer to home, as it were. Thus, when Vasilevich Sr. became sick and died suddenly (heart or stomach ailment, he couldn't remember which), he took the hapless lad on. *Presumably, he'll be as grateful as his dad*, Drydenko reasoned.

"I need to keep an eye on him," Vasilevich Sr. once told his boss. *Well, I did more than that, Vasili*, he chuckled to himself. *I gave him a job — a secure, comfortable one at that. Those are hard to come by and to be valued as much as loyalty...* Vasilevich Jr., no less than Vasilevich Sr., Drydenko believed, would always be loyal. He knew who buttered his daily bread. He supposed that Dimitri would remain his personal assistant once he became head of the KGB and moved to a more prestigious dacha. He'd become used to having him around.

As he thought of Dimitri's status, which he deemed would remain unchanged for the foreseeable future, Drydenko took hold of the rectangular decanter containing the precious cognac and twisted the cork. It gave with a pop. Letting it rest for a moment, he opened the kitchen cupboard door, reached for an elegant balloon-shaped crystal glass, and poured a generous amount. He swished it around the sides of the glass, noted the golden color, let his nose inhale the aromatic bouquet, *a blend of floral and fruit embraced by waves of cinnamon and other spices, perhaps*, and took a sip, letting the liquid settle and languish before swallowing. It hit the spot; a drink to be savored. Indeed, as he clicked the switch on the beta machine, he kept sipping. On further tasting and reflection, he detected a delicate fragrant aftertaste that he couldn't quite identify — unusual for such a discerning palate as his, he thought. Oddly enough, as he watched the porn flick, Drydenko discovered that he was far from aroused. Moreover, he was having trouble focusing and his mouth had an acidic, pasty taste — *surely not the cognac.* Slowly a sense of panic gripped him as he experienced increasing difficulty in breathing and could hardly move...

CHAPTER 38

It was a simple plan — as most desperate plans are. But it took nerve and manipulative charm to pull it off. Klara knew that after that night, when her betrayal came to light, she had to somehow divest herself of her boss. She believed that she would not survive that night and, from her perspective, it was only a matter of time before he went over the edge, before he'd decide that she was expendable.

She didn't know precisely when the idea dawned that Dimitri Vasilevich might provide the means to free herself of Drydenko. He had been chauffeuring her back and forth from her Moscow apartment to the Zhudov 1 complex dacha for almost a year. With each ride the wonder and lust in his eyes grew. She sensed it; could see it when she looked into his rearview mirror.

For a long while he said nothing, and she didn't encourage him. If the truth be known, she was a bit dismissive of him, despite his trim body and handsome, square-jawed features. There was always a polite but terse exchange or two before she'd settle into silence in the back seat of the Volga. Gradually, they talked; first of small inconsequential matters and general trends, slowly expanding in the last few months to more open, more personal affairs. Dimitri proved a good listener with a shrewd, calculating intelligence that belied his strong, silent, stalwart image. She knew that he was increasingly smitten with her and that it could be used to her advantage.

She found the old goat repulsive, she explained to the attentive valet. "The liver spots on his hands, those long, bony fingers ... the scarred face and the dead eye with the peculiar stare; the disgusting folds that hang from his midriff…" Besides, he was cruel and made her do things.

"What kind of things?" he asked.

"Sick things…" He had sexual proclivities, she explained, that ranged from the unsavory to the indecent. The bottom line was that she didn't want to be with him. But she wouldn't be safe if she left him. "What can I do? That's how it works for us below!" she related bitterly. He was her powerful boss and about to become almost invincible.

Dimitri took it all in (in fact, he took all of her in), mulling and grinding the bits she seeded until a convergence crystallized and he popped the question. "How can I help you?"

"I wish he'd just leave me alone … but that probably will not happen."

"No, probably not," he agreed. "Not without an … intervention."

The course of action was consummated in her apartment bedroom. "There is a way," he said softly, stroking her raven hair as they lay naked, side by side. "It could be done."

Having led him through her labyrinth of disturbing stories, she mildly protested, "There has to be another way—"

"No, there isn't," he stated emphatically. Finally, he persuaded her, and she capitulated, giving him her best smile that brought out the deep dimple on her left cheek. She had him.

"How?" she asked.

"He is a creature of habit, quite predictable, and an opportunity will present itself."

So it did via his precious cognac order. Drydenko fancied himself a connoisseur and would be sampling it without delay.

"He can't help himself. He waits with anticipation for each new, exotic flask, which I am in charge of delivering. I'm sure he's into it even as I speak and as fast as he can pry open the cork!"

"He drinks like a fish in general — at home, in his office," Klara agreed. "There's usually a half-empty decanter sitting on the table when I arrive. He insists that I, too, sample what he calls 'the good stuff.'"

"What if one night a particular batch of his 'good stuff' was off —
like bad kvass?"

"What do you mean?"

"Potassium chloride, along with a couple other very potent
ingredients — it wouldn't take a lot."

"Poison. You want to poison him?"

"A lethal dose could easily find its ways into the cognac."

"Wouldn't it be discovered? That he was poisoned — murdered?"

"Actually, no," Dimitri replied confidently. "I had a number of
interesting instructors in military school, including those in
chemistry class that told me otherwise."

"I don't understand?"

"Potassium chloride is a natural biochemical. It is virtually
undetectable, even in the event of a most thorough autopsy. Deputy
Director Drydenko, it will be assumed, died of cardiac arrest."

"And you can get it?"

"Yes … I do have friends with access, but you don't want to know.
It may be harder to artfully get it into cognac, although I doubt that
he would notice a doctored cork particularly. But I will be exceedingly
careful…"

***

"Is — is he dead?" Klara nervously glanced at the prostrate figure, his
kimono askew on the sofa. The tape in the beta box had evidently run
its course.

"I'll check," said Vasilevich in a clipped manner.

As he bent over to feel a pulse, Drydenko's eyes flickered open
and a bony hand twitched as a shiver went through his body.

Vasilevich jumped back, and Klara let out a gasp.

Drydenko's dying eyes recognized him, and he seemed to smile.
*Done in by my scheming mistress — bitch and an ungrateful dork,
undoubtedly led by his dick… As the Americans would say — I didn't
see it coming…*

"What do we do?" Klara asked anxiously.

"Something I had hoped to avoid." He pulled out a syringe and a vial of colorless liquid. "A direct injection of potassium chloride — but wouldn't want any mysterious puncture holes found—"

Suddenly, Drydenko convulsed and seemed to expel a last bubble of air. An eerie silence ensued.

"On the other hand, no further ... intervention may be necessary," Vasilevich announced. "I think he just expired." He tucked the syringe and vial back into his coat pocket.

"*Bohjeh, Bohjeh Moi...* I think I'm traumatized!"

"It's over. The charwoman will find him tomorrow morning. She'll come running and screaming to my quarters. It will look like a heart attack. Perhaps got overexcited — all that American smut did him in..." He smiled. "Give me a minute."

Vasilevich left the room while Klara stood, stunned. He came back from the bathroom with a small mirror. Cautiously, he once again approached the sprawled figure. He placed the mirror close to his open mouth.

"Just want to be sure," he said. "Yes ... he is dead."

"What now?"

"I drive you back to Moscow. I am sure we can find something interesting to do."

CHAPTER 39

Arkady Zhutoff had to decide how to proceed. He had his marching orders and a lengthy dossier to justify them. It was his duty to carry them out, even if the man who gave them suddenly died! After all, Lucovich was a traitor — the documents proved it.

Still, there were aspects that did not sit well with him, including the whole business between Bakinin and Lucovich, to which he was not privy; Lucovich's murky assignment in Canada, apparently at the behest of Drydenko; and his own trip to the UK to fetch Lucovich and bring him directly to the deputy director. Now Lucovich had a rather nebulous existence in one of Moscow's plusher apartment buildings (at least by ordinary citizens' standards). *You've been put on hold for me to deal with*, thought Zhutoff. *But should I? Especially now?* There was something disquieting, unsavory about the whole affair that he couldn't easily put his finger on. On the other hand, if Lucovich truly was a traitor, he could return to London and once again become Woodal and resume his activities. As a conscientious Soviet security officer, he could not allow that to happen — especially since he had his instructions.

No question, Zhutoff had a dilemma. Should he duly carry out his assignment or let it lie for others to sort out? Did it matter that Drydenko was dead? Bad timing, it seemed, but no suspicions of foul play had as yet surfaced. It appeared a natural death. But so had Bakinin's, and it had been only forty-eight hours or so since he heard about Drydenko — the verdict could change. In fact, news of the untimely death of the new KGB chief (designate) was still to be officially released. Zhutoff had his own sources, though.

It seemed like some sort of irony within an irony to Zhutoff as he arrived at his destination, an impressive, albeit modestly sized, five-story red-brick edifice not far from the Dostoevskaya Metro Station. He parked the Volga on a side street. Normally, there would be at least one other colleague getting out of the car with him if they were about to search an apartment and apprehend and detain a suspect. This was a special solo job with no prisoner to be taken in. The only part of this mission in character with more routine KGB operations was that it would be carried out in the dark. The cold February sun had long since set.

Zhutoff walked up the narrow but clean stairs to the third floor. The corridor was wide, with good lighting. The place was indeed more upscale, although he still smelled the sour odor of fried sausages, cabbage, and beer. He stopped at apartment 303, checked that no one was in the vicinity, dug into his overcoat pocket, and fished out what appeared to be a ring with Allen keys attached of varying sizes. Selecting a long, slender one, he quickly inserted it into the door lock. A precise twist was followed by a click, and he was in. The whole procedure took about seven seconds.

Having just left his quarry, Zhutoff knew there would be no one inside. He had followed Lucovich into a local pub a couple of blocks away and left him there staring into his beer. *He will come home when he is ready*, reasoned Zhutoff, *where I will be ready to greet him...*

The bulky agent did not switch lights on but allowed his eyes to adjust to the darkness, only after painfully hitting his shin against a low, solid coffee table in the living room. He surveyed his surroundings, noting that the apartment had the luxury of a balcony, which gave him an idea. *Yes, that will work nicely*, he decided. To this point, he wasn't sure on the how; now he knew.

***

Alexandr Lucovich sat slumped over a cloudy Baltika brew at a dark corner table in one of Moscow's lesser-known establishments. He had finished his supper, a bowl of borscht and a plate of greasy perogies (fish and chips were not on the menu). Taking another swig of the bitter ale, he contemplated his future. According to Drydenko, it was to be another month before relocation to his new posting in Kiev. While at loose ends in Moscow, his mind went blank at the thought of moving. He really didn't know that much about his home region's capital, nor did he have any meaningful connections there. The place was a tabula rasa. He had passed through a number of times; an impressive city of gleaming church domes and tree canopies. Otherwise... He raised his glass in mock salute, chuckling to himself. *Here's to Kiev and to our great bard, Taras Shevchenko... I'd rather be in London.*

It was his last beer. Shrugging into his heavy Napoleon overcoat, grabbing his fur-lined *shupka*, properly aligning the ear flaps and securing it tightly on his head, he waved at Lyonka, the bartender, whom he'd gotten to know over the last few weeks, and strolled out to face the elements. It had plunged to about –25 degrees C with a mild northern wind that nevertheless felt like stinging pine needles on his face.

A brisk walk to his abode would do him good and clear his head — not that he was overly drunk. He'd been distracted lately — for quite some time, actually — as weighty matters pressed. It went without saying that he didn't trust Drydenko. And he was keenly aware that he had the weaker hand to play. In truth, he *was* bluffing when all was said and done. Even if he told his story, released his damning documents, Drydenko, from his position of power, could in any number of ways undercut, minimize, and bury his secret and him. No illusions on that score. But what were his options? He might have some desperate ones in London, but here in Moscow he was feeling ... vulnerable.

"Oh, to be Adam Woodal again," he wished out loud, his breath curling into dissipating fog as he made his way down the deserted prospekt.

***

Lucovich felt the needle plunge into his neck before sensing the salient presence behind him. He knew immediately that he had seconds before numbness and loss of mobility. Zhutoff extracted the needle, satisfied that he had injected enough of the white liquid to do the job. He quickly capped and thrust it back into his coat pocket and then eased his victim down to the floor before closing and locking the door.

He then dragged the immobile man by the armpits and awkwardly propped him up against the wall adjoining the kitchen and living room. He struggled to remove Lucovich's coat, inner jacket, boots, and hat, hanging the clothing on a coat rack near the apartment entrance before placing the boots inside the closet. *Might as well be tidy about it*, he thought. Surveying his surroundings, Zhutoff sighed before refocusing on his subject. He was perspiring profusely, although it was far from warm. "Better get on with it!" he muttered to himself as once again he lifted his prey by the armpits and pulled him across the living room to the glass balcony door.

An acceptable suicide — at least by KGB standards — was a headlong plunge from one's high-rise window (or in this case balcony). Indeed, it was the preferred method used on all manner of deviants, from uncooperative politicians, bureaucrats, and financiers to annoying journalists. With a great deal of straining and grunting, Zhutoff finally deposited Lucovich onto the balcony. *Now to lift him and topple the dead weight over the railing.* However, even as Zhutoff went through the motions (and it was no easy task on his own), another disturbing thought suddenly arose. He was only on the third floor; *suppose he survives — hits a soft snow bank or has a hard head...* This could lead to complications best avoided. Zhutoff, in all probability, would have to explain his botched actions, despite his orders and the dossier. After all, his boss was dead!

Halfway through propping up his charge on the railing, he abruptly dropped him like a sack of potatoes. Why not just leave him? Lucovich was maybe conscious of what was happening (Zhutoff wasn't really sure), but in an immobilized state he couldn't do much about it. In due course, Zhutoff figured, he would simply freeze on the balcony. Suicide by cold was not only viable but less messy than a sprawled body below. The KGB stalwart stepped over the man and walked inside, vigorously rubbing his hands before sliding the balcony door shut. He decided to hang around until early morning just to make sure. Meanwhile, he wondered what Lucovich had to drink.

***

It was both terrifying and liberating to know how your life was about to end. Lucovich sensed himself being dragged about, lifted, propped, and dropped. He heard the grunts, the frosty crack of an opening door, and felt a blast of frigid air. He was on the balcony, pulled across to the edge. He knew what was to come as he was laboriously hauled up against the railing. *Not very imaginative*, he mused in a moment of levity.

Then, abruptly, he was let go and a large figure — *Zhutoff?* — stepped over him and the door closed. *A change of plan?*

The breeze seemed to pick up and swirl about him. The night sky was clear and it was very cold as his plumes of breath indicated. His head was tilted slightly toward the glass, and he saw a smear of color inside through the glare. It wasn't only his reflection but a person — *Zhutoff?* he wondered again. His vision was strained and becoming unfocused. He tried to shout, but nothing came out.

So this is it! he thought, a half smile curling on his lips. Nothing hurt; he wasn't particularly cold now, and serenity descended over him as he closed his eyes.

CHAPTER 40

"Ah, you are awake," Zhutoff said with a hint of joviality.

Lucovich blinked a number of times, and he realized that he was on his sofa, underneath a blanket and his heavy coat. He shifted, feeling sluggish.

"The sedative has almost worn off. Don't worry, it has no lasting effect. That was not the way you were supposed to go," Zhutoff said stiffly. He was sitting in the well-worn love seat opposite the sofa with a drink in his hand.

Helping himself to my booze again, thought Lucovich as he eased his way to a more erect position. His head was pounding; his face and hands felt raw and oddly stretched. He looked down and wiggled his fingers. All seemed in working order.

"Do not worry; nothing froze. I decided to save you before that happened."

"You saved me?" Lucovich frowned.

"*Da*, I did."

"But you put me out there?" Lucovich motioned with his head toward the balcony.

"That is also true."

Lucovich pondered for a moment. "So … why and why?"

"Ah … the first part is easy to answer — I was following orders. The second part — not so easy. I had to wrestle with my conscience and instincts, and you almost lost."

Silence ensued before Lucovich spoke. "So … I guess Deputy Director Drydenko decided to terminate our bargain."

"That I would not know. Obviously, you had some arrangement with the deputy director."

"Which evidently I don't have anymore…"

Zhutoff cleared his throat. "This is true. Deputy Director Drydenko died sometime in the last forty-eight hours," he said flatly. "That is all I know… But he did issue orders." He shrugged. "I came to carry them out, but alas…" He paused and took a gulp of Lucovich's vodka. "Would you like some?" He raised his emptied glass.

"No." Lucovich shook his head and winced. "Help yourself."

"*Spasibo.*" Zhutoff heaved himself off the love seat and made his way to the kitchen table on which rested a half-empty bottle of Stolichnaya. He poured himself another generous portion and returned to his seat.

"Thank you for not … allowing me to die."

Zhutoff swirled his drink. "*Nazdarovya.*" He once again raised his glass. "Here is the thing, Comrade Lucovich." He took a modest sip. "You are wondering why? I need to know that very answer myself, and for that I need a truthful answer. Are you a traitor to the motherland?"

Lucovich sat up, a little more alert, and frowned. "No. What made you draw this conclusion?"

"I have a thick dossier that says so and I have … had my orders to take appropriate actions."

Lucovich nodded. "Provided by Deputy Director Drydenko, I gather." *Just like he provided an enormous file on Glinka.*

"Yes."

"What happened to Drydenko? How did he die?" Lucovich abruptly asked, more out of curiosity than morbid satisfaction.

"Of natural causes, apparently," Zhutoff replied evenly. "If that is what you are asking?"

Lucovich nodded. "I am not a traitor. What manner of spying did I do or secrets I allegedly reveal — to the British, I presume?"

"Oh, a variety — informant for MI6, for instance. Your transgressions are listed, complete with dates, times, and drop-offs."

"I see… Well, rest assured, I was not an informant, double agent, spy, or otherwise a traitor. What I am is … expendable. Drydenko had a secret that would have destroyed his career and him. He used me to make sure that it remained buried. But, by whatever means, Deputy Director Bakinin found out about my mission, hence your visit to London and my hasty meeting with him."

"Yes, yes." Zhutoff waved his hand impatiently. He had ascertained as much and why Drydenko called upon him to honor his debt by the off-the-book sanction of Bakinin. It was a power struggle, and it was personal. That part he surmised; but what were the state objectives? This was unclear, and it bothered him. On the other hand, he did not want to know the specific nature of the Drydenko-Bakinin conflict because, he was sure, it would be distasteful and demoralizing. Perhaps the truth was best left bottled like bad beer after all…

"The reason I changed my mind about fulfilling my orders is because of the unusual circumstances surrounding your relations with both Deputy Director Drydenko and Bakinin. It gives rise to certain doubts and reservations, despite my orders. Yes, in the end … a profound dilemma for me. If you are a traitor, then not following my orders is a dereliction of duty. If, on the other hand, you are not a traitor, then…" Zhutoff splayed open his hands, the glass teetering precariously on the edge of a spill.

"I can give you the details of my dealings with Drydenko and Bakinin and provide the materials Drydenko sought to bury and Bakinin obtained just before he died," Lucovich said in a rush of words. "It was, as you say, both personal and an internal power struggle. I just got caught in the middle and became a loose end for Drydenko. My becoming a traitor is a convenient fabrication, which almost had the desired consequences. If you want to know the nature of Drydenko's secret and why it was so valuable to Bakinin, I'll gladly tell you."

Zhutoff waved him off. "*Nyet*, I do not want to know the details. They would serve no purpose for me, or the state, I suspect."

Lucovich nodded.

"I had to satisfy myself that I was doing the right thing for the motherland when I did not complete Deputy Director Drydenko's orders — that this was the proper action… And after a long debate sitting here while you were out there," he glanced at the balcony, "well, I reached my conclusion. I needed more clarification and verification and with the deputy director's sudden death … perhaps his orders are dead too."

Zhutoff suddenly got up and in one big tilt of his head downed the rest of his vodka.

"I have decided that my actions are correct. I have not compromised the state. I do not know who else has this dossier on you — perhaps nobody or it is suitably hidden — but what I have will be delivered to you anonymously, since destroying state property without proper authorization is not permitted." Zhutoff smiled. "Of course, you can do with it what you like. I think we are done now."

"Just so I am clear," Lucovich prompted. "You do not wish to know Drydenko's secret?"

Zhutoff sighed. "No, I do not. I am sure that I would believe you, and I do not want to be disillusioned."

With that the bulky KGB agent readjusted his hat, buttoned his coat, and quietly went to the door and let himself out. "*Dobre ooytro,*" he said, closing the door.

Lucovich, still quite dazed and only somewhat comprehending the totality of his experience, lay back down, exhausted. Should he ever become Adam Woodal again, he would make sure that Zhutoff's mother received the best boots, gloves, and scarf Harrods had in stock.

Epilogue

It seemed that he was safe. Three weeks after Deputy Drydenko's sudden demise, Adam Woodal reappeared back in London. There had been a change of address, and he was "between jobs," until a suitable position presented itself. Otherwise, it was business as usual.

Lucovich was glad to return to a life of low-level intrigue and leave behind the absurdity of what had occurred. In fact, he tried desperately to deposit those events into a recessed chamber deep in the back of his subconscious. Any disturbing voices that sought some meaning or clarification for what transpired were ruthlessly suppressed. He had, after all, been trained to do just that. Thus, the "Canada mission," the whole Drydenko-Bakinin affair thereafter, and Zhutoff's attempted sanction and abrupt change of mind were dealt with, perfunctorily buried and, as far as possible, forgotten about.

And yet his time in Canada came regurgitating through when he least expected. Or, more precisely, he realized, not so much the place as the person — Irene popped into his mind unsolicited more than she should have. He didn't know why; he had no real feelings for her. Still, her image came and, however tenuous, lingered. His analysis never went further than a question: *What if... What if circumstances were different... What if I could have stayed...* It was a recurring self-indulgent, reflective moment on an abstract notion that he always summarily dismissed almost as soon as it emerged. That it even emerged was the puzzle. He hoped that she didn't think too badly of him — the way he appeared and disappeared from her life. It was ... unavoidable.

***

It took almost six months before his existence as Adam Woodal became unsustainable. At first, he didn't know who was onto him. Had someone in the Komitet read Drydenko's dossier compiled on him? Or was it MI6 counterintelligence? For a couple of weeks he had the prickly feeling that he was being followed — that eyes were on him. Then one of his "shadows" got careless near the Morning Crescent Tube Station; Lucovich spotted him two days in a row. Not a coincidence.

The question of whether it was KGB or MI6 was resolved a few days later when he was summoned to Moscow for a new assignment. *Yes, the proverbial writing is on the wall*, he thought, looking at himself in the mirror as he shaved. *Time to make other arrangements...*

Thus, five days before he was scheduled to fly out to Frankfurt (and on to Berlin and Moscow), he went for a long stroll into the heart of the city. At the appointed time and place, he spotted a man in a bowler hat with a red sash carrying a green Harrods bag. The man choreographed a number of intricate pathways through crowded streets and a series of shops with Woodal discreetly in his wake. They finally found themselves in Boodle's Pub on St. James Street.

"Don't worry, your 'tails' have been rerouted or otherwise detained," declared the tall, thin man in properly modulated English, his bowler hat and bag on the seat beside him. They were ensconced in one of Boodle's darker corners, chatting over a pint. "I'll escort you from here to a 'safe house,' where you will be debriefed. I trust you have put your affairs in order?"

"Yes, yes, I have," replied Woodal, appearing calm, although he was perspiring profusely and his pulse was racing. His only regret was that he could not tell Suzanne, his new significant other, anything. She would discover him gone soon enough — vanished! Pity that. They were, from her point of view, well on their way to becoming a serious item. *I wouldn't have gone quite that far*, he reflected with a touch of melancholy, *still... fate does not ask...*

A new identity and a new life awaited him, provided he was valuable enough to the Brits and the long, patient arm of the Komitet didn't find him. "Speaking of which," he sighed into a half smile, "Zhutoff most certainly will be disappointed."

ACKNOWLEDGMENTS

First and foremost, I am grateful to my wife, Diane, who encouraged me and cheerfully put up with my writing hibernations. And to my wonderful daughters, Alisha and Halyna, who initially vetted the manuscript and provided insightful critiques.

I'd also like to thank Jon Martin for his technical help and Allister Thompson for his careful edits. Huge kudos to Melissa Novak for a great front cover illustration.

Finally, thanks to everyone at Iguana Books, especially Paula Chiarcos and Christine Falcone for their skillful copy edits, comments, and proofreading, and Cheryl Hawley, Meghan Behse, and Greg Ioannou for their support.

Any errors of commission and/or omission are entirely mine.

CPSIA information can be obtained
at www.ICGtesting.com
Printed in the USA
LVHW100428140422
716131LV00001B/61